WOLVES IN SHEEP'S CLOTHING

"We're with the territorial militia," Fry informed him. "We're making calls on every settler in the valley to see how many fighting men we can call on if we were to have Indian trouble." He flashed a wide smile for Cochran's benefit. "Are there more menfolk living here that we can count on in a pinch?"

"Ain't nobody here but me and the missus," Cochran said. "Hell, they coulda told you that in the settlement—saved you a ride all the way down the valley."

Fry's smile returned. This time it was genuine. "No trouble at all. We had to ride down here anyway, to chase the war party off."

"War party? What war party?"

"Why, the one that's fixin' to burn your place," Fry replied and nodded to Pitt.

Without hesitating, Pitt turned the rifle that had been resting across his saddle, pointing it directly at John Cochran's forehead. The look of surprise became a permanent feature of the dead man's face as Pitt's rifle ball made a neat black hole just above Cochran's eyes.

HERO'S STAND

Charles G. West

A SIGNET BOOK

SIGNET
Published by New American Library, a division of
Penguin Putnam Inc., 375 Hudson Street,
New York, New York 10014, U.S.A.
Penguin Books Ltd, 80 Strand,
London WC2R 0RL, England
Penguin Books Australia Ltd, 250 Camberwell Road,
Camberwell, Victoria 3124, Australia
Penguin Books Canada Ltd, 10 Alcorn Avenue,
Toronto, Ontario, Canada M4V 3B2
Penguin Books (N.Z.) Ltd, Cnr Rosedale and Airborne Roads,
Albany, Auckland 1310, New Zealand

Penguin Books Ltd, Registered Offices:
Harmondsworth, Middlesex, England

First published by Signet, an imprint of New American Library,
a division of Penguin Putnam Inc.

First Printing, March 2003
10 9 8 7 6 5 4 3 2 1

PUBLISHER'S NOTE
This is a work of fiction. Names, characters, places, and incidents either
are the product of the author's imagination or are used fictitiously,
and any resemblance to actual persons, living or dead, business
establishments, events, or locales is entirely coincidental.

For Ronda

Chapter 1

"**D**amn you, Caldwell! I told you to hold your fire till we got a little closer. Now they're scattering." Simon Fry jammed his heels into the sides of his big bay gelding, at the same time shouting orders to the rider on his right. "Pitt! Cut them two off before they get to that ravine." Jack Pitt had not waited for instructions and was already quirting his horse mercilessly as he raced to intercept the two Indian women trying to escape. Fry charged toward two young Indian men who were now on their ponies and riding straight toward the hills to the west. In spite of his annoyance with Caldwell for jumping the gun, Fry leaned forward, low on his horse's neck, a look of determination etched on his otherwise expressionless face. "Mendel!" he roared as two more of the surprised Indians scrambled to escape up the valley, one a woman leading a horse that was pulling a travois. Mendel Knox, needing no further orders, tore off after the two, whooping at the top of his lungs, a wide grin spread across his face.

The surprise had been so complete that the gang of white men might have ridden almost into the Indian camp before they were discovered had it not been for Caldwell's premature shot. Even so, Simon Fry's band of outlaws was too close to give the startled Indians any chance to avoid the murderous assault. Quick as they were, the Indian ponies had no time to spring into full gallop before the white men began to cut the riders down. The narrow valley soon echoed with the sharp chatter of rifles as one brave after another was riddled with lead.

Wiley Johnson, following close behind Fry, searched frantically for a clear target, but Fry blocked his view of the fleeing Indians. Yanking sharply on the reins, Wiley swerved off at an angle to get clear of Fry's horse, almost trampling the body of the woman killed by Caldwell's first shot. His horse jerked away to avoid the body, and Wiley, almost thrown from the saddle, regained his balance only to find a terrified toddler in his path. The child screamed in horror as it tried to run for its life. Startled at first, Wiley reined back. But when he realized what had spooked his horse, he spurred the animal straight toward the screaming child in an attempt to trample the life from the toddler. Having a natural tendency to avoid the child, the horse balked, almost unseating Wiley for a second time. Furious at having nearly come out of the saddle again, he turned and shot the infant, then galloped away after the horses.

It was all over in a matter of minutes, and the riders gathered back at the Indian campsite. Fry wasn't satisfied that the job was complete, how-

ever. "There's another one around here somewhere. I counted eight, and I don't see but seven
dead Injuns."

"By God, you're right," Jack Pitt said. "There
was eight of 'em, all right. The other'n musta
crawled down that creek bank."

"Check down yonder, Pitt," Fry said. "Somebody look upstream."

The raiders split up to search the creek banks
while Fry watched from the Indian camp. Only
minutes passed before Trask yelled out, "I got
him! Here he is!" No sooner had he sung out
his discovery than he followed it with a sharp
yelp of pain as an arrow thudded into his shoulder. The cornered Indian quickly notched another arrow but had no time to release it before
Mendel put a bullet between his eyes.

"Damn, Trask," Fry muttered when he rode
up to the wounded man, now dismounted and
sitting on the creek bank. "That was mighty
damned careless." Fry sat on his horse, looking
down dispassionately at the arrow protruding
from Trask's shoulder. "How bad is it?"

Wincing with pain, his teeth tightly clenched,
Trask tried to gingerly pull his shirt away from
the shaft. Each time he bumped the arrow, it
caused him to suck his breath in sharply. "I don't
know," he whined, "but it hurts a damn plenty."

"Mighty damned careless," Fry repeated, then
called back to the rest of the men, who were
already rifling the bodies of the dead. "Clell,
better come take a look at Trask."

Clell Adams looked up and grimaced, obviously more interested in searching for something of value on the still-warm corpse before him. Being the oldest of the pack that ran with Simon Fry, it had more or less fallen upon him to do the doctoring for the gang. He had no training for this position, and he had never volunteered to tend the wounded, but he was old enough to be a daddy to Hicks and Caldwell—the two youngest—so he pretended to know what to do. With some reluctance now, he rolled the Indian's body over in case he had missed anything, then got to his feet.

"Damn, Trask," Clell remarked as he stood over him. "How'd you let that happen?"

"Dammit, Clell, that don't matter," Trask spat back at him. "Just git the damn thing outta my shoulder." The deepening lines on Trask's face bore evidence that the pain was becoming intense, and there was more than a bit of concern in his eyes.

Finding very little of value on their victims, the other men gathered around Clell and his patient. Clell knelt down beside Trask and gave the arrow a stout tug, evoking an immediate yelp of pain from the wounded man. "She's in there pretty solid," Clell stated. Then, with a none-too-gentle touch, he rolled Trask over on his side. "Didn't come clear through, though."

Alarmed by the indecisive expression on Clell's face, and frightened by the throbbing in his shoulder that seemed to increase with each beat of his heart, Trask stammered, "Wh-whad-daya gonna do? My shoulder's gittin' stiff as a board."

Clell scratched his head as he considered the question. "Well, I seen a feller with an arrow in his side once back in '61—Blackfoot arrow, it was. It wouldn't come out, either. So a couple of his partners held him down while another feller drove that arrow right on through. When the head come out, they broke it off. Then they pulled the shaft out the way it come in."

"Oh Lordy," Trask groaned.

"Only way it would come out," Clell added. "Feller died, though. Them Blackfoot had put something on that arrowhead. Made the wound swell all up until it puffed out like a ripe gourd."

"Oh Lordy, Lordy." Trask sighed and lay back against the bank, convinced that his outlaw days were coming to an end. His eyes rolled back until there was almost nothing visible but the whites. His face, as stark as a hatchet blade, blanched nearly as pale as his eyes, and he began to slowly roll his head from side to side in anticipation of the pain that was certain to come.

Growing more impatient by the moment, Simon Fry stepped down from his horse and pushed a couple of curious spectators aside. After taking a closer look at the arrow, he reached out and gave it a quick tug. The force was enough to lift the slender Trask a foot off the ground, but the arrow remained firmly embedded. Dropping the screaming Trask back to the ground, he said, "Drive it through. We can't hang around here all day."

"Gimme a hand here, boys," Clell said as he looked around the creek bank for a suitable rock to use as a hammer.

Almost gleeful in their eagerness to participate in the procedure about to be performed—especially one that promised to greatly add to Trask's suffering—Mendel and Wiley pounced upon the unfortunate man, each taking an arm and pinning him to the ground. The abruptness with which they attacked him caused the already suffering Trask to cry out in pain.

"This is gonna hurt like hellfire," Mendel promised, making no attempt to hide the wide grin on his face.

"That's a fact, Trask," Wiley agreed. "We're gonna see how much sand you got now. 'Course it might be a waste of time. You never know what kinda shit that Injun rubbed on that there arrowhead."

"Wiley's right," Caldwell chimed in. "I heared a feller tell about gittin' jumped by a band of Blackfoot on the Popo Agie. He said them Injuns had mixed up a terrible potion— dog shit, coyote piss, rotten meat, and I don't know what all—so even if you got the arrow out, that mess would kill you, anyway."

Receiving little comfort from his comrades, Trask began a continuous low moan, his eyes rolled back like he was trying to look at the top of his head.

"What the hell kinda Injuns is these, anyway?" Clell asked. "Blackfoot?"

Impatient to mount up and get under way once more, Fry replied, "No, Snakes. Now get on with it." His concern at the moment was whether or not these eight dead Indians had been part of a larger band nearby.

Clell nodded. Selecting a flat rock the size of a dinner plate, he bent over Trask again. "All right, hold him steady, boys." He started to administer the first blow to the arrow shaft, then paused a moment. "Maybe a couple of you other fellers better grab a'holt of his feet. I don't wanna git kicked in the head."

Hicks and Caldwell each sat on a foot, and Clell was now ready to drive the arrow through. Trask screamed out in agony as the first jarring blow sent a searing pain through his body, causing his back to arch up from the sandy creek bank. He withstood three more excruciating blows from Clell's stone before he fainted dead away. Clell continued to hammer, finally splitting the wooden shaft, but the arrowhead refused to budge. Defeated, he sat back on his heels and peered at the unconscious man. "Hell, Fry, it ain't comin' out. It's up agin somethin' solid—bone, I reckon. All I'm doin' is drivin' it in deeper."

"Shit!" Fry exhaled in disgust. "Well, break it off close as you can and tie a rag over it. I reckon he won't be the first son of a bitch walkin' around with an arrowhead in him."

Clell shrugged, took out his knife, and went to work on the splintered arrow shaft. "What about what Caldwell said? About that shit they put all over the arrowhead?"

Fry shrugged his indifference. He was already thinking that Trask would now be a liability.

Jack Pitt, an amused observer to this point, spoke up. "Hell, there ain't likely anything on that arrowhead. This sure as hell weren't no war party, and I don't reckon that Injun would wanna put anything on his arrow that would spoil the meat if he was huntin'." Knowing Fry's concerns, Pitt looked at his partner and added, "He'll be all right, just stiff and sore for a while."

This seemed to satisfy Fry. "All right, then. Throw some water on him, and let's round up them Injun ponies. It's best not to hang around here any longer."

After Trask was revived, he was helped up on his horse by Clell and Hicks. Protesting feebly, he was roughly seated, after which Pitt informed him to hang on or fall off and be left behind. Knowing Pit was deadly serious, Trask lay on his horse's neck, his good hand wound tightly in the animal's mane. They rode toward the south end of the tiny valley, driving the Indian ponies ahead of them, hoping to find a pass that would take them through the mountains ahead.

Pleased with the stroke of luck that had permitted them to encounter the small party of Indians, Fry was already appraising the newly acquired horseflesh. It couldn't have been any better: eight horses, one per man. He, of course, would claim first pick, so he looked the little herd over carefully. He smiled to himself when he reviewed his day's work—eight horses and eight dead Indians, not counting the baby. Nice and neat.

Simon Fry and Jack Pitt had been together for quite a few years: since the spring of '67, in fact, when both men had followed the rush for gold to California. They were not as fortunate as some who had gotten there earlier and skimmed fair amounts of dust from the many obscure streams that showed a hint of color. Both men had soon become disenchanted with the hard physical toil of placer mining. Being of like mind and disposition, they had begun to look for an easier way to obtain the precious flakes that drove so many to labor in the clear, rushing streams.

Fry had never held a fondness for hard work, preferring to use his brain instead—a quality that had enabled him to rise to a vice presidency in a St. Louis bank. His impatience to await the time-honored rewards for long, faithful service to that institution had prompted him to take certain shortcuts to attain his financial goals. He was doing quite well for himself until the senior vice president, Jonah Henderson, had accidentally caught him in the process of diverting funds to his personal account. Faced with ruination, if not prison as well, Fry had offered to cut Henderson in as a partner. But the senior officer was an honest man and had consequently informed Fry that he was bound to report his findings to the board. Without hesitation, and with no feelings of remorse, Fry had laid Henderson out with a poker. Leaving the senior vice president lying on the floor of the bank with a fractured skull, Fry had decided it was an opportune time to join the many adventurers harking to the call of gold in the West. And like many who left the East for reasons less than noble, he had left his real name behind as well: abandoning the disgraced name of Steadman Finch to the gossips of St. Louis, he had taken on the name of Simon Fry.

In Jack Pitt, Fry had found the perfect partner. Big and physically strong, Pitt was a deep-thinking man of few words. And although Pitt normally did his own thinking, he was not averse to letting Fry call the shots as long as he didn't disagree in principle. Unlike Fry, Pitt had never held an honest job, having always found it easier to take what he needed from the physically inferior. The two had established an equitable partnership from the first.

Being smart enough to see that only a small percentage of honest prospectors gained the vast riches that everyone hoped for—and ruthless enough to take advantage of honest men—Fry and Pitt gave up the pan and sluice box and

sought their fortunes with powder and ball. As
Fry so eloquently expressed it, a pick and shovel
were not the only tools with which to mine. A
Winchester rifle and a Colt revolver worked just
as well and raised one hell of a lot less sweat.

At first, the two combed the mountain
streams, seeking out isolated claims and murdering any unlucky miner who happened to
cross their path. As time went on, they picked
up additional partners from the riffraff who followed the gold strikes—unprincipled men like
themselves, who had no qualms when it came
to splitting a lone prospector's skull for a little
sack of yellow dust. Their gang of cutthroats
grew to eight, an optimum number according to
Fry. Any more, and they might become unman-
ageable; yet they were enough to deal with
those prospectors quick to grab their rifles. If
they had been a military unit, Fry would have
been captain and Pitt his lieutenant. The rest
were expendable.

Mendel Knox appeared at the top of the rise,
reined his horse to a stop, and waved the others on.

"Looks like Mendel's found somethin',"
Clell offered.

"I hope to hell he's found a way to get off of
this damn mountain." Fry was in a foul mood.
They had spent a good part of the morning tra-
versing a lofty mountain, looking for a way
through to the western slope. Every trail seemed

to dead-end into the shear side of another mountain whose slopes were a thick wall of lodgepole pines. All morning they could see what appeared to be a gap in the peaks that promised to be a valley, but they had been unsuccessful in finding a pass that might lead them to it.

It had not been a productive summer for Fry's band of outlaws. When things got too hot for them in California, they had followed the late strikes in Montana territory. But they had found the claims too few and too hard to get to, not lucrative enough for their needs. The one sizable strike, at Rottenwood Creek, had looked to be prime pickings until a vigilante committee was formed, making it too risky to remain in that vicinity. So now Fry grumbled to himself as he rode up yet another rise, in need of a place to winter and with a wounded man on his hands.

"What did you find, Mendel?" Pitt asked when the group caught up.

"A way outta these mountains," Mendel answered, a smug grin on his face. "There's an old game trail on the other side of this ridge. It leads through a pass, and that valley we've been lookin' for is on the other side." Fry started to say something, but Mendel cut him off. "And that ain't all. There's a little settlement in that there valley."

This piqued Fry's interest right away. He looked at Pitt and smiled. "This might be a good day, after all. Let's go have a look."

*   *   *

"Whaddaya think, Fry?" Jack Pitt prodded, leaning forward with his foot propped upon a large rock and his elbow supported on his knee. Like his partner, Pitt had been studying the little settlement far below them in the valley. It seemed peaceful enough, with log houses scattered some distance apart on both sides of a strongly flowing river. When Fry didn't answer immediately, Pitt said, "Looks ripe for the pickin' to me."

Fry nodded briefly to acknowledge his partner's comments, but he still didn't answer right away. He was sizing up the homesteads that were visible, wondering how many more were hidden from view in the valley below and estimating the potential for resistance. Behind him, he could already hear comments from the others, anxious to ride down and raid the settlement. When Wiley Johnson voiced the question "What are we waitin' for?" Fry turned and answered, "We're waiting for when I say."

Wiley shrugged but held his tongue. There was no doubt in anyone's mind who called the shots for the gang. To a man, they conceded that Fry was the brains behind their actions, and each knew that any challenge to that fact would be dealt with forcefully by Jack Pitt.

Turning back to Pitt, Fry shared his thoughts on the matter. "I'm thinking we need a place to hole up for the winter. It's already fall. We'll be up to our asses in snow before you know it.

This place looks like it might be just what the doctor ordered. It's damn sure isolated enough, and it looks like a bunch of farmers to me. If there's a rifle in every cabin down there, it wouldn't be enough to cause us any concern."

Pitt saw the wisdom in Fry's thinking. Ordinarily, his philosophy was simply to attack and destroy, but with the coming cold weather, the thought of holing up in a small settlement appealed to him. And this one was so far off the main trails that they could hardly expect any chance of outside help for the settlers when the time came to pillage it. He nodded his head in approval.

"Maybe they got a doctor," Trask groaned, feeling too sick and feverish to gawk at the collection of cabins in the valley. He had taken advantage of the pause to lie down against a tree, resting his wounded shoulder, which was woefully swollen and painful.

"Maybe he could chop that arm off fer ya," Mendel said and laughed. Several of the others laughed with him, totally devoid of compassion for their wounded comrade. "You could keep it to use as a backscratcher."

"To hell with the doctor," Wiley blustered. "Wonder if they got any women down there?" His question was answered with hoots of approval from several of the others.

"Quiet, dammit!" Fry ordered. "Let's get something straight right now. There ain't gonna be no killing and raping—at least, not right away." His words were met with groans of surprise from the men, and he waited for the protests to die down before explaining his decision. "We need a good, warm place to ride out the winter. This place looks as good as any to me. But if we go charging down there, killing and burning, a lot of 'em will get away—especially those on the other side of the river. Even if we killed all of 'em, then we wouldn't have anybody to do the work for us. That's why we're going down there peaceful-like. If we play our cards right, we just might have ourselves a nice, comfortable winter. When the snows close up these passes, we can do what we want. Nobody'll be able to get out of this valley to ride for help. Maybe come spring, things in Montana will cool off enough to hit the gold claims again."

"How the hell are we just gonna ride in and take over if we don't shoot a few of 'em?" Mendel asked. "What's gonna keep some of 'em from taking potshots at us?"

"They're gonna welcome us like saviors," Fry replied, grinning slyly, "because we'll be coming to save them from the Injuns." He paused to see if there were any more questions. When, in spite of the many puzzled expressions, no one spoke, he went on. "Now, let's get those uniforms out of the pack and get ready to give these poor folks some protection from the Injuns."

Stolen from a quartermaster's wagon, the uniforms were an odd assortment—a few garrison tunics, an officer's sword (which Fry strapped to his side), one pair of blue wool trousers that Hicks wore because he was the only one small enough to wear them, and a half-dozen campaign hats. The gang made a ragtag bunch of soldiers, but Fry thought the uniforms adequate to show at least some semblance of military bearing.

When they were all outfitted and ready to ride, Fry told them how they were to answer if questioned by the folks in the settlement. "It's best if you just keep your mouth shut and let me and Pitt do the talking. But if anybody asks, we're part of the Montana militia, and we've been chasing renegade Injuns." He paused, making up his story as he went along. "And we've been ordered to winter here to protect this settlement." He hesitated once more, looking from one face to another. His eyes narrowed as he said, "Now, boys, this might be a real sweet winter with no trouble a'tall if we all mind our manners—and nobody goes off half-cocked. If we play this thing right, we might see the other side of winter fat and sassy. Whaddaya say, boys?"

He was answered with nods and grunts of agreement from all the men. Clell Adams wanted to know what he was supposed to call him. "Captain Fry" was the answer.

"Cap'n it is, then," Clell chuckled, "but don't expect me to do no damn salutin'." This brought a laugh from the others.

"Hell," Pitt snorted, "the only time you ever

bring your hand up to your face is when you've got a drink of whiskey in it." His comment brought another round of chuckling.

"Or when you're a'pickin' your nose," Wiley added.

"All right, then," Fry said. "Let's go down and meet the good folks in the valley. And try to act like soldiers."

Horace Spratte looked up from his work to catch sight of a party of eight riders making its way slowly down the north ridge. Canyon Creek didn't get many visitors, especially this time of year, so Horace was naturally curious.

He and his wife, Effie, had found their way into the valley little more than a year before, having taken over the old Kendall place. They had started out from Council Bluffs with a party headed for Oregon, but Effie had come down with consumption, forcing them to drop out at Fort Laramie. It was late fall before Effie had been well enough to travel again, too late to continue on to Oregon. Luckily for them, they had met an old trapper and guide named Monk Grissom, who had offered to take them to Canyon Creek to wait out the winter.

The Sprattes had been welcomed in the valley, and, since there was a sturdy cabin available, they had found it convenient to settle there until the spring. It had concerned them somewhat that the Kendall homestead was available because of the Indian attack that had resulted in the deaths of John Kendall and his wife. But Reverend Lindstrom had assured them that the threat of Indian trouble was greatly reduced and should not be of concern.

John Kendall had been one of the original settlers to accompany Reverend Lindstrom to Canyon Creek. A tall, rawboned man, he had married a woman from the Shoshoni camp on the far side of the western ridge. They had had a son, Luke. In 1868, Chief Washakie had moved his people to a permanent reservation east of the Wind River Mountains. Not long after, the settlement had been hit with the only raid by hostile Indians it had ever experienced. John Kendall and his wife had both been slaughtered by the Ute raiding party that swept through the valley. The raiders had hit the Colefield place on their way out, killing Robert Mashburn, another of the original settlers. The boy, Luke, was away at the village of his mother's people on the reservation when his parents had been killed. When he returned to find that his parents were dead, his initial inclination had been to return to the Shoshoni village. Rufus Colefield, Robert's father-in-law, had persuaded the boy to remain in the valley and live with him and his now-widowed daughter, Katie. Luke had soon developed a strong bond with the old man and his daughter even though most folks in the valley had figured he would return to his mother's people. Since the Ute raid, there had been no more trouble with Indians.

Katie Mashburn's husband, Robert, the third victim of the Indian raid, was sorely missed in the community. The widow never talked about that dreadful day when the Utes had swept down on their homestead, and Reverend Lindstrom had told Effie that it was best not to bring up the subject. Effie, from her infrequent contact with Katie, would hardly have broached such a subject, anyway. Katie was a strange, lonely woman who kept pretty much to herself. Doing a man's work on the little patch of ground she and her father farmed, Katie never seemed to have time for visiting or socializing in general with the other women of the valley. And she was the only woman in Canyon Creek who constantly wore a pistol strapped around her waist. When Horace commented on it to Monk Grissom, Monk told him that Katie had taken to wearing it after the Utes killed her husband, vowing she'd never be caught without some protection again. According to Monk, Katie believed that if she had been armed on that day, she could have stood at her husband's side instead of hiding in a corner of the garden. Newcomers to Canyon Creek found the young woman with the sad face almost unapproachable. She preferred to keep to herself, mixing only with her father and Luke Kendall, the halfbreed boy who lived with them.

When spring came, Horace and Effie had decided to settle in the valley permanently in spite of the sad history associated with the prime piece of bottomland by the river. The little settlement hadn't grown much in the last few years, a fact that troubled Reverend Lindstrom, who still envisioned a proper town there someday. Monk Grissom speculated that the lack of growth was probably a contributing factor in their friendly relations with the Shoshoni village beyond the range of mountains to the west.

Now that the strangers were closer to the valley floor, Horace could see that they were not Indians, although the horses they drove before them looked like Indian ponies. Effie, just then noticing that Horace was staring out across the river, paused to see what had captured his attention. "What is it, Horace?" she asked, shielding her eyes with her hand as she strained to identify the riders. After a moment, when her husband did not answer, she spoke again. "Are they soldiers? Some of 'em's wearing army hats." She picked up her pan, half-filled with the last of the fall peas, and walked over beside Horace.

"I don't know," Horace said. "Ain't nobody I've ever seen before." For a brief moment, he considered going to the cabin to fetch his rifle but thought better of it. The men were on the other side of the river. Besides, they had never had cause to fear white visitors to their little valley. Why appear unfriendly by meeting strangers with a gun in hand? There were eight of them, anyway. He couldn't do much about it if they were hostile, so he stood watching as they crossed over the meadow and turned down the river. "Headed for the reverend's place, I reckon," Horace decided. When the riders reached a point directly across the river from where the Sprattes stood watching, the leader looked their way and gave them a brief wave of his hand. As they passed on by, the men following made no gestures but stared openly at the man and his wife.

"The one in front is sure settin' in a fancy saddle," Horace commented, noticing the high cantle and pommel of Simon Fry's Spanish saddle.

"One of 'em looks like he's got a bad arm," Effie remarked as the last of the riders passed from their view.

Not waiting for his wife to suggest it, Horace unhitched his mule from the plow, hopped on its back, and headed downriver to cross at the ford just above the church. By the time he reached Reverend Lindstrom's place, the strangers had already found the preacher working to repair a hole in the roof of the log structure that served as the valley's place of worship. As soon as he forded the river, Horace met Whitey Branch coming from the small gathering of men in front of the church.

"Soldiers," Whitey called out excitedly as Horace approached. He pulled up to talk. Ordinarily, Horace, like most folks in the valley, would have stopped and humored Whitey. The poor devil was a mite slow-witted. Some thought he had been kicked in the head by a mule when he was a boy. But Whitey had no family to attest to that, so nobody knew for sure. Sometimes a nuisance, but harmless and always friendly, he showed up at everybody's doorstep on a regular basis.

Horace was intent upon hearing the news of the valley's visitors firsthand, so he didn't even slow down when he passed Whitey, tossing a "Howdy, Whitey" at his disappointed neighbor and urging his mule up the riverbank. Horace found the reverend talking to two of the men while the others turned their horses out to graze on the ample valley grass.

"Here's another one of our citizens now," Reverend Lindstrom said as Horace rode up. "This here's Horace Spratte. Him and his wife live up the river a piece." He waited for Horace to slide off his mule. "Horace, this is Captain Fry of the . . ." He turned back to Fry. "What was it?"

"The Montana Territorial Militia," Fry answered. "Pleased to meet you, Mr. Spratte."

"Seen you go by my place," Horace replied, offering his hand.

Lindstrom went on. "Captain Fry tells me that he's been sent out here to give us protection from the Indians."

This puzzled Horace. "Protection? We ain't had no trouble with the Injuns."

"Well, you might have some before the winter's over," Fry replied. "'There's been some bad raiding north of here, and not too far north at that."

This wasn't pleasant news to Horace. "Is that a fact? Who was it? Bannocks? Koutenai?"

"Both of 'em," Fry quickly replied, "and Snakes, too." He glanced at Pitt beside him, and Jack nodded silent conformation.

"Snakes?" Horace couldn't believe his ears. "Are you sure? We ain't had no trouble with Chief Washakie's band of Shoshonis since I've been living here." He looked at Lindstrom for conformation.

The reverend nodded and said, "That's what I was telling the captain here. We ain't had no trouble with the Snakes."

"Well, I guess you got some now," Fry replied, getting a mite testy at being questioned. "I know damn well that Trask over there has a Snake arrow in him, and we damned sure took care of the party that done it." He started to say more, but Jack Pitt's warning glance reminded him to hold his temper. "I reckon this bunch must have been renegades," he allowed, his tone taking on a friendly quality once more. "At any rate, we've been ordered to operate out of this valley this winter."

Reverend Lindstrom was pleased that his little congregation had been selected for special attention. "It's been over fifteen years since I brought the first of these people over the divide to this valley. This is the first time anybody outside the valley has cared one way or the other what happened to us."

"Well, we've been spread mighty thin," Fry responded, building on the lie. "But I reckon it's high time we got some men over here to protect you folks."

Horace was busy eyeing the six soldiers now taking their ease near the corner of the church building. After a moment, he turned back to Simon Fry. "For soldiers, you boys sure ain't got much in the way of uniforms."

Fry was quick to answer. "We don't put too much stock in spit and polish when we're fighting Injuns. And like I said, we're not regular army. We're volunteers in the Montana Territorial Militia." Seeing that the lack of uniforms had been noticed, he felt it the opportune moment to broach another subject, one closer to his concern. "Funds are mighty scarce for my brave men, who've left their families and homes to take care of the Injun problem so folks like you can live in peace. But the other settlements we've been quartered in have been generous in sharing food and grain with us."

Lindstrom and Spratte exchanged brief glances. After a long moment, the reverend finally spoke. "I guess I speak for the folks of Canyon Creek when I say I'm sure we can provide some food and grain to help you out." Being a Christian man by faith and occupation, Lindstrom began to warm more toward the idea of sharing with these good soldiers the longer he thought about it. "Of course, we'll be glad to help," he decided. "Won't we, Horace?"

"I reckon," Horace answered but not with the enthusiasm now displayed on the preacher's face. "Maybe we can talk about it during prayer meeting tomorrow night," he suggested.

"We'll need a place to set up camp," Fry said.

"We could use a doctor, too," Pitt put in. "We got a wounded man that needs some lookin' after."

"I'm sorry. We ain't got a doctor, but I'll be glad to take a look at him—help him if I can." Lindstrom started to say something more, when he heard the sound of horses approaching from behind the church. He turned to see Rufus Colefield round the corner, followed by the half-breed boy, Luke Kendall. Rufus hopped down and, handing his reins to Luke, strode over to meet the soldiers while the boy stood back a respectable distance and listened to the men talk of supposed Shoshoni renegades.

Rufus Colefield was enthusiastic about any military presence in the little valley, even if there had been no trouble from the Indians in a long time. He welcomed Fry and Pitt warmly, although his eagerness to receive them waned somewhat when the conversation returned to the topic of provisions for the eight men. He was somewhat more helpful when Fry repeated his need for a base of operations.

"You could set up camp in Jed Springer's old place," Rufus suggested. "There's a cabin already built, with a good fireplace, and it ain't no more than a quarter of a mile from my place."

"That's right," Lindstrom said and explained to Fry that Jed Springer, an old trapper who had settled in the valley, had been killed some time back. "Jed got liquored up one night and fell off his horse—broke his neck."

"That just might do at that," Fry said and winked at Pitt. "Yes, sir, that sounds like the perfect place to set up my headquarters."

Rufus beamed his pleasure at having suggested the place. "We can show you how to get there, can't we, Luke?"

The boy said nothing; the only indication that he had heard Rufus was a slight nod of his head. He found the militiamen a curious lot, with the nondescript items of military clothing—a few hats, a shirt or two. He remembered the soldiers he had seen two years before, when he had lived with his mother's people for a while and journeyed to Fort Laramie for the treaty talks. Those soldiers had all been dressed in identical blue uniforms and rode in military file. Not like these men, sprawled now on the ground while their horses pulled up grass from the reverend's pasture.

Luke gave the horses a longer look. He was especially interested in the fancy hand-tooled Spanish saddle on the captain's horse. The initials *SF* were tooled on the skirt. Luke had never seen such a fancy saddle before. Aside from the eight saddled horses and four packhorses, there were eight more that looked to be Indian ponies. While Rufus talked to the two soldiers and Reverend Lindstrom, Luke moved over toward the grazing animals. They were Shoshoni ponies—he was certain of that. One in particular, a spirited little buckskin, looked just like one that Little Otter treasured. He had heard the soldiers tell of a fight with a party of renegade Snake Raiders, but he found it hard to believe that any of Chief Washakie's band had been involved. He had been to the Shoshoni camp recently enough to know that there were no such renegades. Chief Washakie would not tolerate it. Maybe, like most white men, they didn't know one Indian from another. Luke decided that he didn't like the looks of these so-called soldiers. Though young in years, in spite of Rufus Colefield's open acceptance of the strangers, Luke Kendall relied upon his own sense of judgment.

Katie Mashburn filled the basin with water from the wooden bucket beside the back door. To bring it to a comfortable temperature, she added a bit more of the boiling water from the kettle hanging in the fireplace and tested it with her hand. Throughout the summer, she had bathed down at the river after working in the field. Today there was a definite chill in the air, so she had decided to take her bath in the cabin since her pa and Luke had ridden over to the reverend's place. Whitey Branch had passed the cabin an hour before with news that some militiamen had come to Canyon Creek. Whitey had appointed himself as the unofficial town crier of the settlement, and Katie knew that he had a tendency to exaggerate on occasion. Her pa had decided to see for himself, so he'd saddled his horse and, taking the boy with him, had gone to gawk at the soldiers.

When the water felt right, Katie sat down and pulled her boots off. Laying them aside, she sat still and listened for a few minutes. There was not a sound to be heard outside the crude log house. Still she listened. There was nothing but the sound of the clock on the mantel, its constant ticking tediously counting off the moments of the day. It was a small clock to be so loud, or maybe its ticking merely seemed especially loud when contrasted with the heavy silence inside the cabin. It was a melancholy sound that seemed intent upon reminding her of the ticking away of her youth. It suddenly struck her that she could not recall a time when she had been really young—childhood, maybe—but never a young lady. But then, out here no one was a young lady, it seemed. You were either a child or an old woman, and you went from one to the other overnight. Although she perceived herself as an older woman, none but her own eyes saw her that way. In the short span of her years, she had known enough hardship and pain to age her in mind as well as in spirit.

Sighing, she got up from the chair, unbuckled

the wide leather belt, and laid her heavy pistol aside, making sure it was within easy reach if needed in a hurry. Ever mindful of that horrible day when they had been suddenly surprised by a Ute war party, she did not feel comfortable unless the pistol was handy. Her eyes lingered a few moments longer on the Colt revolver that Monk Grissom had acquired for her by means she was discreet enough not to question. He would only venture to say that the army had more than they needed in a large shipment of Colt's new model. Called the *Peacemaker*, it was a vast improvement over the single-action revolver she had worn before. She had never had occasion to use either weapon, but she had promised herself that there would be no hesitation to do so if it became necessary.

Katie had long ago decided that she could count on no one but herself, although in recent months she had begun to rely on Luke. Rufus, her father, was a hardworking man but not a brave one. He had run when the Indians came that day. He couldn't help it, she had decided, and had forgiven him for it, although she knew that the poor little man had never forgiven himself for his actions on that day. What could he have done against a raiding party of that size? It would have been a foolish waste of life if he had attempted to stop them. Still, it might have made a difference if he had stood against them with her husband. *Who am I to judge anyone?* she asked herself. *I was hiding in the corn rows.* Her hand dropped to rest upon the handle of her Colt .45. *Next time, it'll be different.*

"So, here you are, Katie-girl, dressed like a man, doing a man's labor, taking care of your pa instead of the other way around—and raising John Kendall's bastard son." As soon as she said it, she felt ashamed of herself. She knew that young Luke Kendall's mother, a full-blooded Shoshoni, had been as much a married woman as she was. And Luke was a good boy, although he was a handful sometimes. But he was a bright youngster as well. She had seen that right off; otherwise, she would not have agreed to look after the boy after his folks had been killed. With Robert gone, she and her father had needed an extra hand around the place, anyway.

Realizing that if she dawdled much longer, she would need to heat more water, Katie took off her shirt and trousers and began to clean some of the field grime from her body. After she had dried herself, she picked up the mirror from the shelf. Holding it so the crack down the middle was not in the way, she took a serious look at the image reflected back to her. What she saw in the mirror did little to encourage her. She could not honestly say that she was homely, but there were wrinkles and worry lines around her eyes and nose that testified to her many hours in the sun and the certain toll life on the frontier took on all women. "What the hell do I care?" she blurted and put the mirror down.

When she had put on some clean clothes, she

walked to the door of the cabin and threw the
gray bathwater out. She had already started fixing supper when she heard horses approaching.
Picking up her pistol, she went to the door to
make sure it was her father and the boy.

Rufus Colefield was anxious to tell his daughter the good news. He left the horses for Luke
to put away while he bounded through the
cabin door to find Katie. "Maybe you can stop
worrying so much about Injuns now," he
started. "The territorial governor sent a militia
unit to winter in the valley."

Katie paused when hearing this. "Territorial
governor? I didn't know there was such a person out here."

"Well, I reckon there is, 'cause the captain
said that was who sent him and his soldiers."

"Really? How many soldiers?"

"There's eight of 'em, but one of 'em's bad
wounded," Rufus replied. "They're gonna set
up camp right downriver from us in Jed Springer's old place. Me and Luke showed 'em where
it was."

Katie turned to face her father. "Eight?" she
asked incredulously. "Is that all? Are there
more coming?"

"Reckon not. Leastways, they didn't say so."
Seeing the skeptical look in his daughter's eyes,
he quickly added, "But they all look like they
could handle theirselves—except that one with
the arrowhead in his shoulder."

This piqued Katie's attention right away. "Arrowhead?" she asked. "Where did they have a run-in with Indians? What kind of Indians? Did they say?"

"They said Shoshoni," Rufus replied, casting a sideways glance to see if Luke was in earshot before he continued. "The captain said there had been a lot of Snake raiding parties between here and the Wind River Mountains. Said they had run down a bunch of 'em a couple of days ago, and that's where that feller picked up the arrow."

The story didn't make sense to Katie. The Shoshoni had been peaceful for a long time now, and there had been no incidents that she was aware of that might have destroyed that peace— certainly no conflict between the folks of Canyon Creek and Chief Washakie's band. Young Luke Kendall's presence in the valley had been an important link in the friendship between the Shoshonis and the white settlers, since his mother had been a member of the tribe. It didn't hurt that Monk Grissom had a cabin in the valley, either. Monk had been a friend of the old chief's for a long time. For these reasons, Katie wasn't comfortable with reports of Shoshoni raiding parties in the area. It just didn't make sense. When Luke came into the cabin after taking care of the horses, she questioned him on the subject.

"You heard what the soldiers said? That the Shoshoni are raiding?"

Luke nodded.

"What have you heard when you visit your uncle, Angry Bear?"

"There has been no talk of war parties on the reservation," the boy replied. "My uncle told me that Washakie is disappointed that the white man's government has not provided the tools and seed they promised, or the help to breed better animals, and the many other things to help our people. But there is no talk of war. I don't think the soldiers know what they're talking about."

Katie studied Luke's face for a moment, considering his opinion, one that agreed with her first reaction to her father's story. She had learned in the short time that Luke had lived with them that the boy was especially astute for a youth of fourteen. With Katie's blessing, Luke was allowed the freedom to go to the Shoshoni village to visit his relatives whenever he chose. Since he had just returned from a visit only two days before, Katie felt he would surely have learned of any recent war parties. The boy was honest to a fault, so she never doubted anything he told her. John Kendall had never discouraged his son from spending time with his mother's people. To the contrary, he had believed that it was good for the boy to know the way of the Shoshoni. As a result, Katie now saw more Indian than white in Luke.

"I guess we'll just have to wait and see about these soldiers, but I think you're probably right.

I don't believe the Shoshonis have been raiding white folks.'' She reached out and smoothed down a wild shock of hair on the boy's head, smiled, and said, ''Sit down at the table while I fix supper, and we'll work some more on your reading this evening.''

A silent observer to the interaction between his daughter and the half-breed boy, Rufus Colefield realized that the only time he ever saw Katie smile was when she was talking with Luke.

Chapter 2

Over two thousand miles east of Canyon Creek, on a hot July morning, young Jim Culver held the plow steady with one hand while he took the reins from behind his neck with the other. "I've been turning that rock over from one side of the furrow to the other for two years. I'm tired of looking at it." Pulling back hard on the reins, he called out softly, "Ho, Henry, ho—ho back." When the mule continued its steady pace down the row, Jim's voice took on more authority, and he jerked back on the reins with force. "Ho, dammit, Henry, you old, wore-out bag of bones!" Nearing the end of the row and the shade of three tall poplars at the edge of the field, the mule decided it more sensible to pause in the shade. Knowing it useless to argue with the cantankerous old mule, Jim decided to let Henry have his way. Leaving the mule standing in the shade, he walked back up the row. Setting his feet solidly under him, he bent his knees and got a firm grip on the sizable rock. Gritting his teeth and exhaling loudly, he straightened up, bringing the rock with him. Then, carefully placing one foot after the other, he carried it to the edge of the field.

He took off his hat and squinted up at the sun—close to noon, he figured, and he still had about a half-acre left to plow. He paused for a few minutes to let the warm sun caress his face. It felt good. He turned toward the south field, where he could just see Stephen following along behind Red, the three-year-old mule their pa had bought last spring. *He's almost at the end of the field*, Jim thought. He glanced back at Henry and shook his head slowly. That was the way of things when you were the youngest. You plowed with the old mule.

"I don't give a damn," he announced to the mule, which studied him now in mournful contemplation. "I ain't staying around this place much longer." In the past two years, there hadn't been a day that passed without his either saying it or thinking it. But this day was different, he told himself. Today was his birthday—twenty-one years old. It was long past time for a man to set out to find his place in the world. It might make it a little harder for John and Stephen, but they seemed more in tune with the farm than he was. He was more like Clay, his eldest brother, who had left the farm eight years ago. John and Stephen could handle it, even without much help from Pa—and there hadn't been much help from him for over a year. He had never quite recovered from a bout of pneumonia a year ago this past December.

Raymond Culver never said much to his youngest son about the itch that some men have for the horizon. But he could see it in Jim's eyes whenever the boy looked with longing at the sun setting in the west. And there was no denying that of the three sons still at home, Jim was the one most at home in the woods, hunting any critter he could find. Raymond had lost a son and a daughter to the western frontier already. Still, he would never tell Jim not to go. He would never kill the boy's spirit, although it would be hard to see him go. It had been eight years since Jim's brother, Clay, had left for Dakota territory—eight years with only an occasional word—from places like Fort Benton, Fort Laramie, and Fort Hall, and once even from Fort Lincoln—to let them know he was still alive. Raymond Culver was resigned to the fact that he would never see Clay again, and, with his health failing so rapidly, he might probably say the same in regard to Jim if the boy was determined to leave.

"Come on, Henry." Jim plopped his hat back on his head and grabbed the reins. "Let's get this field done. I've got some plans tonight. I need something pretty to look at after staring at your hind end all day." He took a firm grip with both hands as the plow took hold, leaning hard to his left to compensate for Henry's tendency to stray. "John will be out here looking at these furrows," he reminded the indifferent mule.

At a little past seven o'clock that evening, Jim guided his horse to the end of the long hitching post beside the Virginia Hotel and tied on next to a bay gelding. There were only a few horses tied at the rail. Most of the guests were arriving by carriage, the men's fancy shoes and the ladies' frilly dresses protected from the dusty street by a scarlet carpet leading from the cobblestone curb to the entrance of the hotel. Fredericksburg was determined to demonstrate her elegance as the gentlemen and their ladies came out to celebrate the annual Summer Cotillion.

Having no illusions whatsoever that he belonged to this handsome throng, Jim glanced down at the engraved invitation in his hand as he entered the building. He couldn't help but smile. No Culver had ever been invited to attend one of these grand affairs. John and Stephen had both advised against attending the dance, but Jim had insisted on going. After all, it was his birthday. Fredericksburg's high society might just as well provide him with a celebration. His friend Alan Cranston had presented him with an invitation and all but dared him to come. Jim was sure it was thought to be a great joke, but he had decided to call Alan's bluff. So here he stood, in clean homespun shirt and woolen morning coat, looking for all the world like the country bumpkin.

Smiling graciously and bowing his head politely to each couple as they entered the hotel ballroom, a tall, thin doorman welcomed Fredericksburg's elite. Knowing most of the guests, and recognizing pedigree in those he did not, he opened the door wide as the luminaries of local society traipsed by in their finery. Jim stood off to the side of the lobby, watching the parade of silks and satins for a few minutes, hoping to spot Alan Cranston. It was quite a show, he had to admit, the ladies in their ballroom gowns, on the arms of their escorts, laughing and chattering to friends and acquaintances—most of them discarding their light evening wraps as soon as possible in order to better display their gowns.

There were quite a few unaccompanied gentlemen as well, young and dashing in their dark formal wear. Several were army officers, no longer regarded as forces of occupation but as part of the social scene of a city they had once bloodied in battle. The war had been over for nine years, but Jim still found it ironic that the town so embraced the army it had once hated.

Nearly half an hour passed while Jim stood in one corner of the lobby. The last of the arrivals had passed through the doors, and the first lively strains of a reel drifted through to the lobby. He had to assume that Alan and his sister, Violet, had come earlier. As the call for the first dance was heard, he glanced back to see the doorman step inside and pull the doors closed behind him. Taking the invitation from his coat pocket, Jim made his way across the carpeted lobby.

The tall, stern-faced doorman turned when he heard the door open behind him. Immediately flashing his welcoming smile, he quickly extinguished it upon encountering the homespun attire of the strapping young man standing before him, invitation in hand. "May I help you, sir?" he offered in skeptical coolness.

Jim favored him with a wide, friendly smile. "No, thanks. I don't need any help. I'm just going to the dance." He handed the invitation over and prepared to step around the doorman.

"Sir, this is the annual Summer Cotillion, invited guests only." Without looking at it, he held Jim's invitation as if it were a piece of dried manure. The young man was clearly out of his element.

His friendly smile still firmly in place, Jim said, "That's a fact. That's why I just handed you my invitation."

The doorman was about to protest when a voice behind him intervened. "Well, by damn, I didn't think you'd come," Alan Cranston called out as he hurried to greet his friend. "Charles, this man is my guest."

Genuinely astonished, Charles turned to face Alan. "Why, of course, Mr. Cranston." He stepped aside while the two young men shook hands, and Alan, grinning from ear to ear, pounded Jim on the shoulder. By the expression on his face, it was apparent that Charles still found the situation offensive to his nostrils.

Brushing past the exasperated doorman, Alan took Jim by the arm and led him away toward a table across the room. "Come on, Jim, and I'll introduce you to my friends."

Alan led him to a large round table close by the dance floor, where a young lady sat with three couples. All eyes at the table, as well as most in the entire ballroom, were upon Jim as he crossed the floor. He was already beginning to have misgivings about his decision to attend this highly sophisticated social function. It had seemed like a splendid lark when Alan had first suggested it. Now he looked about him, unable to find one solitary soul who wasn't dressed in formal attire.

Jim looked around the table at the amused smiles that greeted him as Alan introduced him to his friends. "This is Jim Culver," Alan announced, beaming his pleasure. "This is the fellow I was telling you about. He literally rescued me from perishing in the deep woods on the Rapidan."

Jim nodded to each one as they were introduced. Smiling warmly, he responded to Alan's praise. "I just happened along at the right time. I doubt that Alan would have perished."

"I'm not so sure," Alan protested. He turned to explain to his friends. "My horse stepped in a muskrat hole and broke his leg. He went down so quickly that I couldn't get my boot out of the stirrup." He paused to make sure everyone understood the gravity of the situation. "Well, I ended up with my left leg firmly pinned beneath about twelve hundred pounds of horse, and I couldn't persuade the hard-headed nag to get off of me." He grinned as he turned toward Jim.

"Then along came Jim from out of nowhere and rescued me."

The four young ladies at the table all applauded, making Jim feel extremely foolish. But in spite of his embarrassment, he tried to smile politely as Alan directed him to a seat next to his sister, Violet. Alan went on to tell his friends that he had come to know Jim over the course of the summer, when he had occasion to inspect some farmland that his father was negotiating with the bank to buy. Jim had not only given him some excellent advice on the value of the land in question, but he had turned out to be a first-rate woodsman. "I think Jim is more at home in the forest than many of the animals that live there," he said.

The party at the table seemed friendly enough to Jim at first, asking him many questions about himself and his home near the banks of the Rapidan. As he answered each question, looking into the amused faces that studied him, it began to dawn upon him that Alan might have invited him as a curiosity to entertain his friends. It could be that he was wrong, but the more inane the questions became, the more convinced he was that he was a pawn to Alan's intention to display his backwoods acquaintance. While the idea irritated him, he decided to ignore the open rudeness Alan's friends displayed and make an effort to enjoy the dance. After all, he decided, it was his birthday, and he had been determined to enjoy himself.

When a lull finally came in the conversation, he turned his chair to watch the dancers as they whirled around the floor. Two of the couples at the table got to their feet to join in the next dance as another reel was called. "Why don't you give it a try, Jim?" Alan suggested. "Violet is fairly accomplished. She could show you the steps."

Out of the corner of his eye, Jim caught the stern frown Violet aimed at her brother. If looks had steel points, Jim allowed that Alan would have been pierced through the brain with that one. "Well, that would be mighty generous of Violet," he said, glancing at the now-passive face of Alan's sister, "but I guess I'll just watch." The look of relief on the young lady's face was hard to disguise. She was soon radiant again, when a young lieutenant, properly dashing in his dress uniform, invited her to dance. Jim had to admit they made a handsome couple as they swirled to the strains of a waltz. The lieutenant returned to "borrow" Violet several more times during the evening until the band called a short intermission, whereupon the two disappeared through the doors to the veranda.

His mind now made up that he had made a giant mistake in coming to the affair, Jim decided it best to take his leave during the intermission. He figured his entertainment value was about exhausted, anyway. The others at the table were already diverting the conversation inward, to the exclusion of the bumpkin. *Might as well finish the punch and this dinky little piece of cake, though.*

Alan seemed genuinely disappointed when Jim told him he was going, but he made no real effort to dissuade him. Saying a quick but polite good-bye to the others seated at the table, Jim nodded once more to Alan, then took his leave. Feeling relieved to be done with his only venture into the world of Fredericksburg high society, he made his way to the entrance, grinning at the dour face of the tall, skinny old man still standing by the door.

The cool night air felt like a tonic to his lungs, and he filled them, breathing in deeply to flush out the scent of perfume. He walked around to the side of the hotel where he had left his horse. The patient Morgan stallion raised his head and whinnied softly when he saw his master approach. Still absorbing the refreshing chill of the evening, Jim stood at the rail and scratched the horse's forelock while he reflected back on the hours just spent in the company of Alan Cranston and his fancy friends. "Time would have been better spent in the woods coon hunting, Toby," he told his horse as strains of a lively tune from inside the ballroom faintly floated on the chilly air, announcing the end of the intermission. As if suddenly feeling trapped, he reached up, undid his tie, and pulled it off.

With a sigh of relief, he prepared to step up into the saddle, when he thought he heard something in the darkness. He paused to listen.

Then he was sure of it. He had heard something. It was a girl's voice, and it had come from the rear corner of the building. Thinking nothing of it, he stepped up on Toby and backed the obedient animal away from the rail. He was just about to give the horse a nudge with his heels when another sound stopped him, and he strained to listen. It was the girl's voice again, but this time there was a definite tone of alarm in it. He turned Toby toward the rear of the hotel, slowly walking the animal toward the sounds in the darkness.

"No. I mean it, sir," Jim heard the girl say as he silently approached the figures he could now make out in the deep shadows. "I think we'd better go back to the dance now."

Her escort grabbed her arm, holding her against the side of the building. "I think we'd better stay out here a while longer," he stated confidently. "You know you want the same thing I do. You've been swishing that little tail of yours in front of my nose all evening." Before she could protest again, he pushed his body against her, forcing her up against the side of the hotel. She fought to keep his mouth from finding hers, but he was much too powerful for her frail attempts.

Close enough now to clearly see the couple, Jim recognized the tall lieutenant who had monopolized Violet's evening and realized that the lady in distress was Alan's sister. He could also clearly see that she was earnest in her protests and was desperately trying to escape the young soldier's mauling. So intent upon his desire to have his way with the young girl, the lieutenant was unaware of the man on the horse directly behind him.

Jim took but a moment more to assess the situation before taking action. Unhurriedly, but with no loss of urgency, he untied the long rawhide whip he carried on his saddle. Remaining in the saddle, he let the coils fall loosely to the ground, relaxing the muscles in his arm so that he could feel the weight of the knotted end as it danced along the hard-baked dirt. Then, in one swift motion, he cocked his arm and cracked the whip smartly. The sound of the rawhide ripping the chill night air was as loud as a rifle shot, so loud that it caused Toby to flinch. The crack of the whip was followed almost instantaneously by a cry of pain from the young officer as the rawhide knot burned a hole in the seat of his pants.

Whirling about in response to the pain in his rear, in a confused state of anger and surprise, the lieutenant reached for his revolver, only to realize he wasn't wearing it. Still confused for a moment and thinking that he had been shot, he was desperately trying to understand what had happened. When he was able to realize that the dark figure on the horse was holding a whip and not a gun, rage overcame the panic of moments before. Forgetting the terrified young girl still huddled against the wall, he started to charge toward the man on horseback. He had taken no more than a step when Jim stopped him cold, laying a welt across the officer's neck that knocked him off his feet.

Jim pulled lightly on the reins, causing Toby to sidestep around to a position behind the lieutenant, who was now on his hands and knees. "Go on back inside now, Violet," Jim directed, his voice calm and deliberate. Frightened and tearful, she did as she was told, almost stumbling in her haste to reach the safety of the lighted terrace. Jim returned his attention to the man at his horse's feet.

"You rebel swine," the soldier spat, enraged by his humiliation. "I'll kill you for this. You're a dead man!" He started to get up on his feet.

Jim didn't speak, preferring to let his whip talk for him. It being his opinion that the brash young officer was in need of a good whipping for his assault on Alan's sister, Jim proceeded to administer the punishment. He snapped his whip around the officer's ankles and jerked him off his feet again. Then he methodically tattooed the unfortunate soldier's back and buttocks with a series of stinging stripes that would take some time in healing. Satisfied that the lady's honor had been avenged, he left the lieutenant cowering in a fetal position and pointed Toby toward home.

Stephen Culver looked up from the harness he was mending when he heard the dogs barking.

He immediately turned his gaze toward the river and the shallow ford near the corner of the north pasture. *Well, here they come,* he thought and laid the harness aside. He counted four mounted soldiers led by two officers and a civilian, and they were heading straight for the house. "Pa! John!" he called out. "Soldiers coming!" He got up and walked to the edge of the yard. In a few minutes, his father and brother emerged from the barn and walked over to join him.

"They didn't waste no time, did they?" John said, shielding his eyes against the morning sun with his hand.

"I didn't expect they would," his father answered. He had expected the sheriff early that morning, so he had sent Jim off before sunup to lay up in the woods for a while until things cooled off. He was mildly surprised to see the detachment of soldiers, although he might have known it was a possibility. Jim had recounted the entire incident when he came in the night before. Raymond knew there would most likely be some ramifications as a result. But he figured at most Sheriff Thompkins would ride out to hear Jim's side, and that would be the end of it. He also figured that if Jim wasn't here, Barney Thompkins wouldn't put himself to the trouble of trying to find him.

"Ol' Barney's got himself quite an escort," Stephen commented. The two brothers and their pa stood waiting by the fence for the party to get within hailing distance.

"Well, Barney," Raymond Culver called out as the detachment pulled up to the fence, "things must be pretty dangerous in these parts if you need that much protection to come visit."

"Morning, Raymond," Sheriff Thompkins replied. He had known Raymond Culver since a long time before the war. It was obvious that he didn't enjoy his business with his old acquaintance on this morning. "We come to see Jim. He got into a little scrape with the lieutenant here last night."

"It was a little more than a scrape, Mr. Culver," one of the officers interrupted. He wore a captain's bars. "Your son made an attempt on the life of an officer in the United States Army." He glanced briefly at the lieutenant beside him. "I'm not going to stand for any bleeding-heart rebels attacking my men."

Thompkins waited patiently for the captain to finish before calmly continuing. "Well, that's one side of it, Raymond. Is Jim about? I'd like to hear his side of it."

"If Jim had'a tried to kill that soldier, I reckon he'd be dead," Stephen blurted.

"Hush up, son." Raymond quickly silenced him. Turning his gaze on the lieutenant, he asked, "Is this fellow the one you say Jim attacked?"

The lieutenant flushed scarlet, although not to the point where the dark red welt on his neck was disguised. "Yeah," Thompkins replied. "This here's Lieutenant Ebersole."

"Well, he don't look to be in too bad a shape to me," Raymond said. Directing his comments solely to Thompkins, he went on. "Barney, what are you bringing all these soldiers out here for? Is Fredericksburg under martial law again? Jim told me exactly what happened last night. Your fancy lieutenant here tried to force himself on a young lady, and Jim just gave him a little whipping for it. It was lucky for her that Jim come along when he did."

"That's a damn lie!" Lieutenant Ebersole blurted. "The lady and I were taking a rest from the dance, and your son attacked me without warning."

Again, Thompkins waited for the lieutenant's outburst to end before continuing. "That's one side of it, Raymond. I'd like to hear from Jim now."

"Jim ain't here. He cut out this morning. Don't know where he was heading. Besides, I just told you what happened, just like he told me, and you've known Jim long enough to know he don't lie."

Thompkins frowned his disappointment. Plainly, he was hoping to settle the issue between the two parties right then and there and let that be the end of it. That might have been possible if Jim was there. Now he feared the lieutenant was going to demand that something be done about it. One glance at the faces of the two officers confirmed his suspicions, but he made an attempt to defuse the situation. "I don't reckon there's much to do about it since Jim ain't here." This he directed toward the captain. "Raymond's right; there don't seem to be much harm done, just a little fuss between two young fellows. Probably best to just forget about it."

"Like hell it is," the captain fired back. "We're not going to pass this off as some schoolyard fight between two little boys. If you think I went to all the trouble to ride out here just to say 'boys will be boys,' you're sadly mistaken. One of my officers was attacked. If I let this go unpunished, it'll send a message to every other hot-headed rebel around here."

"Why, you pompous son of a . . ."

That was as far as John got before his father silenced him with a firm hand on his arm, holding him back. At the same time, Raymond Culver shot a warning glance at his other son. When he was satisfied that John and Stephen would contain their anger, he again calmly addressed Sheriff Thompkins. "Barney, I understand that these soldiers are upset over what happened last night. But I think it's pretty plain that it didn't have nothing to do with the Union army being unwelcome in our country. What it boils down to is your young lieutenant there not knowing how to treat a lady, and him and Jim got into a tussle over it. Looks like to me, it's his word against Jim's. What did the young lady say about it?"

"I don't rightly know," Thompkins confessed. "Her momma put her on the early train to Richmond this morning."

"Well, that don't help matters much, does it?" He looked up at the captain. "Jim's gone, too. I don't know when he'll be back. I don't see that there's anything we can do about it. Might as well let it go."

"That's about the way I see it," Sheriff Thompkins concurred, looking over at the captain for his reaction.

The look in Captain Thomas Boyd's eyes told Raymond Culver that the officer was embroiled in the middle of a mission he wished he had not embarked upon. In fact, Boyd was beginning to suspect that maybe Culver's version of the incident might actually come closer to the truth. Trent Ebersole was known to be quite the rakehell around town. It would not surprise Boyd to learn that the lieutenant had forced his affections upon a young lady. The most expeditious thing to do would be to call it a closed incident. Culver was right. Ebersole wasn't really injured beyond his pride. On the other hand, the captain was reluctant to ignore the lieutenant's charges for fear it might give his men the impression that their captain did not back them in disputes with the civilian population. He didn't like it, but he felt he had no choice. "I'm afraid this isn't the end of it, Sheriff." He looked back at Raymond Culver. "We'll be back, Mr. Culver. If you're smart, you'll tell your son to report to either my headquarters or to Sheriff Thompkins. I promise you he'll get a fair hearing, but he'll have to answer for his actions."

Raymond's face did not hide his disgust at the captain's statement. "A fair hearing, huh? A military hearing, you mean." He looked up at the smirk on the lieutenant's face, then back at Thompkins, who shook his head in a helpless gesture. He took one step backward and said, "I reckon you've stated your business." He nodded toward the river. "There's a shallow ford beyond that stand of oak trees. That's the quickest way for you to get off my land."

Approximately one hundred yards upriver from the stand of oaks that his father had pointed out, young Jim Culver knelt in a clump of wild myrtle, watching the confrontation at his father's front gate. Too far away to determine what was being said, he could still guess how the meeting had concluded. He had seen that posture in his father many times when Raymond Culver was not pleased with something— taking a step backward and standing firmly in a wide stance as if ready to fight. It was easy to assume that the soldiers were not going to let it go. Jim had always felt responsible for his actions. For that reason, he had argued, although briefly, when his father had told him to leave that morning. Now he felt that he must take responsibility for the whipping he had given the lieutenant. He feared that the army might somehow seek to punish his father for something he had done. His mind made up, he backed out of the myrtle and walked back to his horse.

*　　*　　*

Captain Boyd leaned forward on his horse's neck to stay in the saddle as the red roan scrambled up the riverbank. A moment later, he was obliged to rein his mount to a sudden stop as soon as it had gained level ground. Waiting on horseback squarely in the middle of the narrow path before him, was a young man with a Winchester cradled casually across his arms.

"Whoa!" Boyd called out as the sheriff and the others pushed up behind him. The thickness of the brush and saplings on either side of the path made it difficult to spread out, a fact that Boyd noted. *He picked a good place to face us. They're all jammed up behind me.* The lieutenant and Sheriff Thompkins tried to force their mounts up as close to Boyd as they could manage, but the brush made it impossible to flank him.

"I guess you'd be looking for me," Jim said. He looked beyond the captain and nodded his head. "Sheriff Thompkins," he acknowledged.

"Howdy, Jim," Thompkins answered, not waiting for Boyd to speak. "I reckon you know what we're about."

"I reckon," Jim replied. Toby stamped nervously in the presence of the other horses.

"It would help if you'd back that horse up a little so we could all get outta the river," Thompkins said.

Jim smiled. "Let's talk a bit first." He turned his attention back to Boyd. "What can I do for you, Captain?"

Boyd didn't care for the position he found himself in. Jim might have found the one place where he could hold all seven of them at bay. He didn't want to suggest this to Jim. He just hoped those behind him realized their vulnerability and refrained from doing anything foolish. He would be the first one to get a bullet from that Winchester cradled in Jim's arms.

"Mr. Culver," Boyd stated, "we're obliged to take you in for questioning on the incident at the Virginia Hotel last evening." He hastened to add, "At this point, it's just for questioning, but there are charges against you that have to be addressed."

Jim listened patiently while also keeping an eye on the lieutenant, who was struggling with his horse in an effort to push up to a better position behind Boyd. "Let's address 'em right here," Jim replied. "What are the charges?"

"You are charged with assaulting Lieutenant Ebersole."

"All I did was keep that fancy-pants behind you from forcing himself on a lady. I'da been a poor excuse for a man if I hadn't. As far as you taking me in, I ain't going anywhere with you, now or any other time. You've got the truth of the matter now, and I consider it closed." He started backing Toby slowly away while keeping a sharp eye on the captain.

Boyd was somewhat at a loss for words. He had not expected outright disobedience to a representative of the United States government. He was about to protest Jim's stance on the issue, but the shot rang out before he could speak. The events that took place in the next few seconds would greatly alter the course of two lives and directly affect many more.

During the discussion between Jim and Captain Boyd, Lieutenant Ebersole had slowly eased his revolver from its holster. When Jim started backing away, Ebersole saw his chance. He suddenly shoved Boyd aside and fired at Jim. The shot caught Jim in the left shoulder. The impact almost knocked him off his horse but did not prevent him from returning fire. It was Jim's shot that Barney Thompkins would talk about afterward. In the brief second that Captain Boyd was trying to recover from Ebersole's shove to the side, Jim ripped a .45 slug from his Winchester under Boyd's outstretched arm and into Ebersole's heart. The brash lieutenant was dead before his body crumpled to the ground.

Startled by the sudden shots, the horses bolted, dumping two of the troopers back into the river. The others fought with their mounts to keep from joining them. The tight confines of the thicket made it difficult to keep the horses off each other. Seeing his chance to escape, Jim kept pulling Toby back until the brush gave way to a cleaner riverbank. Once he had room to turn, he set the big horse off at a gallop.

Fighting with his horse to keep from trampling Ebersole's body, Boyd finally managed to get his mount under control. By the time he did,

Jim had a sizable lead. Barney Thompkins spurred his horse up behind the captain. Looking down at the body, he lamented, "Oh Lord, it shouldn't have come to this. There'll be hell to pay now."

"You're right about that," Boyd said as he tried to get his men organized to go after the fugitive.

"You might as well save your breath," Thompkins advised. "He's got a pretty big head start, and that horse knows these woods."

The captain deemed it his duty to go in pursuit, anyway, but the sheriff proved to be a credible prophet. After an hour of chasing around in the timber, they were forced to admit they had lost him. Captain Boyd pulled up beside the sheriff. "I guess you'd better go back to the Culver place and tell the old man that his son has twenty-four hours to turn himself in. After that, there'll be army patrols looking for him."

Thompkins cocked an eye at the captain. "I'll tell him," he replied. "But as you saw for yourself, Jim Culver probably ain't likely to cotton to that suggestion."

Boyd was not impressed. "Well, he'd better. There'll have to be a hearing. First he bullwhips an officer, then he kills him. I think a military court will want to look into this."

"It was self-defense, pure and simple," Thompkins protested. "The lieutenant shot him first."

"Maybe so," Boyd allowed, "but I believe that

young firebrand pushed him to do it. At any rate, my duty is clear. Any time a civilian kills an officer of the U.S. Army, a military court will need to look into it." Having stated his intentions, Boyd wheeled his horse and headed back to escort Ebersole's body.

Jim Culver sat on the dark riverbank, his back against an old oak tree as he gazed up into a deep black sky that seemed overburdened with stars. The familiar night sounds of frogs and insects surrounded him with their symphony for the rising moon. Jim sat up straight and listened when the serenade suddenly stopped. In a few moments, he heard the sound of a night bird. Smiling, he returned the call and got to his feet.

"I figured you'd know where I was," Jim said as he went to meet his brother. Since they were small children, he and his brothers had considered this spot on the river their private swimming hole. A piece of rotten rope still hung halfway down from a large limb of the old oak, never replaced after it had broken with Stephen in midswing and landed him unceremoniously on his backside some ten feet short of the water.

"Figured you might be hungry," John said as he dropped down off his horse. "I brought you a piece of cornbread."

"Much obliged. You coulda brought a piece of ham with it," Jim joked.

John grunted, then replied, "I ate that on the way up here." He laughed, then became serious.

"Barney Thompkins came back to the house. He said you killed that soldier."

"It was self-defense, John. The lowdown son of a bitch threw down on me without any warning. I didn't have much time to think it over. I wasn't gonna wait for him to shoot me again. His aim might have got better the second time."

"I know. Barney said it was self-defense. Are you hurt bad? Ma's worried about you, 'fraid you were off in the woods somewhere dying. You don't look too bad to me. Where'd he get you?"

"Shoulder," Jim replied, placing his right hand over the wound. "It ain't bad. I think the bullet went right on through. At least, it don't feel like it's in there."

"Let me have a look," John said, turning his younger brother around in an effort to see by the light of the rising moon. "Hard to see, but I think you might be right. There didn't seem to be much bleeding."

Jim questioned his brother while John examined his wound. "So, if Thompkins said it was self-defense, then I guess that's the end of it. Right?"

" 'Fraid not. He said the army's giving you twenty-four hours to turn yourself in. If you don't, they're coming looking for you."

Jim didn't reply at once, thinking it over. His initial reaction was not to trust the army's intentions. It was cut-and-dried as far as he was concerned; the lieutenant shot him, and he shot back. If he willingly surrendered to a bunch of army officers, there was no telling how they might turn the incident around before it was over. His mind made up, he said, "I don't reckon I'll be turning myself in to no damn military court."

"That's what I figured you'd say," John said. He knew his brother well. "What are you gonna do? You can't hide out here in the woods forever."

"I guess I'm gonna do what I've been thinking about doing for a while now. There ain't no reason for me to stay around here anymore, and there's damn good reason to leave. I'm heading for Montana territory. Clay's out there somewhere. I'm gonna find him." When his brother did not respond at once, Jim went on to apologize. "I hate to leave the farm work on you and Stephen. I know Pa ain't been able to do much to help. But, dammit John, I just don't have farming in my blood."

John smiled. "I know it, Jim. Frankly, I've been expecting you to take off before now. Don't worry about the farm. Stephen and I can handle it just fine." He paused. Giving his younger brother a little pat on the back, he couldn't resist teasing. "Besides, me and Stephen were getting tired of planting in those crooked rows you plow." He laughed and took up his horse's reins again. "Come on. Let's go back to the house and see about scraping up some possibles for you. We need to take a look at that wound, too. There ain't no soldiers here now, but they might be coming back in the morning." He didn't express it, but he also wanted Jim to say good-bye to their mother and father. He knew it was likely to be the last time they saw him.

Raymond Culver watched silently as his wife applied a clean bandage to the shoulder of their youngest son. Rachael Culver solemnly went about her task, her eyes devoid of tears in spite of the knowledge that Jim was preparing to follow in his older brother's footsteps. She never let the boys see her cry, saving her tears for the deep hours of the night when she thought no one would know, not even her husband. They had known other young men, and some women, who had left Virginia to go west. No one ever came back. They might as well be dead. There were messages from time to time from her eldest son, Clay, but it was still like hearing from someone who had passed on. She held no hope that she would ever see his face again. And now, Jim.

She looked up at him and smiled, indicating that the bandaging was complete. His ready smile could always warm her heart, even on this occasion. She followed his every move as he got up from the kitchen table and pulled on a clean shirt. Jim, the baby, was her favorite. She admitted that to herself. It was only natural that a mother always favored her youngest. She glanced at her husband and realized by his smile that she had been caught admiring her son. She didn't care.

Raymond watched as Stephen and John helped Jim pack some clothes in a bedroll. He couldn't help but admire his sons, all tall and strong. Jim had turned out to be the biggest of the three—as big as Clay, as best Raymond could remember, his eldest having been away these many years. He had watched Jim fill out during the last two years—strong as a mule but with no love for the land. *Well*, he thought, *I got no love for the land myself, but I never had much choice.*

"Well, I guess that's it," Jim said, looking around to see if he had forgotten anything.

"Mighty slim provisions to start out to Oregon on, especially this late in the season," Raymond Culver commented as he watched Jim hitch up the string on one of the bags he planned to carry behind the saddle.

"I don't need a whole lot," Jim replied, smiling. "I've got my rifle and plenty of ammunition. I reckon I'll eat."

Raymond shook his head in mild exasperation. "The Good Lord is supposed to take care of fools and young men. I'll leave it up to Him to decide which one you'll be." Seeing that Jim was ready to walk out the door, he stepped up, placed his hand on his shoulder, and said, "You take care of yourself, Son."

"I will, Pa." He turned to his mother and tried to smile. "I'll be seeing you," he said, knowing there was no way he could guarantee it. He kissed her on the cheek and hugged her.

Stephen led Toby up to the porch as Jim walked out. "You might wanna check that girth yourself," he advised. "I don't know how you tolerate this hard-headed cuss. He blowed on me twice, trying to keep me from drawing it up tight."

Jim laughed. "I'll check it." Toby didn't like anybody saddling him but Jim. The horse did have some cantankerous ways, but he and Jim always understood each other.

Never fond of drawn-out good-byes, Jim stepped up on Toby, nodding to John and Stephen. He paused briefly to fix one last image of his parents in his mind. Then he wheeled Toby and headed west.

Chapter 3

Monk Grissom guided his dingy gray mare through the thick belt of pines that ringed the mountains guarding the northern end of the valley the reverend had named Canyon Creek. He had taken to riding the mare a lot more in recent months. Her gait was considerably more gentle than the buckskin's, making it much easier on his rheumatism after a day in the saddle.

It would be good to get home to the valley and off a horse for a while, a fact that irritated him more than a little. For most of his life, it had been the other way around. He was feeling old age gaining on him more and more as each summer ended, a fact Monk didn't share with anyone. He was too proud to admit that his wild days were not only behind him but too far back to remember clearly. Sometimes he got confused when trying to recall something that had happened in the past. He didn't consider it serious, but still aggravating—like just that past week, when he couldn't remember if his old partner, Browney Hawkins, had died at the last rendezvous on the Green River or during the year of the big storm at Popo Agie. Katie Mashburn probably noticed that Monk was showing signs of wearing out, but if she did, she didn't let on. Katie didn't miss much.

Dammit! he thought. *I just peed not more than thirty minutes ago, and I've got to go again. Gittin' old is a first-class pain in the ass.* He reined the mare to a stop at the edge of the pines. Stiff and aching in his joints, he slowly threw a leg over and stepped down. "Damn!" he uttered when the persistent pain shot through his groin as he untied his buckskin britches. "Just hold your horses!" Fumbling furiously with the rawhide strings, he just made it before his insistent flow released on its own. After a few short seconds, he was done. "Is that all?" he snarled at the offending organ. "I just about bust a gut over a few little ol' drops?" Thoroughly disgusted with his obvious state of deterioration, he tied his trousers again.

Monk had roamed the mountains and prairies for most of his life, free and wild. He had been a free trapper, a scout, and a guide—and his strength and toughness had been his pride. Old age was a bitter pill to swallow, and Monk had been fighting it for the past five years. The medicine man in Chief Washakie's village had told him to chew on raw camas roots to help his bladder problem, but they didn't seem to give him any relief. He sometimes wondered if Browney was the lucky one, getting killed before he got too old to live in the mountains.

"Don't do no good to complain about it," he sighed and climbed up in the saddle again.

Home was less than an hour away. His thoughts were distracted by the cry of a red-tailed hawk high overhead, and he paused to squint up into the clear blue sky. The sight of the winged hunter automatically reminded him again of his younger days, when he had felt as free as a hawk with the whole Rocky Mountains to range in. Ornery as a grizzly and cunning as a fox, he had kept his topnotch for a heap of years. In those days, it had never occurred to him that he would ever grow old. He figured that when his number came up, it would be delivered in the form of a Blackfoot arrow or an angry squaw's knife.

Starting down through the last of the trees, Monk caught something that seemed out of place out of the corner of his eye. A thin column of smoke was threading its way up toward the mountains. He stopped to get a bearing on the location. It appeared to be coming from Jed Springer's old place on the river. *Now, that's mighty curious*, he thought. *Best have a little look-see at that.* Keeping an eye on the smoke, he continued down the slope toward the valley floor.

"Somebody's coming."

Clell Adams rose up on one elbow. "Where?"

"Yonder," Hicks replied, pointing out toward the meadow.

Clell remained up on his elbow, staring at the lone rider approaching from the northern end of the valley. When it became apparent that the rider was indeed headed straight for them, Clell sank back to his position against the side of the cabin. "You better go git Fry, I reckon."

"Go git him yourself, old man," Hicks replied, remaining seated on the other side of the cabin door. Like Clell, Hicks was taking his ease in the warm sun that was reflected from the logs of the cabin. Both men had come outside to escape the constant moaning of Trask, whose wound was paining him considerably.

"Fry!" Clell yelled out. "We got company!"

In a few moments, Simon Fry was standing in the doorway, squinting out at the lone figure riding toward the cabin. "Who is it?"

"Well, now, how in the hell do I know that?" Clell returned.

Ignoring Clell's snide retort, Fry continued to stare at their visitor. "Looks like an old trapper," he said. He waited in the doorway while Monk approached the cabin.

Monk took inventory of the cabin as he neared the shallow branch that ran in front of Jed's old place. They sure as hell didn't look like homesteaders. There was no sign of women or children, and, from the number of horses grazing in the small pasture, Monk figured there had to be more than the three men he could see.

"Howdy," Monk called out as he rode up before the cabin.

"Howdy," Fry returned. "What can I do for you?"

"Nothin' much, I reckon," Monk drawled. "I

got a little place just on the other side of Rufus Colefield's. Been gone for a spell. How long have you fellers been camping in Jed's old cabin?" He glanced over at the two men lounging on each side of the doorstep. The younger one eyed him with bored curiosity, while the older man had shoved his hat down over his eyes and appeared to be sleeping.

"A few days," Fry answered. "We're in the Montana Territorial Militia. I'm Captain Fry."

"The Montana Militia?" Monk repeated. "That's a new one on me. I ain't never heard of the Montana Militia. What in the world are you doin' over in this part of the territory?" When Fry offered his concocted story about trouble with the Shoshonis, Monk was sincerely surprised. "You can't be talkin' about Chief Washakie's crowd," Monk said. "They ain't caused no trouble for a long spell. Where was they raidin'?"

"North of here a piece," Fry replied.

"Forevermore," Monk exclaimed. "That's pretty hard to believe." He glanced at the two lounging men again. "How big a detail was sent?" When Fry informed him that there were eight men in his command, Monk shook his head, amazed. "That ain't much of a detachment." He scratched his head thoughtfully. Monk had spent considerable time scouting for the army at Fort Laramie, and he knew that eight men weren't enough to make up a normal patrol. "I expect if you run into a war party, eight men wouldn't stand much of a chance." The idea seemed absurd to Monk. "Eight men! Where'd you fellers come from, anyway?"

"Virginia City," Fry answered.

"Virginia City?" He marveled. "I didn't know there was any soldiers at Virginia City. I heard they'd moved the capital there about a year ago, but I never heard tell of a soldier fort there. I've been over that way more'n a few times. There wasn't never no soldiers there."

"Well, there are now. Like I told you, we're volunteers in the territorial militia. We ain't been organized very long." Fry was getting irritated. This old mountain rat was as full of pesky questions as Horace Spratte had been.

Monk sensed the irritation in Fry's voice. The captain didn't seem to like being questioned about the particulars of his mission to the valley. "It seems a mite peculiar to me that any territorial governor would send a detachment as small as your'n to chase a Snake raiding party. You sure they was Snakes?" He didn't wait for an answer. "Everybody knows Washakie's people have been friendly to the whites for a long time. Maybe that raiding party was Sioux; they've been riled up lately in a few spots." He shook his head and scratched his beard thoughtfully. "Eight men. Hell, if Washakie's Snakes were on the warpath, they'd run through you fellers like shit through a goose."

Monk could see that his comment wasn't well received by the man standing in the doorway, but he didn't particularly care. As far as he knew, there wasn't any such thing as a territorial militia in this part of the country. Their story might have been easier to swallow if there were about fifty of them instead of just eight. Judging from the two lolling around the doorstep, they were a pretty sorry-looking lot. They may have been part of a militia at some time, but if that were the case, it was Monk's guess that they were most likely deserters now. It was his guess that they had just happened upon Canyon Creek and decided to lay up here for a while. *No skin off my back,* he figured, *as along as they keep to theirselves and don't cause no trouble.*

"Mister," Fry warned, "you ask a helluva lot of questions. If I said the raiding party was Snake, then, by God, they were Snake." He was about to say more, when Pitt moved up behind him to get a look at Monk.

"The captain here just told you we're spread pretty thin. We're just the advance party. There'll be others before long. We was sent out here to help you folks. Have you got a problem with that?"

Monk eyed the big man standing behind the "captain." He stood almost a head taller than Fry. A husky brute, Monk figured he must be the stud horse of the outfit. Taking his time to answer Pitt, Monk craned his neck to look beyond Pitt, trying to get a glimpse at whoever else might be in the cabin. "Nope," he finally said. "I ain't got no problems a'tall. You boys just look like a pretty ragged bunch of soldiers to me."

"Why, you old son of a—" Pitt started when a wail from Trask interrupted him.

"Pitt, ask him if there's a doctor here'bouts," Trask yelled. "I need a doctor, dammit!" Trask's swollen shoulder had only gotten worse since Reverend Lindstrom had given it a cursory glance and rubbed some bag balm on it, reasoning that the salve would reduce the soreness since it worked so effectively on his cow's udder. But it had reached a point where Trask was suffering constantly with the pain.

Not waiting for Pitt to convey the question, Monk asked, "What's wrong with him?"

"He took an arrow in the shoulder, and the head's lodged in there," Fry answered, then pointedly added, "A Snake arrow. He's been bellyaching ever since. I asked your preacher if there was a doctor here. He said there wasn't."

"I've took a few arrows out from time to time. Bring him out here, and I'll take a look at him," Monk said.

"Anything to stop his whining," Fry replied after thinking about it for a second. He looked back over his shoulder. "Bring him on out here."

In a few seconds, Mendel and Wiley carried the suffering man outside and laid him on the ground beside the front step. Trask was in such pain that he cried out when they put him down. Monk dismounted and knelt down to take a look at the wound. It was a nasty-looking wound, swollen and festering. The skin had tried to heal over it, but it was so full of pus that it had formed a lump the size of a small melon on the unfortunate man's shoulder.

"What was you aimin' to do? Just wait till his arm dropped off?" Monk asked sarcastically. "That arrow shoulda come outta there."

"Hell, we tried. It wouldn't budge," Clell said, raising up on his elbow to watch the fun.

"Well, he's got to be cut. That thing's gotta come outta there. If it don't, he's gonna lose that arm, maybe worse. I seen a trapper with a wound no worse than that. It was back in '56 or '57—don't remember which—at the Bayou Salade, near the head of the Arkansas River. He died."

"Oh Lordy," Trask moaned. It was not what he wanted to hear.

"Hell," Monk grunted, "it looks like it's wantin' to pop out, anyway. Won't take much to cut it out." He looked at the faces gawking at the wounded man. When no one gave any indication of taking on the job, he asked, "Want me to do it?"

"Yeah," Fry quickly replied. "Cut him."

For the second time since he had been shot, Trask was pinned down to the ground by his comrades. Monk drew his long skinning knife and wiped it on the side of his leg to make sure it was clean. With a nod to the three men holding his patient, he got down to business. When he took hold of Trask's shoulder, the man cried out in pain. "Damn, son, I ain't cut you yet," Monk said, then cut the shirt away to give himself some room to work.

After another look at the wound, Monk didn't waste much time. With one quick move of his knife, he slashed the yellowish-green center of the swelling, instantly releasing a thick, foul-smelling fluid that caused the circle of spectators to back away a few feet. Trask yelped in pain, stiffened, then relaxed, perspiration beading his forehead. "Well, hell," Monk exclaimed. "No wonder it was hurtin' so bad. There's a three-inch piece of the wood shaft still in the stone head. Just like a big ol' splinter, it was trying to work its way out, but the arrowhead wouldn't let it." With little warning, other than a curt "This is gonna hurt like hell," Monk sank his knife deep into the muscle until he felt the blade strike the arrowhead. Trask screamed and fainted dead away.

"Damn," Clell commented dryly, "I think you kilt him."

"Naw," Monk replied as he worked away at the arrowhead. "He's just passed out. It'll be easier on him. Anybody got any whiskey? This dang hole's got so full of blood, I can't see what I'm doin'."

All seven of the other members of the gang had now gathered around to watch the mutilation of Trask's shoulder. No one budged until finally Fry told Caldwell to fetch a jug from inside the cabin. Caldwell did as he was told, handing the jug to Monk upon his return. Monk was about to uncork it, when Mendel protested.

"You plannin' to waste good whiskey on his shoulder? Hell, old man, there's a whole damn river behind the cabin. Wash it out with water."

Monk uncorked the jug. "Whiskey works better'n water. Besides, whiskey'll make the blood strong . . . if it's the right kind of whiskey," he added with a grin and tilted the jug up to his lips, taking a long pull of the fiery liquid. Unable to speak for a moment while the fire burned in his throat, he fought back the tears and tried to smile. "It's the right kind," he finally rasped. Pouring generously, he splashed the whiskey over the arrowhead. Able to see again, he poked at the stubborn arrow shaft, trying to determine why it was so reluctant to back out. "Somebody musta tried to drive it on through," he decided. "Wedged it up against his rib." With one more cut, he slashed the muscle holding the arrowhead tightly against the rib, allowing the missile to move away from Trask's rib cage. One simple tug of the broken shaft, and he was able to extract the offending arrowhead.

Simon Fry stood over the unconscious Trask, his arms folded in front of him as he gazed at the stricken man. Trask was ashen, blood flowing freely from the messy wound in his shoulder. He looked for all the world as if he were dead. In a tone completely devoid of pity, Fry asked, "Is he dead?"

"No," Monk said, wiping his bloody hands on Trask's pants, "but he soon will be if you don't stuff something in there to stop that bleedin'." While Caldwell went inside to find a rag, Monk held the arrowhead up to examine it. There was not enough shaft left to identify it—it could have been Shoshoni as they had claimed. "If he wakes up, he might wanna keep this here arrowhead. It might bring him luck. Anyway, that's all I can do for him. Just depends on how strong he is."

"Well, old man, I reckon ol' Trask there owes you a word of thanks," Fry said. "That is, if he ain't dead." A wry smile creased his face. "He wasn't much use to us laying around moaning, anyway."

"No trouble a'tall," Monk replied. "I reckon he'll most likely heal up after a while." He matched Fry's smile with a knowing smile of his own as he finished cleaning up. After a few minutes watching a crude bandage being applied to Trask's shoulder, Monk walked over to his horse and stepped up into the saddle. "I expect you need all your soldiers, being so short-handed. You never know when old Washakie might send about two hundred armed warriors raising hell through this valley."

The comment was intended to give Fry and his men something to think about. Monk knew that Washakie was at peace with the white settlers in the valley. In fact, the old chief was encouraging his people to learn to speak English and plant crops—a development that Monk was disappointed to see. As far as Monk was concerned, Indian ways were better.

His natural instincts cautioned him to be careful about showing his back to men such as these, so he backed his horse slowly away from the cabin, keeping an eye on the seven men gathered around Trask. Then, turning, he rode off across the branch and headed for his own cabin.

"He's a feisty old cuss, ain't he?" Pitt said as they watched Monk ride off down the valley.

"I'm not so sure he believes we're militia," Fry decided. "We might better keep an eye on him. He might cause trouble."

"It's his funeral if he does," Pitt replied.

The next morning found Monk in better spirits after a restful night sleeping before his stone fireplace. After seeing to his horses, he took an inspection tour around the crude shack he now called home to see if any repairs were required before winter set in. He was a bit more mindful of the condition of the cabin from a standpoint of defending it against attack than he would have been before his meeting with the valley's most recent visitors. Satisfied that his walls were stout enough, he decided that there wasn't much more he could do to improve them. There were a few thin places in the chinking between the logs that could stand a little reinforcing. He knew he should take care of them soon, but there was a little time yet before the first icy winds would come sweeping through the valley. So he merely made a mental note to work on the cabin walls before too long. His chores done, he focused his attention on himself: more specifically, on the growling in his stomach. Ordinarily, he would have already sliced off a slab of salt pork and put on a pot of coffee. But he had been on the trail for the past week, and his mind had been filled with thoughts of some hot biscuits and fresh-churned butter. And he knew the place to go for them. It was still early enough. He could saddle up and make a friendly little visit to his neighbor, Rufus Colefield. If he didn't waste any more time, he should get there at about the time Katie would be pulling the biscuits from the stone oven he had helped Rufus make.

"Well, lookee yonder what the wind blowed in," Rufus called back over his shoulder.

Katie, a heavy iron skillet in her hand, walked over to stand in the doorway behind her father. "Monk Grissom," was all she said, but she stood there for a long moment watching the old trapper as he guided his horse around the lower end of the garden. Probably the only person other than the boy who could bring a smile to her face was Monk. Always a welcome sight, he had been a close friend to her late husband, and she knew that he never came empty-handed. If he had been hunting, it would be a slab of buffalo hump or the hindquarter of an elk. She knew that he had been to Fort Laramie, so it would most likely be something other than fresh-killed meat. After a moment longer, she turned and went back to the table to make up extra dough. They would need more biscuits.

Rufus stepped outside the door to meet Monk as he pulled up before the hitching post. "I swear, you never know what's gonna show up on your doorstep these days," Rufus joked loudly.

"Howdy, Rufus," Monk said, grinning broadly as he stepped down from his horse. "I figured I'd better come see if you folks had packed up and gone back east yet."

"The only reason I ain't is because I ain't got the money," Rufus replied, laughing at the thought of making the long, arduous trek back across the country. "Come on in the house. You're just in time for breakfast."

"Is that a fact?" Monk did his best to look genuinely surprised. "I wouldn't wanna put you out any. I thought I'd stop by to thank Luke for watching out for my horses while I was gone. Where is that boy, anyway?"

Rufus laughed. "Right behind you."

Monk almost jumped when he looked around to discover Luke standing silently a few feet away. "I swear, Rufus, we're gonna have to hang a cowbell around that boy's neck." He reached back and gave Luke a playful slap on the shoulder. "How you makin' out, son?" He was answered with a warm smile. Monk looked fondly upon John Kendall's son. Like his father, Luke moved quite easily between the Indian's world and the white man's, although at this stage in young Luke's life, he was still probably more Shoshoni. Further thoughts on the subject were put aside when he heard Katie call from inside the cabin.

"I'm putting breakfast on the table. Pa, you and Luke get your butts in here before it gets cold." There was a slight pause before she added, "You can bring in any other strays that might have lost their way, too."

Luke and Rufus looked at Monk and grinned. They filed through the cabin doorway to find Katie standing by the table, hands on hips, a contrived expression of impatience on her face.

"Howdy, Katie," Monk said, pulling his hat off his head. "I hope you don't mind me bustin' in on you at mealtime."

"You're always welcome, Monk," Katie returned, letting her stern expression slip just a little.

"I brung you a sack of coffee beans from Laramie."

"Well, that was mighty thoughtful, Monk. We can sure use 'em. Now sit down and eat your breakfast."

Not a word was spoken for several minutes, until the edge was taken off Monk's appetite. Once the second biscuit was downed, he slowed enough to tell them the news from Fort Laramie. "Another wagon train of Mormons come through while I was there—last one this year, I reckon. It's gittin' a mite late for another'n to start out." He paused to consider what he had said, then continued as if thinking out loud. "Them Mormons just keep coming, but there ain't many big parties anymore, not since '68 or '69. I expect most of 'em rides the train since the railroad was built.

The Injuns is still pretty quiet, just a few little set-to's from some of the younger bucks from time to time. Come to think of it, though, there was a hot little fight down at the river. A bunch of Sioux decided to take over the ferry again. The soldiers had to go over and take it back. Killed two or three young Sioux—didn't amount to much."

"What do you think about our detachment of soldiers here in the valley?"

Monk didn't have to spend much time considering the question. "I reckon I don't think too much of 'em. They don't look much like soldiers to me."

Having been genuinely happy to see the arrival of even a small number of fighting men whose job it was to protect the settlers, Rufus had been hoping to hear a more positive response from Monk. In an attempt to justify his faith in Simon Fry's men, he offered a possible explanation for their presence in the valley. "Well, you've got to remember, these boys ain't regular soldiers. They're militia, volunteers, more'n likely got farms like us somewhere. Captain Fry himself said they didn't think much of spit and polish."

"Maybe so, Rufus," Monk said, shaking his head, "but you ain't got nothin' to go on but their word. Even if they are militia like they claim, eight men don't make much of a unit. I don't know how much help they'd be if we had some honest-to-God trouble. I just hope they don't go stirrin' up no fuss with Chief Washakie."

Showing more than casual interest in the topic of conversation, Katie put her dish towel away and sat down at the table to listen. Her father, reluctant to dismiss his positive view of the valley's newest arrivals, insisted, "I know eight ain't many, but Captain Fry said there'd be more coming later on. You know the army ain't got enough men to keep the peace out here. The only way to do it is to use volunteer militia like these fellers." He shifted his gaze to his daughter for a second. "I know I feel a sight better with some added protection here in the valley."

Monk sat there looking at Rufus for a few moments. Finally, he shrugged and said, "All I'm sayin' is, I'm damn shore gonna watch my back around them boys. They don't look like farmers to me." He wondered if the other folks in the valley were as trusting of Simon Fry and his gang as Rufus seemed to be. Could be they were right, and he was just being overly suspicious. When he thought about it, there wasn't much to draw a gang of outlaws to Canyon Creek, if indeed that's what they were. There was damn little to steal—horses, maybe, and a few family heirlooms that might be worth a little. *Hell, maybe they are militia.* More likely, though, his earlier thoughts were closer to the true story, and they were probably just deserters or other riffraff looking for a warm place to hole up for the winter and live off the charity of honest folks.

"Well," Katie interrupted, "you men can sit around the table and talk all day. I've got work to do." With that, she got up from the table, took off her apron, and strapped her pistol on again. Her actions served to end the breakfast discussion.

"Much obliged, Katie," Monk said as he got to his feet.

"Anytime," Katie replied. "Here, stick a couple of these cold biscuits in your pocket."

He grinned as he graciously accepted the offering. "Thank you, ma'am," He leaned closer to her ear and spoke softly. "I hope my talk about them militia boys didn't worry you. Your pap is probably right, but, just the same, you watch yourself around that bunch."

Katie smiled at the old mountain man. "Don't worry, I will." She stood in the doorway while her father walked out to the hitching post with Monk. She was momentarily overcome by a deep feeling of regret—not for herself, but for her father. Watching his animated conversation as Monk stepped up in the saddle, she knew he was still trying to convince Monk to change his mind about the militia. Katie knew deep down that Rufus was trying to convince himself as well. He chose to see their arrival as a blessing for the settlement because he wanted so badly for it to be just that. It was a sad thing to see, but Katie also knew that her father was frightened. He refused to even admit the possibility that the group of men were not militia as they claimed but were here to do harm. Rufus Colefield had been living in fear from his first exposure to the dangers of this wild territory and living in shame ever since Robert had been killed and he had lacked the courage to stand and fight. She felt a deep compassion for his pain, but there was nothing she could do to alleviate it. She never blamed him for it. What could he have done against the Ute raiding party? Watching him now, as he stood back to give Monk's horse room to turn away from the post, she shook her head slowly. *I'm sorry I ever talked you into leaving Ohio*, she thought, for she knew she had been the driving force behind that decision.

Chapter 4

Mendel Knox sat on his bedroll in the corner of the little cabin that was now the official headquarters of the self-proclaimed unit of the Montana Territorial Militia. A broad smile spread across his face as he watched Simon Fry buckle on the shiny officer's sword. "I swear, Simon, I almost believe you're a damn soldier myself. You mighta missed your callin'."

Fry smirked in response. "I might have considered the military if they made me a general or something, but the pay ain't good enough." He straightened his coat and brushed the dust from the campaign hat. "I reckon I'm soldier enough for this bunch of farmers, though."

Seated in the one chair at the table, Jack Pitt had also been watching Fry's preparation for the town meeting. Although Canyon Creek could hardly be called a town, being no more than a church and Nate Wysong's general store, still Reverend Lindstrom insisted upon calling it one—betting on the come, as Clell put it. The reverend had spread the word around the valley that this was an important meeting, to get acquainted with the detachment of Montana volunteers. It was in everyone's interest to attend the meeting, the reverend said. Ever mindful of his higher calling to administer to the lost sheep of Canyon Creek, Reverend Lindstrom had conveniently scheduled the town meeting to follow immediately after prayer services on Wednesday night.

Silently watching, Pitt couldn't resist teasing his partner a little. "You know, Fry, if you don't shake a leg, you're gonna miss the prayer meetin'."

"Huh," Fry snorted. "Don't think I couldn't stand right up there with the rest of the sinners." He jerked his head around so that he was looking at Hicks and Caldwell lying on their bedrolls. "Maybe I ought to take a couple of you younger fellows with me." This brought the two youngest members of his gang to immediate attention. "Don't get all riled up," Fry said before they could protest. "I'd be afraid the roof might fall in if you two sinners walked in."

On a more serious note, Fry sat down on the edge of the table to discuss their plans for the evening. "According to what that fat ol' preacher told me, most everybody in the whole valley will be at this meeting. This would be a good time for you and the boys to nose around a little, see if there's anything worth taking." Pitt grunted. He had already had the same idea. Fry continued. "If anybody sees you sniffing around, you can tell 'em you're scouting the valley to see how best to protect 'em." He shot a sharp glance in Wiley Johnson's direction while reminding Pitt of their overall plan to keep the peace for the time being. "Keep in mind that all you wanna do is look the pickings over for when the time is right."

Pitt snorted, slightly resenting the inference that he might have been stupid enough to steal or plunder before they were ready to depart the little valley in the spring. "You go on to your prayer meetin'. Me and the boys'll split up and scout around a little."

Fry waited outside the log building until the sounds of the last hymn faded away and a handful of young children burst through the doorway, anxious to escape the watchful eye of the Reverend Lindstrom. He knew the prayer meeting was over then. He carefully folded the square of the soft suede he used to polish the handwork on his Spanish saddle and put it away in his saddlebag. While waiting, he had taken special notice of the number of horses and wagons tied up in front of the church. From what he had seen of the little settlement since he and his men had stumbled upon the valley, he speculated that most of the inhabitants of Canyon Creek were indeed gathered here at the meeting.

"Well," Reverend Lindstrom announced as Fry walked in the door of the church, "here's Captain Fry now." He walked up the short aisle to greet Fry. "I was afraid we had got mixed up on the day." He glanced behind Fry as if expecting someone else. "I was hoping you'd attend the prayer meeting, maybe bring some of your men as well." Lindstrom was clearly disappointed.

"Sorry, Reverend, but you can understand a soldier has duties to attend to." He started to say that Sergeant Pitt was leading the men on a patrol, but then he couldn't remember if Pitt had been a sergeant or a lieutenant when they had first talked to Lindstrom. So he simply said, "Pitt took the men out on patrol."

"Well, that's a shame, but I'm sure you have to do your duty."

Several of the men in the congregation, led by Horace Spratte and Rufus Colefield, came forward to welcome Fry to the meeting. They introduced him to those he had not met. It was a warm welcome from the tiny gathering of homesteaders so long isolated from other settlements in the territory. For Fry's part, he was at his glib best, telling the folks what they most wanted to hear in a manner both sincere and articulate—he and his men were there to help and protect them; they were but the vanguard of larger troops to follow; there were even plans to build a fort nearby. He assured them that all these things were in the territory's future.

His words were met with hearty approval by a breed of people which thrived upon hope alone; otherwise, they would hardly have made the long, hard passage across the continent to this remote valley. Lindstrom beamed. He could envision a thriving little town with an army post nearby. Rufus Colefield literally glowed with enthusiasm, while others in the meeting beamed at each other, transmitting their approval with nods and handshakes. There was never a hint of skepticism, except for one person in the back of the room.

Seated on the last wooden bench, near the door, Monk Grissom listened to the glowing oratory of Simon Fry. He offered no comment on the captain's speech. But to his way of thinking, what Fry had foretold didn't make a great deal of sense. In the first place, why would the army want a fort in this part of the territory? Forts were built where the people were, on the main trails and rivers, where the mainstream of settlers passed through the country. Canyon Creek was almost totally isolated. It was on the road to nowhere. In the second place, they weren't having any Indian trouble to speak of. And even if they were, eight motley-looking volunteers would be of little value. In the third place, this bunch didn't look like soldiers, didn't act like soldiers, didn't smell like soldiers, and, if you cut a slice out of one of them, Monk would bet he wouldn't taste like a soldier, either. In short, Monk wasn't buying what Fry was selling, but he held his tongue. *We'll just wait and see*, he told himself. *This so-called captain is workin' the churn pretty fast. We'll just see if there's any butter when he's done talkin'.* He got to his feet and moved quietly out the door. *I wonder what the rest of his boys is doin' while everybody's settin' here in the church.*

The men whom Monk wondered about were, at that moment, taking an inventory of the homesteads closest to the center of the valley. One pair, Wiley Johnson and Mendel Knox, were even then seated upon their horses at the far end of Rufus Colefield's garden. Through the open door of the cabin, backlit by the lantern glow, the figure of a young woman standing by the kitchen table had captured their attention.

"Damn a'mighty, Mendel. Look at that!" Wiley slid off his horse and moved up through the garden to get a better look. When Mendel moved up beside him, Wiley whispered, "I knew there had to be some young women in this little valley."

Inside the cabin, Rufus's dog emitted a low growl and got up from his place beside the fireplace. Katie, immediately alert, looked quickly toward the corner of the room, where Luke was laboring over a book that she had given him to read. The boy had already sensed something, and met her gaze. Without a word, he picked up his bow and quiver and slipped out the back window into the night. Katie walked to the door and closed it, then took down the rifle from over the fireplace.

Outside in the darkened garden, Wiley uttered an oath. "Damn. She shut the door."

"Dog spooked her," Mendel said. As soon as he said it, the dog began to bark. "We better git our hides outta here."

"Hold still," Wiley whispered. "Let's wait a

minute." He craned his neck, trying to see into the darkness. "That's the first young-lookin' woman I've seen around here." He inched his way a few feet closer to the edge of the garden. "There don't seem to be anybody else around. Her old man must be at the meeting with everybody else. I'm gonna have me a better look."

"You know what Fry told us about gittin' into trouble," Mendel reminded him.

"Hell, what Fry don't know won't hurt him," Wiley replied, his eyes riveted on the door of the cabin. "Maybe you don't need a woman, but it's been too damn long for me."

Mendel was not comfortable with the situation. Wiley's overheated condition was bound to bring trouble for the whole gang. The continuous barking of Rufus's dog didn't help matters any. "Dammit, Wiley, how in hell will Fry not find out about this if you go botherin' that woman?"

"Mendel, you worry too much. Hell, how do you know she ain't willin'? Even if she ain't, she won't likely tell nobody with her throat cut." Wiley smiled at the prospects before him. "Ain't nobody done nothin' to shut that dog up. I bet she's all alone. Who's gonna say it was us?" At the end of the garden now, he placed a hand on the wooden fence and prepared to climb over.

Startled by a solid *thump* on the fence rail, Wiley looked down to discover an arrow neatly embedded in the wood between his thumb and index finger. Before he could snatch his hand

away, there was another *thump* on the rail inches
from Mendel's leg. "Jesus!" Wiley screamed.
Not waiting for the next arrow, both men fled
for their lives. Running, stumbling over the garden rows, they beat a panicked retreat to the
lower end of the garden, where their horses
were tied.

Standing motionless in the shadow of the
trees that framed the shallow branch, Luke
watched the two intruders as they whipped
their horses back down the wagon track. After
a few moments, he left the cover of the trees
and went to retrieve his arrows. Calling to the
dog, he quieted the animal with one sharp command. Katie opened the door and waited for
Luke to come in; she was still holding the rifle.

"Maybe I should have killed them instead of
just giving them a warning," Luke said after
telling Katie what had happened. "It was two
of those soldiers who just came to the valley."

Katie studied the boy's face for a few moments before commenting. Luke was completely
calm about the incident. She had no doubt that
he would not have hesitated to kill both men.
"No," she finally said, "you did the right thing.
They were probably just snooping around."

When Fry returned to Jed Springer's old cabin
after the town meeting, Pitt was waiting to tell
him some news. "Looks like we might have some
Injun trouble, after all. Mendel and Wiley was set
on by a war party at the Colefield place."

"Can't say for shore," Wiley piped up. "But there was a bunch of 'em. Me and Mendel just got outta there by the skin of our teeth."

"Damn," Fry swore. This was not welcome news. He had returned from the meeting smug in the belief that the valley was his for the taking. Indian trouble would only complicate his plans and, depending upon the size of the raiding party, might pose too great a risk for him to hang around. "Dammit," he swore again. "Could you tell what kind of Injuns they were? There's not supposed to be any trouble with the Snakes."

"It was too dark to tell," Wiley replied. "Arrows was flying too thick and fast. I warn't about to wait around for no introductions."

Fry walked back to the door of the cabin and looked out into the night, half-expecting to see the glow of a cabin burning across the river in the direction of Rufus Colefield's place. "I ain't heard no gunfire. They must not have any rifles, or maybe they're trying to keep it quiet." Turning back to face his men, he said, "All right, then. I guess we'd better stand a guard out tonight in case that war party is planning on sweeping through this whole valley. We'll just have to wait till morning to see if it was just a hit-and-run raid. Trask, you can take the first watch."

"Ah, hell, Fry, I'm still stove up pretty bad."

"You ain't been worth a shit for nothing since you took that damn arrow. At least you can sit on your ass and keep your eyes open."

From Fry's tone, Trask knew it would be useless to protest. He roused himself out of the corner and walked slowly out the door. After Trask was gone, Fry detailed the rest of the guard roster.

"Injuns! Run for your lives!" Pitt yelled at the top of his voice while standing directly over a sleeping Clell Adams. At the same time he yelled, he administered a stout kick squarely on Clell's backside that brought the startled old man lurching to his feet from a sound slumber. Snatching at the bushes beside the cabin for support, he scrambled up wildly while trying to orient his still-numbed senses, only to go crashing to the ground again, the result of having his ankles hobbled with a short piece of rope. Figuring he was done for, he rolled over and over until he came to a stop at Pitt's feet. Only then did the befuddled man realize that the hoots and laughter he was hearing were coming from his own comrades and not wild Indians.

Incensed, Clell sat up and began working at the knotted rope around his ankles. "You son of a bitches, that was real damn funny. You're damn lucky I didn't come up shootin'."

The others continued to laugh at Clell, but Pitt wasn't smiling when he warned, "Next time you're on guard, and I catch you sleeping, I'm gonna cut your damn throat."

Knowing Pitt did not waste words on idle threats, Clell was immediately contrite. "Ah, hell, Pitt, I only closed my eyes for a few minutes right at sun-up. There wasn't nobody in sight nowhere. Honest to God."

"That's the only warning you're gonna get," Pitt stated evenly. No one doubted his word.

Fry watched the reprimand from the doorway of the cabin. While Clell got to his feet and removed himself from Pitt's menacing glare, Fry walked outside and stood looking first in one direction and then the other. "If there was a war party moving through this valley last night, they were mighty damn quiet about it." He turned to look at Pitt. "Whaddaya think, Jack?"

Pitt scowled and glanced at Wiley before answering. "Nobody heard anything all night. I don't see no smoke anywhere up or down the valley. I think Wiley and Mendel got spooked and just thought they was seeing Injuns— more'n likely it was just a coon or some varmint."

Both men immediately got their backs up at that. "Wait a minute, Pitt," Wiley protested. "I reckon I know a damn arrow when it's stickin' in a fence rail right beside my hand. And I ain't never seen a coon that was handy with a bow and arrow. Hell, Mendel almost got one in the leg."

"That's a fact," Mendel exclaimed. "It damn shore warn't my imagination. It was Injuns, all right."

Fry thought about it for a moment. There was certainly no indication that a war party had raided the settlement during the night. There was only one way to get to the bottom of this. "We'll saddle up after breakfast and ride over to Colefield's place."

Katie Mashburn stood at the corner of the corral watching Luke work with a black-and-white paint that had been given to him by his uncle, Angry Bear. Luke was quite skilled in working with horses, and Katie enjoyed watching him. He was able to stay on the wildest of mustangs, and yet he had a gentle touch when breaking them. As a result, the two ponies that belonged to him followed him around like puppies.

On this morning, Luke was working with a halterlike bridle on the paint to train the pony to respond to the reins. One hard pull, and it cut the animal's wind off, causing it to stop. It didn't take long before the paint got the message and was soon responding to a light touch of the reins.

Deciding she had dallied too long, Katie turned to go back to the cabin, when she caught sight of the line of riders rounding the corner of the cornfield and coming up the wagon track. *The militia*, she thought, and she glanced back at Luke. He had seen them before she had and was already walking toward the corner of the corral, where his bow lay on the ground.

Katie rested her hand on her ever-present pistol, unconsciously reassuring herself. She had hoped to avoid ever having to meet the valley's newest arrivals, preferring to let her father fawn over them. But first thing that morning, Rufus had gone over to Nate Wysong's store to pick up some supplies, so she supposed she was going to have to see what the soldiers wanted. Maybe, she thought, they would pass on by. But she discarded that thought when the lead horse turned off the track at the corner of the garden and headed up the path toward the cabin. "Damn," she murmured and took a couple of steps away from the corral to stand waiting for Fry and his men.

"Good morning to you, ma'am," Fry called out. "Is this the Colefield place?"

"It is," was Katie's succinct reply.

"Are you Mrs. Colefield?" Fry asked, aware of the obvious difference in ages between the young woman facing him and the man introduced to him earlier as Rufus Colefield.

"Hardly," Katie replied evenly. Anxious to speed them on their way, she said, "If you're looking for Pa, he ain't here." She didn't like the way the eight men had spread out in a line and seemed to be looking the place over.

"I'm Captain Fry, ma'am," Fry went on, still trying to charm his way past the obviously cold reception from the young woman. "We're just out on a patrol this morning, trying to make sure all you folks up this way are all right." His words were met with a dispassionate stare. "I heard you might have had some trouble with Indians last night."

"No trouble," Katie stated flatly, staring un-blinking at Fry, her hand still resting on her pis-tol. Luke climbed over the top rail of the corral and moved to her side, his bow in his hand.

Recognizing the boy as the young half-breed who had accompanied Rufus Colefield to the church that first day, Fry began to form a clear picture in his mind of the "war party" that had attacked Wiley and Mendel the night before. It might have amused him had he not felt such disgust for the stupidity of the two men. He glanced at Pitt, and Pitt met his gaze with a slight nod of his chin. He, too, had focused on Luke's bow and the quiet confidence displayed on the boy's face.

Knowing then that the woman and the boy knew full-well that two of his men had been snooping around their cabin the night before, Fry felt he should offer some form of explana-tion. "We had several scouts out last night look-ing for signs of Indian raiders. Two men checked on your place just to make sure you folks were all right."

Katie could not suppress the hint of a smile that nudged the corners of her mouth. "Well, now, that's mighty reassuring, Captain," she said, making no attempt to hide her sarcasm. "I'll give you and your men some advice. Folks who don't have mischief on their minds usually call out to identify themselves before coming up to the cabin. If they come sneaking around after dark, they stand a good chance of getting shot."

Fry wasn't at all comfortable with the dressing-down he was taking from the young woman, but he was resolved to watch his manners for now. "Yes, ma'am," was all he trusted himself to respond, then, "If you folks are all right, we'll be leaving now."

As the riders wheeled about to leave, there were two who lingered a moment longer than the others. There was no mistaking the lust in the eyes of Wiley Johnson. He found himself intrigued by the joyless face of the young woman. While Wiley gawked at Katie, Mendel was sizing up the half-breed boy at her side, realizing that he and Wiley had turned tail and run from a fourteen-year-old with a bow. It didn't sit well with him, for he knew he and Wiley were going to take a real ribbing from the others. After glaring at Luke for a long moment, he reined his horse around and called to his partner, "Come on, Wiley."

Katie stood watching the eight self-proclaimed soldiers until they loped out of sight around the corner of the cornfield. Then she turned to Luke and said, "You watch yourself around that bunch, Luke. I don't like their looks. I think Monk's right; that's just a bunch of riffraff looking to leech off of the valley all winter."

Luke nodded. He didn't voice it, but he had not missed the lust in Wiley's eyes when the dingy-whiskered degenerate had leered at Katie. He felt reasonably certain that Wiley was one of the men who had snooped around the cabin the night before. Luke decided it might be a good idea if he kept an eye on this so-called militia unit.

"If you two ain't a pair of jackasses," Fry snarled in disgust after they had ridden out of sight of Rufus Colefield's place. "So you were attacked by a whole war party of wild Injuns, were you? Arrows flying thick and fast, right?" Several of the men grinned, anticipating the tongue-lashing Fry was about to administer to Wiley and Mendel. Trask snickered, delighted to see someone else take the brunt of the gang's scorn for a change. Fry went on. "Injuns raiding the whole valley! Well, there was your war party back there. A snotnosed young'un with a bow and arrow sent you two a'running." The more he ranted, the more the stupidity of the two galled him. "Dammit, Mendel, I told you not to let anybody see you scouting around. I know Wiley goes loco when he gets the scent of a female, but I thought you had enough sense to keep a rein on him."

If Wiley was insulted by Fry's remark, it wasn't evident by the lecherous smile on his face. He was already fantasizing about the melancholy young woman with the .45 strapped around her waist. *She must have some mighty fine stuff she's trying to protect*, he told himself. The thought brought a smile to his face. He closed his eyes for a second while he fantasized Katie helplessly forced to submit to a lustful attack.

The image held a great appeal for Wiley, for he could picture himself as the perpetrator. The scene excited him, and he would play it over and over in his mind during the next few days. Right then, however, his fantasy was interrupted by the harsh scolding from Fry, and he was forced to bring his mind back to the present.

"Dammit, Wiley," Fry was saying, "if you foul up before we're ready to clean this valley out, I'll shoot you myself." Fry and Pitt had huddled several times over the prospects of sacking the little settlement. They both agreed that it was prime for the plucking, but, as long as their militia ruse was successful, there was a good argument for staying with their original plan of laying up here for the winter and not striking until spring. The only thing that might ruin it would be if one of the men pulled some damn-fool trick like Wiley had almost attempted. Most of the inhabitants of the valley had accepted Fry and his men with childish faith. But there were a few who were openly skeptical. The woman they had just left and the old trapper, Monk Grissom, came to mind.

"We need something to make these people think we're really protecting them," Fry said, thinking out loud.

"We need an Injun raid," Pitt returned. He had been thinking about Wiley and Mendel's frightened retreat from Colefield's cabin the night before. When Fry's expression questioned the seriousness of his remark, Pitt continued. "You said there was one man that didn't come to the meetin' the other night because he had a place way down at the south end of the valley." Fry nodded, already seeing where Pitt was going. Pitt went on. "Why don't we take those Injun ponies we took from them Snakes and pay him a little visit? We burn him out, and I'll bet the rest of these folks'll feel real good about having some militia around."

"Especially when we go up there and chase the Injuns away," Fry replied, smiling.

John Cochran filled a basin with water from the wooden bucket by the step. He dumped the few little knotty potatoes he had dug up from the garden into the basin to wash. "That's about it for the potatoes," he said to his wife, who was watching him from the door. "Them last two or three hills on the far end of the row just kept on making potatoes, but I reckon they finally played out." When she made no comment, he looked up to find her gazing past him toward the pasture.

"Somebody's coming," she said then.

John turned and squinted into the setting sun, shielding his eyes with his hand. "Seven . . . eight of 'em," he said. "Now, I wonder who that could be." A few years ago, his first concern would have been Indians, but he was not worried about Indians at the present time. He had made his peace with the band of Shoshonis on the western side of the pass and was accustomed to occasional visits from small parties from the reservation. The riders crossing the pasture now appeared to be white men, possibly from the settlement. But if they were, he didn't recognize any of them. "Stay inside, Ruth, till I find out who they are." His wife stepped back inside the cabin and pushed the door shut. John walked out from the front step to meet the strangers.

"Evenin'," Simon Fry called out as they reined their horses to a stop a few feet from Cochran.

"Evenin'," Cochran returned. "What brings you fellers out this way?" He looked the eight men over from left to right and back again. There was something strange about the way they stared back at him with almost identical blank expressions, save for a slight smile here and there. John found it odd that several of the men seemed to be having trouble controlling their horses— horses that looked like Indian ponies.

"We're with the territorial militia," Fry informed him. "We're making calls on every settler in the valley to see how many fighting men we can call on if we were to have Indian trouble." He flashed a wide smile for John's benefit. "Are there some more menfolk living here that we can count on in a pinch?"

Cochran was too surprised to answer Fry's question. Instead, he exclaimed, "Militia? Well, I'll be go-to-hell."

Fry waited a long moment for John's response, his smile still in place while Cochran scratched his head in wonder. When Cochran still did not answer, Fry asked again, "How many rifles can I count on here?"

Ignoring the question again, John asked one of his own. "Is the Injuns raidin'? I ain't heard nuthin' down this end of the valley."

Fry could hold a phony smile for just so long before he began to lose his patience. "Dammit, man, are you the only one here or not?"

Fry's impatience did not faze Cochran's unhurried manner. He took a moment to marvel once more at the eight men looking down at him before he finally responded. "Ain't nobody here but me and the missus. Hell, they coulda told you that in the settlement—saved you a ride all the way down the valley."

Fry's smile returned. This time it was genuine. "No trouble at all. We had to ride down here anyway, to chase the war party off."

"War party? What war party?"

"Why the one that's fixin' to burn your place," Fry replied and nodded to Pitt. Without hesitating, Pitt turned the rifle that had been resting across his saddle, pointing it directly at John Cochran's forehead. The look of surprise became a permanent feature of the dead man's face as Pitt's rifle ball made a neat black hole just above Cochran's eyes.

The sudden report of the rifle set off a chorus of hoots and wild laughter as the rest of the men exulted in the bloodletting. Without waiting for further word, they sprang from their saddles, intent upon the looting that was to follow. Just for the pure enjoyment of it, both Hicks and Caldwell fired their pistols into the body of the mortally wounded settler.

A muffled gasp from inside the cabin, followed by the sound of a bar falling into place behind the door, triggered a wild look in Wiley's eyes. "Let's git a look at the missus," he sang out in joyous lust and led the charge toward the door of the cabin. He was only a step ahead of Mendel and Clell.

Finding the door closed tight and barred with a piece of pine timber, the mob's fever only became more intense, and it turned into a playful competition to see who could break into the cabin first. Soon it became a frantic contest as they circled the cabin, trying to break through the locked shutters, throwing their shoulders desperately against the door. Hicks and Caldwell scrambled up on the roof in an effort to dig through from above.

Patiently watching the chaos that had developed around the rude log structure, Fry and Pitt remained in the saddle. "If they don't break into that cabin pretty soon, we'll burn it down," Fry remarked casually. "I don't intend to hang around here all night." Dismounting, he said, "Let's take a look around to see if there's anything worth keeping."

There wasn't much. John Cochran, like most

of the settlers in Canyon Creek, had barely been scratching out enough to survive, hoping to eventually realize the potential offered by the fertile bottomland. It didn't take more than a few minutes' time to see that the raid was not going to produce any stock worth keeping. Other than a half-dozen chickens, there was a saddle horse and a team of oxen. Fry decided to simply shoot the oxen, so he and Pitt put them down while the other six men continued their frantic efforts to gain access to the cabin. "We can say we recovered the horse," Fry said, "if anybody gets nosy."

John Cochran had constructed a solid door for his cabin, mounted with strap hinges on the inside that were fashioned from the rims of a wagon wheel. And it wasn't until Mendel discovered Cochran's ax by the woodpile that the gang of outlaws was successful in chopping their way through. There was little doubt about who among them lusted most for something female. That was Wiley. For it seemed that his every waking thought was below his belt. But Mendel had an urge, too, and he was the one wielding the ax. He was as determined as Wiley to have first crack at the woman.

As Mendel chopped away at the thick pine door, Wiley flinched with each blow of the blade as it took bigger and bigger chips from the wood. His eyes wide with anticipation, he trembled with impatience, unable to contain his lust. "Let me spell you a while, Mendel," he begged.

"Just stand back and gimme some room," Mendel replied with no thought of stepping aside when he could feel the ax working at the last remnants of resistance. Two more solid blows, and he was through. Even as the last chunk of wood fell away, Mendel quickly reached through the hole and lifted the bar.

There was a mad scramble to be first to squeeze through the open door, but Mendel managed to edge in ahead of the others, with Wiley right behind. Mendel's reward was to come face-to-face with John Cochran's terrified wife, allowing him no more than a split second before Cochran's rifle went off almost in his face. The sudden discharge of the weapon startled the surge of leering renegades for only a few seconds before Wiley sprang forward and snatched the rifle from the terrified woman. Behind him, the others crowded in, stepping over Mendel, who lay choking to death from the wound in his throat.

Wiley pulled the woman back toward a corner of the cabin. "Sorry, boys, you're just gonna have to wait your turn. I reckon I got her first." He nodded his head toward his friend lying in agony on the floor. "Maybe somebody better take a look at ol' Mendel there."

"Just git on with it, Wiley," Clell Adams said. "You ain't the only one's rutty, and you ain't got the only claim on the woman." He stepped back and bent down to take a look at Mendel. The wounded man's eyes were bulging wildly as he grasped his throat with both hands in an effort to stop the blood that was strangling him. Clell gazed at him dispassionately for a few seconds before announcing, "Ain't nuthin' we can do for him. He's chokin' to death." He turned his attention back to Wiley and the woman in the corner, leaving Mendel trying to beg for help but unable to speak through the blood in his windpipe.

The four men gathered around to watch Wiley as he wrestled with the struggling woman. She was older than Katie Mashburn. A gaunt, bone-thin woman, her face was lined with evidence of years of hard labor. But as long as she was a female, she would do to satisfy Wiley Johnson's needs.

Wiley giggled as she fought his every move, enjoying the fight she attempted to wage. He had almost succeeded in ripping away her undergarments when she suddenly managed to free her hand long enough to pull a small pistol from her skirt pocket. Wiley at once jerked back, throwing his arms up before his face in an effort to protect himself. But the shot he expected did not come. Instead, she thrust the pistol against her breast and pulled the trigger.

She immediately crumpled to the floor. Wiley sprang back upon her, cursing vehemently. "Damn you! What'd you have to do that for? Dammit, don't you die on me." But the mortally wounded woman was already sighing her final breaths. Untying his trousers, he wedged himself between the lifeless legs and proceeded to answer his barbaric call.

"Dammit, hurry up, Wiley," Clell urged. "You ain't the only one with a need."

"Damn," young Hicks exhaled. "Not me; I ain't got no need to jump on a dead woman."

"Me, neither," Caldwell added.

"Well, I ain't so fussy," Clell said. "Hurry up, Wiley."

With interest immediately lost, the others turned their attention to looting the cabin while the macabre activity continued in the corner. Like Fry and Pitt had discovered outside, there was very little of value inside the cabin. The Cochrans' possessions consisted mainly of pots and pans, tools and harness. There were a few sentimental things of value only to the dead couple—pictures of family back East, a silver comb, a Bible, a few other trinkets—but nothing that could turn a profit for the likes of the bloody butchers that had descended upon the unfortunate couple that day.

"We better scalp 'em," Pitt pointed out as the gang prepared to leave. Fry nodded his agreement, and Pitt grabbed Hicks by the arm. "You and Trask scalp 'em, and do it neat, like an Injun." Looking back at Fry, he asked, "Whaddaya wanna do about Mendel?"

"We oughta just leave his ass where it is, the dumb bastard." He thought for a minute. "I expect we'd better take him back and bury him. If we don't, people might start asking questions."

He gave the matter a few moments more thought, then changed his mind. "No, let's leave him here. Let the good folks of Canyon Creek get a look at him so they'll see we lost a man trying to protect 'em."

Fry looked around him for a few moments, surveying the scene they would be leaving. "Caldwell, look inside there and find a broom. It might be a good idea to sweep over some of these boot tracks you damn fools left around the cabin." He reached into his saddlebags and pulled out a pair of moccasins he had kept after the raid on the Shoshoni camp. "Here, Hicks, your foot's the smallest. Put these on and walk around in front of the cabin so there'll be something besides boot tracks around here."

While the last details were being taken care of to cover what had actually taken place, Clell chased down a couple of chickens that had wandered back to the cabin. Grinning his satisfaction, he said, "It's been a helluva long time since I've had a chicken dinner." He tied them on his saddle.

"All right, burn it," Fry ordered.

Chapter 5

Monk Grissom cocked his head to one side and put an ear to the wind. He was right; there was a horse approaching. *Now, who the hell is that?* he wondered, irritated at having been interrupted in his morning toilet. Groaning with the effort, he stood up and peered out through the branches of the willows. "Whitey Branch," he grumbled as he recognized the familiar figure approaching the shallow ford below Monk's cabin. He wasn't in the mood to suffer Whitey on this crisp fall morning. His rheumatism was protesting the coming of winter, and he didn't feel like visiting with anyone, especially Whitey, who seemed to have little more to do than ride around the valley drinking up everyone's coffee.

Clothed in nothing more than his long underwear and his boots, Monk made his way unhurriedly back along the path to his cabin. Looking back toward the river, he noticed that Whitey appeared to be in a hurry, whipping his horse repeatedly as the animal climbed up the low riverbank. "Monk!" Whitey sang out when he spotted the grizzled old trapper. "Injuns!"

This immediately stopped Monk in his tracks, and he turned to wait until Whitey galloped up.

"Where?" Monk demanded, looking behind Whitey, half-expecting to see a war party chasing the excited man.

Yanking back so hard on the reins that Monk winced, Whitey pulled his horse to a sliding stop a few feet away. "Cochran's place!" Whitey blurted. "War party raided the place last night! Burnt him out! Killed John and his wife!"

"Sweet Jesus!" Monk exhaled. He didn't know John Cochran very well. He had really spent very little time talking to the man, but, on the few occasions he had, Cochran had seemed to be a decent enough sort. He and his wife worked hard on the little piece of land way down on the south end of the valley. "Who found 'em?" Monk asked.

"Soldiers," Whitey replied, stepping down from the saddle. "A couple of 'em just happened to be on their way back from a scout when they seen the fire. They run the Injuns off, but one of 'em got shot. The captain is on his way down there with the rest of his men to see if they can pick up a trail. I'm on my way down there now—thought you might wanna take a look."

"What band was it? Did they say?"

"The soldiers that run 'em off said it was too dark to tell for sure, but they suspect it was Snakes."

"Snakes?" Monk replied. "I find that damn hard to believe." This was the second report of attacks by Shoshoni war parties. It didn't make sense to Monk. Chief Washakie was on peaceful terms with the white folks in Canyon Creek, had been for a long time. And it wasn't likely some of the younger bucks on the reservation were staging killing raids on their own. Chief Washakie maintained a firm control over his people. Monk decided he would have to scout Cochran's place himself. It had to be some other band that had made the raid. Then, too, it was possible that Whitey had gotten the message confused. "Let me git my clothes on and saddle my horse. We'd best go take a look," he said, forgetting the discomfort of his rheumatism for the moment.

"You got any coffee left?" Whitey asked as he followed Monk to the cabin.

It was close to midmorning when Monk and Whitey crossed the pasture and rode toward the smoking ruins of John Cochran's cabin. Simon Fry and his men were already there, as well as a few of the valley folk, including Reverend Lindstrom and Horace Spratte, who were busy digging a grave. Monk noticed that the soldiers were sitting in a group, lounging before a crackling fire kindled from the charred timbers of John Cochran's cabin. They made no effort to help with the grave-digging, and it struck Monk as rather curious that Captain Fry did not detail a couple of men to handle that chore.

"Mornin', Monk," Reverend Lindstrom said, pausing to lean on his shovel. "It's a sad morning for the valley, I'm afraid. We've lost Brother

Cochran and his wife. It's just terrible—a savage attack after so long at peace with the Injuns." He shook his head sadly. "I reckon he took his chances, living so far from the settlement."

Monk stood for a moment, silently appraising the scene around the burnt-out cabin, glancing at the carcasses of the dead oxen in the pasture, back to the two bodies lying side by side under a single blanket, and finally to the group of so-called soldiers sitting idly by. "Snakes, I heard somebody say," Monk spoke.

"That's right," Lindstrom answered. "Captain Fry said there was no doubt they were Snakes. They killed one of the soldiers." Lindstrom paused a moment while Monk was obviously considering what he had just been told. "I guess it was lucky for the rest of us that the soldiers were able to get here quick enough to chase 'em away—hard luck for John and Ruth, though."

"Yeah, hard luck," Monk replied, a generous portion of skepticism in his tone. He didn't voice it to the reverend, but Monk didn't like the look of this Indian attack, even though the news that one of the militia had been killed caused him to reconsider his first suspicions. "I think I'll take a little look around."

"There ain't much to see," Lindstrom said, taking up his shovel again. "Me and Horace decided to lay John and Ruth to rest together in the same grave. I'll say a few words over 'em after we get 'em in the ground."

Whitey offered to take a turn with a shovel

while Monk walked over to view the bodies. Kneeling down beside them, he pulled the blanket away from their faces. Monk had seen more than his share of dead folks in a lifetime that spanned more than six decades. But he had never become callous to the point where he did not feel the frailty of his own mortality whenever he was met with the cold, lifeless eyes of a corpse. His body rigid with death's final paralysis, John Cochran lay with a rifle ball in his brain, as evidenced by the ugly black hole in his forehead, his face still testifying to the surprise he must have felt. It was obvious to Monk that Cochran never saw the attack coming.

Shifting his gaze to Ruth Cochran's face, Monk read the lines of desperation etched into her final expression. Drawn and tired, it had never been a beautiful face. But on the few occasions he had talked with the woman, Monk remembered that it had been a kind face. He glanced up at the ragged patches on her scalp where hair had once been, now crusted black with dried blood. A single shot in her breast had taken her life. The circle of singed cloth around the wound told him that the gun had been held close against her skin. He wondered if perhaps she might have taken her own life. He shook his head slowly as he imagined the horror the poor woman must have suffered in her final moments on this earth.

"It's too bad we didn't get here before they had a chance to scalp them."

Monk looked around to find Simon Fry standing over him. He squinted up at him for a few moments before responding. "Yeah, it's a dirty shame," he finally said. Looking back at the corpses, he commented, "It's about the raggedest job of scalpin' I've ever seen." He shifted his gaze back to Fry once more. "Looks like they tried to take the whole top of their heads off, don't it? 'Stead of just slitting it neatly from the back to the crown like an Injun usually does it."

There was just a slight rising of Fry's eyebrows, the only hint of irritation registered. "I guess they were in too big a hurry to do it neatly," Fry said evenly, "what with me and my men hot on their tails."

"That musta been it," Monk commented dryly, noting the irritation in the captain's expression. He pulled the blanket aside, revealing the bodies completely. He didn't comment again for a long time while he studied the unfortunate couple. When he finally spoke, it was as if he were thinking out loud. "Mighty peculiar for an Injun massacre, just that one shot in Cochran's head, couple more in his belly. Ain't no arrows stuck in him." He glanced up at Fry again. "You find any arrows anywhere?"

Fry shook his head. "No. I reckon they all had guns."

"Yeah," Monk replied, "they musta." He continued his musing over the bodies. "No mutilation. Injuns usually mess up a body pretty bad, so's the dead man can't find his way to the spirit world."

"Like I said," Fry replied curtly, "they were in a big hurry."

"That's probably it." Monk scratched his head as if seriously thinking about it. "Something a little peculiar 'bout Mrs. Cochran, too. They was in too big a hurry to mutilate the bodies, even to do more'n a half-assed job of scalpin' 'em. But they had time to rape this poor woman."

Monk was beginning to get under Fry's skin. The old mountain man was picking away at the scene Fry had set, and he was afraid Monk might plant some doubt in the minds of the other residents of Canyon Creek if he kept up his nosing around. Fry decided to end the discussion. "Well, my men and I have more important things to do than sit around here trying to figure out why an Indian does what he does." That said, he turned on his heel and returned to his men.

Monk covered the bodies again and got to his feet. He wanted to take a close look around the cabin. *I reckon shootin' off my mouth didn't do much to endear me to that phony son of a bitch. I better damn shore watch my back from now on.* He took a moment to cut himself a chunk of tobacco from a plug he had made up from kinnikinnick and molasses.

Fry's men continued to lie around by the fire, unconcerned with the burial ceremony taking place less than thirty yards away. Their own dead, Mendel Knox, still lay where his body had been dragged before they set fire to the cabin,

his hands still clutching his throat in death. One
of their number, however, was not as indifferent
as his companions. Jack Pitt had watched Monk
closely the whole time Fry had been talking to
the mountain man. Pitt could see trouble coming
with Monk's suspicious mind. "Now, what the
hell's that old son of a bitch lookin' for?" he
voiced when Monk began a careful search
around the burnt-out cabin.

"I wouldn't worry about that old fool," Fry
replied.

"Yeah? Well, I would. We don't need that
snoopy old bastard puttin' ideas in their heads."
Pitt got to his feet and headed toward the stone
step where the front door had once stood, and
where Monk was now poking around in the ashes.

"What are you lookin' for, old man?" Pitt
growled. He walked up close, almost stepping
on Monk's toes. "I expect it would be best to let
us worry about them Injuns."

The gruffness in Pitt's voice was not lost on
Monk, nor was the obvious intent to intimidate
as Fry's enforcer towered over him. But Monk
Grissom had stood up to grizzly bears and men
as mean as grizzly bears. He wasn't likely to be
cowered by the likes of Jack Pitt. Monk took his
time in responding, shifting his chew of tobacco
over to the other side of his mouth. "That so?
Well, I expect you'd best back up a step. I need
room to spit." With that, he launched a long
brown stream of tobacco juice that just barely
missed the toe of Pitt's boot.

Pitt jumped back quickly to avoid getting splashed. "Why, you old—"

"Is that what you boys is doing?" Monk interrupted before Pitt could finish the threat. "Worrying about the Injuns that done this?" He glanced over at Pitt's companions gathered around the fire. "Seems to me you ain't lookin' too damn worried. I mean, with an Injun war party so close around."

"Old man, we'll take care of the damn Injuns. You know, if you keep snoopin' around, you're just likely to run into a whole lot of trouble— maybe git yourself kilt." Realizing his admonishment was sounding like a direct threat, Pitt attempted to soften it a bit. "That's what we was sent out here for: to handle the Injun problem so folks like you can tend to your farmin'."

"Huh," Monk snorted. "I don't do a helluva lot of farmin'." He spat another stream of brown liquid to sizzle on the smoking timbers of John Cochran's cabin. "Don't worry yourself about me, though. I don't intend to git in your way. I'm just naturally curious is all, 'specially when I see things that don't look natural—like the ground around this cabin. Don't it strike you as mighty peculiar that them Injuns, in their all-fired hurry, decided to sweep over most of their tracks? I mean, I can't find more than a few moccasin tracks around this cabin. And they was from a mighty small foot—like a boy or a woman." He squinted up at the huge man. "Reckon they had women along on a war party?" Pitt declined to answer, so Monk went on. "There are some tracks of unshod horses—Injun ponies, all right. But it's hard to say how many there was."

Like Fry, Pitt soon lost patience with the quiet, relentless manner of the weathered old mountain man. Monk asked too many questions, and nothing seemed to escape his notice. Had it not been for the presence of Lindstrom and the others at the cabin, Pitt might have been tempted to settle Monk's hash right then and there. As it was, however, he had to restrain himself and wait for a later opportunity to permanently shut the old trapper's mouth. "Well, we covered the ground around the cabin pretty good. I reckon we probably covered up most of the footprints." Seeing the look of doubt on Monk's face, Pitt tried to form a smile on his face as he spoke in a low voice that only Monk could hear. "It's best if everybody stays out of the way, so's us soldiers can take care of the Injuns. I wouldn't want any of you folks to git hurt."

A thin smile parted Monk's lips. He stepped around Pitt and walked over to the corner of the corral where Mendel's body lay. Like a surly yard dog, Pitt turned and followed behind him. Out of the corner of his eye, Monk noted that the rest of the militia soldiers were also watching him carefully. There was little doubt that they didn't appreciate his scouting around the scene of the massacre, and Monk was becoming more and more convinced that his gut instincts about this rough-looking gang had been accurate all along. *Militia, my ass,* he was thinking as he stood over the late Mendel Knox, *this whole story smells to high Heaven.* He could feel the presence of Jack Pitt's hulking body standing over him as he gazed down at the grisly corpse. If there had not been so many witnesses—now in the process of interring the bodies of John and Ruth Cochran—Monk would not have turned his back on Pitt. As it was, he continued to ignore the belligerent bully while he took a good look at Mendel's wound.

"Looks like your man got shot at pretty close range," was Monk's only comment. He rose to his feet once more and, without another glance at the imposing figure of Jack Pitt, turned and walked over to join Reverend Lindstrom and the others. He had an uncomfortable feeling about the Indian raid on the cabin. And it was damn sure apparent enough that these so-called soldiers didn't appreciate his curiosity. There was damn little sign to tell for sure what had happened here. Maybe what Fry and Pitt said was the straight of it, but Monk had a nagging suspicion that the *Injuns* that done it might still be sitting over by the corner of the burnt-out cabin. *Mighty peculiar,* he thought, *that they didn't get a shot at the Injuns, but they managed to capture Cochran's horse.* He decided that before he voiced his suspicions to Lindstrom and the others, he'd ride over to the Snake village for a little talk with Chief Washakie.

*   *   *

Washakie, Shoshoni Chief, got to his feet, stood for a moment watching the lone rider making his way through the outer ring of lodges, then walked slowly forward to meet his visitor. A wide smile spread slowly across the old chief's face as he recognized the buckskin-clad figure exchanging greetings with familiar faces he passed on his way to Washakie's lodge.

"Ah . . . What brings White Feathers to visit me this morning?" Washakie called out, greeting Monk with the name the Shoshoni knew him by—the name inspired by Monk's full shock of snow-white hair.

Monk mirrored Washakie's grin as he threw a leg over and slid to the ground. "I just wanted to see if Chief Washakie had grown so old that he was rooted by the cookfire," Monk joked.

Washakie laughed. "When I am as old as you, then I will sit by the cookfire."

The two old friends clasped arms in greeting. Then Washkie led Monk back to his lodge. While the chief's wife scurried around to place some boiled meat before them, they exchanged casual conversation about the season and the hunt. This continued for a little over half an hour before Monk broached the reason for his visit to the Shoshoni village.

There was genuine surprise in the lined face of the old chief when Monk told him that there had been reports of raiding by Shoshoni war parties within the last week. "None of my young men have left the village on war parties," Washakie said with no uncertainty. "We have no time for war now. We are at peace with the white man. Now is the time for hunting. Soon the mountain passes will be clogged with snow. You know this, White Feathers. We do not make war on the white families in the valley."

"I know this," Monk replied. "I didn't say I thought your young men had killed a white couple. I said there had been reports that it was done by Shoshonis."

"Some of our own people are missing," Washakie said. "Nine from our village have not returned from a visit to our friends the Bannocks. Walks Big and his wife and son, his brothers and their families—all should have been back many days ago. I fear our enemies, the Crows, may have killed them. For several days now, we have sent scouting parties out to look for them, but we have found no sign of them." He shook his head. "No sign at all." Then he shrugged. "The Bannock village is on the Wind River— nowhere near the little valley where the white families live."

Monk was sure this was the straight of it. He had known it before riding up here, but he had wanted to hear it confirmed by Washakie's own words to be doubly sure. There was no doubt in his mind now who had murdered John Cochran and his wife. He resolved to see to it that Simon Fry and his sorry bunch didn't get away with it even though he had no actual proof. The more he thought about it, the madder he got. *That lowdown collection of saddle tramps and cutthroats . . . The way that slick Fry has the people of Canyon Creek eating out of his hand . . .* It made Monk's blood boil. *Well, I'll fix their murdering asses.* He couldn't do it alone—he knew that—but when he got all the men of the valley together, there ought to be enough for a hanging party.

At Washakie's insistence, Monk lingered a while longer to visit with the chief. But as soon as he deemed it not impolite to do so, he said his good-byes after offering his hopes that Walks Big's family would soon be found. Promising that he would return soon for a longer visit, he stepped up into the saddle and was soon moving back down the trail at a serious pace.

Chapter 6

"**H**ere he comes!" Hicks announced in a loud whisper as he scrambled down from his perch on the rocky ledge above the six lounging men.

Jack Pitt pushed his hat up from over his eyes and sat up. He kicked Wiley's boot to awaken him. "Git up, Wiley!" Turning to the young man sitting against a scrubby pine trunk behind him, he said, "Bring up the horses, Caldwell. You and Wiley hold 'em till I git back." With a nod of his head toward Hicks, he signaled for the lookout to follow him. "Let's go have a look."

Crawling out on the ledge where Hicks had stood watch, Pitt flattened his huge body against the rocky shelf. Far below, entering the north end of the narrow pass, Monk Grissom urged his horse along the old game trail.

"There he is," Hicks whispered.

"I see the old fart," Pitt shot back. "Been to see his Injun friends, and they probably told him they didn't kill nobody—like you could believe anything an Injun would tell you." He watched Monk's progress for a few moments more before pushing back away from the edge of the ledge. "I reckon he figures he's gonna tell all his neighbors that there wasn't no Injun raid," he said sarcastically.

"He can't prove nuthin'. It's our word against his'n," Hicks said. "Why, hell, when Fry gits through sweet-talkin' them folks, they ain't gonna believe that old coot."

"Maybe so, maybe not," Pitt replied, never taking his eyes off the lone rider entering the pass. "I know one thing for sure: he ain't gonna find many folks to talk to if we send his nosy ass to hell." Backing away from the edge of the rock, he got to his feet. "Come on with me, Hicks. We'll ride over to the other side of the canyon. The rest of you boys git down there in the rocks on this side."

When a man has survived in Indian territory as long as Monk Grissom, it's damn certain that it's due to a lot more than pure luck. This is especially true in the lofty mountain ranges of the Rockies, where there is no shortage of things to put a man under. In addition to hostile Indian tribes, there are grizzlies and rattlesnakes. There are snowstorms and blizzards in the winter, shale slides and raging rivers in the spring. Monk had known men to die from a simple fall from a horse while trying to follow a hazardous mountain trail. He knew that he had received his fair share of luck over the years. He also knew that his thick shock of white hair was well-rooted to the top of his head because of a sense of danger that served to alert him when there was no physical evidence to warn him. Some might call it instinct. Monk simply knew it as a sudden uneasy feeling deep in his gut that told him things weren't as they should be. Making his way through the narrow pass, he had that feeling now.

Reining his horse back to a slow walk, he scanned the ridges on each side. Hard impersonal walls of gray granite rose above the fringe of aspen to stand silently watching him with no sign of life, neither bird nor beast. It was as if the ticking of the celestial clock had paused, and time stood still, with nothing moving about him and his horse. He felt his gut draw in and a slight tension throughout his entire body. Something wasn't right. The buckskin confirmed it and would have warned him earlier if Monk had been paying closer attention to the horse's ears. Monk noticed them now. Pricked up sharply, flicking all around, the horse's ears searched for the source of sounds inaudible to Monk.

Monk squinted hard as he continued to search the ridges on each side, trying to force his aging eyes to a sharper focus. There was no feeling of fear. Monk had long ago outgrown a dread for the long, dark trail that sooner or later every man was obliged to take. For this reason, he never considered the option of turning around and hightailing it back the way he had just come. Another reason was the fact that cutting through this pass was the quickest way back to warn the people of Canyon Creek. To go around would add two days to the trip, and Monk felt an urgency to get back and put a stop to the murderous plans of Simon Fry and his *militia* before they killed someone else.

Approaching the south end of the pass, he pulled his rifle from the deerskin case and laid it across his saddle. The muffled thud of his horse's hooves on the beaten-down grass of the old game trail seemed to be the only sound in the entire valley. Moments later, his horse snorted, the buckskin stallion sensing the presence of other horses.

Monk didn't wait for further signs. He promptly jerked the reins over to his right and kicked his horse into a gallop toward a stand of aspens at the base of the ridge. Shots immediately rang out behind him from the rocks on the eastern side of the pass, and lead balls snapped through the air around him like angry bullwhips. Lying low on his horse's neck, Monk urged the buckskin on. The trees and cover were only fifty yards away now. *I might make it*, he thought just before the lead ball smacked into his horse's belly. The buckskin screamed and kicked its hind legs high in the air before bucking and stumbling, throwing Monk over its head.

He landed hard, the wind knocked out of him for several minutes. The excruciating pain he felt when he tried to scramble up told him that he had broken some ribs. Ignoring the pain, he hobbled to his feet and went for his rifle, which was lying a few feet away. Rifle in hand, he limped toward the safety of the trees, now only yards away. The salty taste of blood in his mouth now told him that something more than ribs must have busted inside, and he silently cursed the luck.

I'm gittin' too damn old for this, he thought as he struggled to gain the cover of a large boulder at the base of the trees. The thought had barely registered, when he was confronted with a new danger. From behind the very boulder Monk sought for cover, a man stepped out to face him. In that instant, Monk recognized the insolent sneer of the youngest of Simon Fry's gang. Both rifles fired at almost the same time. Monk's Winchester may have been a half-second behind, but it put a hole in Hicks's belly before Monk himself stumbled to the ground with a bullet lodged deep in his right thigh.

"Damn fool," Jack Pitt uttered as he stepped out from behind the boulder. Unconcerned with his partner, who was now seated on the ground, doubled up in agony, Pitt calmly walked over to stand beside Monk, his rifle now pointing directly in the face of the old trapper. "All right, boys," he called out, "this old coon is treed." Looking down at Monk, he said, "I told you to keep your nose outta our business. Now you've done shot one of my boys." He glanced back at Hicks then. Still holding his hands over the hole in his stomach, trying to stop the profuse flow of blood, the wounded man rolled over on his side, moaning. Pitt looked back at Monk. "Gut-shot. I reckon you kilt him." There was no indication of concern in the matter-of-fact statement.

Monk stared defiantly at the muzzle of the rifle no more than a foot from his nose. *Well, what the hell are you waitin' for?* he thought, surprised that Pitt hadn't already put him under. His buckskin britches were soaked with the blood from the wound in his thigh, but he felt more pain from his broken insides. Feeling tired and old, he accepted the obvious fact that he was about to cash in his chips. It was not a thought that overly alarmed Monk, but he did regret the fact that he had been unable to warn the other folks in Canyon Creek about their *militia*. At least he was now free of the one thing he feared most: dying of old age, helpless and feeble, dependent upon the kindness of others. *What the hell is he waitin' for?*

While Pitt continued to stand over him, a self-satisfied smile on his broad face, Monk began to slowly move his hand up across his chest, as if to hold his broken ribs. When Pitt glanced away momentarily as Trask walked up, leading the Indian ponies they had ridden, Monk made a sudden move to pull his pistol. For such a big man, Pitt's reactions were unusually fast. He put a lead ball into Monk's brain before the old trapper could clear his pistol from his belt.

"Well, I reckon that's one old buzzard that ain't gonna bother nobody no more," Clell Adams commented as he stooped over Monk's body. "He sure ain't carryin' much of any value, and that's a fact." He picked up Monk's pistol and examined it.

"If you weren't such a lousy shot," Wiley Johnson said, sneering, "we coulda had a good horse."

Pitt, still standing over Monk's body, looked up at that. "I shoulda knowed that was your shot that hit the damn horse," he said, glaring at Clell. "It's a wonder you didn't hit me and Hicks."

The mention of Hicks called their attention to the wounded man lying several yards away. Clell, anxious to end the discussion about the dead horse, immediately got up and went to look at the young outlaw. "How bad is it, boy?" he asked, kneeling down beside Hicks.

"It's bad," Hicks forced through gritted teeth. "It's hurtin' awful bad. I got to see a doctor." The words had no sooner left his lips than he convulsed in a sudden spasm, causing him to dry-heave as if his stomach were trying to empty itself of the blood that had filled it.

"A doctor!" Clell exclaimed. "You know there ain't no doctor around here." While still kneeling beside Hicks, Clell looked up at the others, who had now gathered around their wounded partner. "He's been gut-shot. There ain't nothin' anybody can do for him. He's as good as dead." Looking back at the horror-stricken young man, Clell callously asked, "You got any strong feeling's 'bout who gits that little bay of your'n? I kinda fancy that horse myself."

"I reckon I'll decide who that horse belongs to," Pitt quickly inserted. "You can have his pistol—since you can't seem to hit what you're aiming at with yours."

"This old codger was carryin' a right nice rifle," Wiley Johnson commented, having picked up Monk's weapon. "A Winchester 66, and in damn fine condition, too."

"I reckon that rifle belongs to me," Pitt quickly informed him, "seein' as it was me what shot him." Still standing motionless over the body, he added, "Anybody got any objections?"

"Why, hell, no, Pitt," Wiley immediately replied. "I ain't got no objections." He stepped forward at once and handed the rifle over.

Taking Monk's rifle in hand, Pitt propped it against the rock he and Hicks had hidden behind, his gaze shifting back and forth, looking for objections from any of the others. There were none. Not even Fry would chance going up against his massive partner when Pitt's mind was set on something.

"Seems fair to me," Wiley said. "Let's take care of Hicks and git the hell outta here. Somebody mighta heard them shots. We ain't too far from that Snake camp." He elbowed Clell aside and bent down to look Hicks close in the eye. The wounded man's eyes were glazed with fear and the terrifying realization that he was dying. "We've got to git moving, boy."

Hicks's eyelids fluttered nervously, his words halting and choked by the blood threatening to strangle him. "Don't leave me, Pitt. . . . Don't leave me. . . . I can ride." His words trailed off.

"Why, hell, no, son," Pitt replied, his voice suddenly soothing. "I ain't gonna leave you." He glanced up at Clell and nodded.

Understanding Pitt's signal, Clell stood up. At the same time, the others, who had gathered around Hicks, backed away a step or two so as not to chance a spattering of blood. Without any more hesitation, Clell pointed Monk's pistol directly in Hicks's face and pulled the trigger. The pistol failed to fire. Clell cocked it again and tried again, with the same results. Hicks cried out in horror. His eyes, glazed and unfocused moments before, were now wide with frightened clarity.

Clell, unconcerned with the terror that clutched at Hicks's very soul, held the pistol up and examined it. "If that don't beat all," he said. "Hell, it's loaded. Maybe the firing pin is broke." He stuck the barrel back in Hick's face again and tried once more, with still no discharge of the pistol.

"Shit, Clell," Pitt uttered in disgust. He pulled his own pistol from his belt and shot Hicks in the back of the head. "Let's git mounted."

"Ain't we gonna bury 'em? At least, poor ol' Hicks." This was Caldwell, who had been closest to Hicks, primarily because he was about the same age as the deceased.

"What if somebody finds 'em?" Clell wondered. "It don't seem like a good idea to have 'em find Hicks a'layin' right next to that old trapper. They'd know fer sure it was us what done it."

"You can stay here and dig him a hole if you want to," Pitt said as he reloaded his pistol. "Damned if I'm gonna do it. Thinking better of it after a second thought, he turned back to face Clell. "You're right," he said. "It wouldn't do for one of the town people to find the two of 'em here." He looked around him at the barren walls of the pass. "Drag 'em both over behind those rocks. The buzzards'll take care of 'em before anybody finds 'em."

"What about the horse?" Clell wanted to know.

"Hell, leave it lay. The buzzards'll make short work of it out in the open like that."

Young Luke Kendall walked his pony slowly up the path from the river. The gray mare hobbled across by the water's edge nickered a familiar acknowledgment, and Luke's pinto answered. The two horses knew each other well. "Monk!" Luke called out. There was no answer. He called out several times—still no answer. Luke was puzzled to find the mare still hobbled where he had left her the day before. Monk had evidently not returned from the Shoshoni village. He had said he would return from Washakie's camp before sundown the night before. *He and Washakie must have gotten started talking about the old days,* Luke thought.

He slid down from his pony and removed the hobbles from the mare so she could run a little bit before he hobbled her again. "You two can visit for a while," he said, leaving the horses to run free while he walked up to the cabin. He wasn't concerned that they might run off somewhere, leaving him afoot. The pinto wouldn't stray far and, upon hearing a low whistle from Luke, would come to him immediately.

It occurred to him that Monk might have returned that morning and decided to leave the mare hobbled where she was. But after checking the cabin and finding nothing but cold ashes in the fireplace, he concluded that Monk had not been back. *It's a good thing you got me to watch the place for you*, Luke thought and made himself comfortable while he sat watching the horses run.

As he sat there, the daylight began to fade away with the sinking of the sun below the mountaintops. Soon the lengthening shadows would engulf the chilly river valley, and it would be pitch black. A worrisome thought invaded Luke's reverie. *Why isn't Monk back?* Maybe his visit to Washakie's camp was so enjoyable that he had forgotten he had a place to look after in the valley. Monk was long in the tooth, but he still liked to stomp and snort once in a while, especially if he happened upon some firewater. Washakie himself did not approve of the white man's whiskey, but some of the younger bucks would occasionally sneak off to imbibe the fiery liquid. Monk may have joined in. Still, Luke began to feel uneasy about Monk's absence. *If he isn't back by tomorrow night, I'd better go to the village to find him.* With that thought, he got to his feet and whistled for the pinto.

The next morning came with still no sign of Monk. Luke had halfway expected the old mountain man to show up at their doorstep to get more of Katie's biscuits. When he didn't, Luke expressed his concern to Katie. "It ain't like Monk to come back later than he said he would. You reckon I'd best go see if I can find him?" Even though he had planned to give Monk until dark that day, he was becoming more and more aware of an uneasy feeling inside.

Katie didn't answer at once. She glanced at her father, who was intent upon putting an edge on his ax and was oblivious to the conversation. Luke's concern about Monk gave her pause to consider some of the events of the past few days. Monk had shown an open contempt for Captain Fry and his soldiers, a contempt that Katie shared, but she had not been as vocal about it as Monk. Without conscious thought, she picked up her belt and holster from the table and strapped it around her waist. There seemed to have been an unusual amount of Indian trouble in the valley since the arrival of the little militia unit—without any real Indian sign. Luke might be wise to be concerned for Monk.

"Maybe you'd best go over to the Shoshoni

camp," she finally answered. "That old fool might have fallen off his horse or something," she added in an attempt to hide her apprehension. Her concern was also for her father and his childlike acceptance of Simon Fry's word. Rufus Colefield was not made of especially strong fiber, and Katie saw no need to give him something else to fear before it became necessary. She walked with Luke to the corral. "You mind your back, Luke, and stay outta sight of any of those soldiers. I don't trust them any more than Monk does." It was unnecessary advice, for Luke's native Shoshoni instincts had taught him to recognize a rattlesnake no matter what form it came in.

As a precaution, Luke crossed the river and passed Jed Springer's old cabin on the other side so as not to be seen by any of the soldiers who could usually be found lounging around their so-called headquarters. After he was certain no one had seen him, he crossed back over and took the trail to the Shoshoni village.

The old game trail was frequently used by Shoshoni hunters, so Luke was not surprised to discover tracks from many horses—some old, some relatively fresh. They could have been made by a hunting party from the Shoshoni camp, he supposed. But he had a gut feeling that told him they had most likely been left by the valley's uninvited militia unit. The fact that none of the horses were shod did not influence his thinking. Simon Fry had a string of Indian ponies.

Entering the south end of the narrow pass that led to the western slopes of the mountains, Luke sharpened his senses to be especially alert, a natural impulse when riding through a pass so prime for ambush. He had ridden no more than fifty yards into the pass when his pony snorted, having detected a scent offensive to its nostrils. Luke searched the walls of the narrow valley, his eyes quickly darting from one side to the other. A few yards farther along, the trail became a bit wider, permitting a broader view of the entire valley. At once, he discovered what the confining entrance to the pass had obscured—buzzards feasting on the carcass of a horse.

Luke immediately nudged the pinto, and the pony sprang to a full gallop. Waving his bow back and forth over his head and yelling loudly, he charged down upon the macabre banquet. The belligerent scavengers scattered reluctantly, waddling only a few yards away from their feast. Squawking raucously, flapping their wings defiantly, they refused to depart the scene entirely even when Luke reined up beside the carcass. One glance at the half-shredded remains told him what he had feared. It was the buckskin that Monk had ridden.

To a boy born to the mountains, there was plenty of sign left to tell the dark story of the evil work that had taken place there. Many tracks

led across the narrow valley, leading toward the
boulders at the base of the trees. There had been
an ambush. That was plain to see. And Luke
knew immediately that the old trapper who had
befriended him—the white-haired, craggy old
friend of his father—was no longer among the
living. He saw the obvious trail of a half-dozen
or more horses that led to the rocks, and he
dreaded what he might find behind them.

As he had feared, the old man was there,
lying face-up, his lifeless eyes staring at the sun,
an ugly black hole near the middle of his forehead. His body had been stripped of everything
but his blood-crusted buckskins. No more than
five feet from Monk's body lay another corpse.
Luke recognized it as one of the men who rode
with Simon Fry. Like Monk, Hicks's body had
been stripped, except for his shirt—which had a
bloody hole in the middle of it—and a dingy
pair of long-handle drawers.

It was easy to imagine what had taken place
in this narrow pass. There was no doubt in Luke's
mind. Monk had been bushwhacked on his way
back from the Shoshoni reservation. The *soldiers*
had succeeded in silencing Monk—as Luke and
Katie had feared they might—but Monk had
managed to take one of them with him. Staring
down at Monk now, Luke felt the heavy sorrow
of the old man's passing. He had known Monk
for most of his young life and he was thankful
that he had found him before the buzzards became distracted from their feast on his horse.

The question now before the fourteen-year-old boy was what he should do. There was no proof that Simon Fry's gang of outlaws were not connected to any military group. Monk had been confident that their only intention was to prey on the helpless farmers of Canyon Creek. There was no doubt in Luke's mind that his father's old friend had been right. His lifeless body surely attested to that. He must warn Katie and her father—and the others in the valley. His first reaction was to seek revenge for Monk himself, but he knew he might be successful in killing only one, or possibly two, of the outlaws before they killed him.

Struggling to keep the anger in his heart from rising to the point where he could not think rationally, Luke tried to make up his mind about what he should do. Looking back at the half-eaten carcass of Monk's horse, he decided that the first thing he had to do was to take care of Monk's body. His first inclination was to take the old man back to Katie's cabin. On second thought, he decided it best to get the body into the ground right away, before he had to fight the buzzards for it.

With nothing with which to dig a grave, he had to settle for scratching out a shallow trench with his knife. When it was finished, he dragged Monk's body as carefully as he could manage, taking care to keep the old-timer's head from bumping over the rock-strewn earth. With Monk resting in the shallow grave, Luke said a silent farewell to his father's old friend. Then he began covering the grave with rocks until he had constructed a solid mound that would keep predators away. He paused but a moment to consider Hicks's body, then decided the buzzards could have it.

His sorrowful chore finished, Luke's thoughts now focused on the immediate action to be taken. The news of Monk's death would be devastating to Katie Mashburn, for she was quite fond of the old man. But he was closer to the Shoshoni camp at this point than he was to Rufus Colefield's cabin. Maybe he should seek help from Washakie and his mother's people. Monk was a friend of the old chief's as well. *No,* he decided, *I've got to get back and tell Katie and her pa what happened.* The next step to be taken could be decided at that point. Katie would know what to do.

Chapter 7

Luke was right: Katie Mashburn was devastated to hear the news of Monk Grissom's death. When Luke arrived at the cabin, after a hard ride from the rocky pass where he had laid Monk to rest, she knew Monk had met with tragedy even before Luke spoke. She stood silent, ashen-faced, while Luke told her and her father how he had found the old mountain man's body hidden in the rocks of the pass along with that of one of the militiamen.

After Luke told them how he had followed the signs that led to the discovery of the bodies, and of the many fresh hoofprints that covered the trail through the pass, Katie sat down heavily at the kitchen table. For several long moments, she said nothing, simply staring at the cabin wall, thinking about the old mountain man who had become like a member of the family. Monk gone? It was almost impossible to accept. Monk was as durable as the mountains he loved so dearly, and like the mountains, she had thought he would always be there. She suddenly felt old. It was going to be a grave winter without Monk around.

Realizing that Luke and her father were staring at her, waiting for her to speak, she finally looked up and said, "I knew he was gonna have trouble with those bastards. He wouldn't keep his thoughts to himself. I told the old fool to keep his mouth shut." She tried to affect an angry tone in an effort to hold back her tears.

Rufus Colefield was beside himself. The news was especially disturbing to him. He grieved for the loss of a man who had been a true friend to him and his daughter. But more than that, the distressing news that one of the soldiers had been found dead right beside Monk brought added concern to worry him. Always the fearful man, Rufus had purchased Simon Fry's story one hundred percent because he so wanted it to be true. His tormented mind would never let him forget the Ute raid that had claimed the life of his son-in-law and caused his daughter to wear a pistol strapped to her waist for most of her waking hours. Simon Fry said he had come to protect the people of Canyon Creek. He said there would be more soldiers coming. Rufus wanted to believe him. He wanted to believe there were more soldiers coming. *He had to believe him,* because Rufus knew he could not protect his daughter in the event there was another raid by Indians. If what Luke said was true, then he might have to face up to protecting his daughter from Fry's men. But maybe Luke had read the sign wrong. There was probably some explanation that would clear it up. There had to be. Surely, he thought, if the soldiers had been responsible for the ambush, they would not have left one of their own to be found there.

"We need to have a meeting with the other folks in the valley," Katie said. "We're going to have to work together to get rid of Simon Fry's gang."

"Hold on a minute, Katie," Rufus quickly responded. "We don't know that things are exactly the way the boy saw them. We need to be sure of what we're doing here. The soldiers came here to help us."

Katie shot an impatient glance in her father's direction. She had long ago accepted Rufus's lack of backbone and had forgiven him for his reluctance to face up to his fears. But at this point in time, she didn't have the patience to placate him. She placed unconditional trust in Luke Kendall's instincts and ability to read sign. To Luke, the picture was clearly that of an ambush by Simon Fry's murderous bunch to silence Monk Grissom. It was obvious to her that their settlement had been taken over by a deadly gang of scavengers bent upon feeding off the people of Canyon Creek. First John and Ruth Cochran, now Monk. If they didn't take action soon, there was no telling who might be next.

"Pa, we can't take any chances on that outlaw gang destroying our valley—sitting on our hands while they kill us off one by one. We need to call a meeting of our neighbors right away. They need to know about Monk." She directed her words toward the boy. "Luke, you need to ride out first thing tomorrow morning—get the word out to everyone in the valley. Tell 'em there's a meeting at our place tomorrow noon. Tell 'em to keep shut about it and don't tell anybody." The boy nodded that he understood. Looking back at her father, she said, "We've got a nest of skunks setting up in our valley, and we'd best get rid of 'em."

Rufus was not at all comfortable with his daughter's grasp of the situation. "I don't know, Katie. I hope you're doin' the right thing. Maybe we should talk to Reverend Lindstrom first before we get everybody riled up."

"He'll be here tomorrow with everybody else. We'll talk to him then." Unconsciously reaching down to shift her pistol holster to a more comfortable position on her hip, she warned Luke, "You watch yourself, boy. Don't let any of that ragtag bunch of Fry's see you." It was an unnecessary warning.

In spite of Reverend Lindstrom's plans to develop Canyon Creek into a thriving valley whose residents would number into the hundreds, there were now only eight families, plus Whitey Branch, in the fertile river bottom. Monk Grissom was gone. So were Jed Springer, Luke's parents, and the Cochrans—all victims of violent deaths. When Luke Kendall spread the word that there was to be an important meeting at the Colefield place, all eight families responded by sending at least one member; in half the cases, the whole family piled into a wagon and drove over, anxious to see what could be important enough to call them away from a day's work. Nate Wysong was away, having gone to Fort Laramie to pick up a wagonload of merchandise for the store. But his wife attended with their three children. As expected, the first to arrive was Whitey Branch. With no family of his own, Whitey usually showed up early to most any function. He had made a sizable dent in the contents of the big metal coffeepot on the corner of Katie's stove by the time Horace Spratte and his wife, Effie, arrived. The last to arrive, at a little past noon, was Henry Lindstrom. As soon as the reverend had greeted everyone, Katie got down to business.

It was apparent to all as soon as they arrived that this was not to be a social affair, for there was no meat on the spit, and no tables were set with tablecloths. There were refreshments, however, for Katie had spent most of the morning baking apple pies, exhausting her supply of the dried apples Monk had brought from Fort Laramie, and there was coffee and cider to wash it down.

Knowing that her neighbors would be anxious to start back to their homes before dark, Katie wasted little time getting the meeting started. As soon as Reverend Lindstrom had greeted the others, she called for everyone's attention.

A genuine and profound sense of sadness captured everyone when she told them of Monk

Grissom's death. There was not a person there who had not counted Monk among their closest friends. A surge of horror raced through the assembly when Katie related the scene of Monk's murder as told to her by Luke.

"Lord have mercy!" Reverend Lindstrom gasped; like Katie, he had figured Monk would be around forever. No one spoke out at first, although there was a great deal of murmuring among the families crowded into Rufus Colefield's cabin. After a moment, Lindstrom voiced the fear that was on everyone's mind. "That's a mighty serious accusation, Katie. Do you know for sure that Monk was killed by the soldiers?"

"That's what I was wondering," Rufus Colefield interjected, undermining his daughter's purpose. "I think we ought to be dang sure before we go off half-cocked."

Katie shot her father an impatient glance before answering. "Who else could it have been? Everybody here knows that Monk was making Fry pretty uncomfortable, asking questions that he didn't care to answer."

"That ain't hardly enough to make him want to kill a man," Horace Spratte offered. "Them soldiers was sent here to protect us. It don't make sense they'd kill anybody, 'specially a good man with a rifle—in case we had some Injun trouble."

Katie had never credited Horace Spratte with a great deal of common sense, but she forced herself to maintain a patient attitude. "Has anybody seen one scrap of proof that that gang of bullies are who they claim to be? They just came riding in here one day saying they were soldiers, and we just sat back and swallowed it. They don't look like any soldiers I've ever seen."

"They's volunteers," Whitey Branch started, but Katie cut him off.

"I know the story," she interrupted. "Listen, folks. All I'm saying is open your eyes. Luke scouted the whole area in the canyon after he found Monk and that other fellow. There was no Injun sign. It was pretty obvious what had happened."

All eyes shifted toward the young son of John Kendall. There was an ample measure of doubt in many of their faces. Luke, after all, was no more than a boy. True, he was half-Shoshoni and known to be as truthful and reliable as his father had been. Still, there was plenty of room for doubt. This was a serious and fearful accusation that Katie was making, one that the whole of the congregation desperately wanted to be unfounded.

"Why is the boy so sure?" Reverend Lindstrom asked. "After all, one of the soldiers was killed, too. It sounds more like the work of Injuns to me." A few heads in the group nodded in agreement with him. "All of us here know that Luke has relatives in that Shoshoni camp, and it's only natural that he wouldn't want to blame the killings on them." He turned to look at the boy standing by the front window. "No offense, Luke. I'm just saying it's the natural thing."

"Luke said it was not the work of Injuns," Katie stated calmly, "and I trust his ability to read sign." She looked around the room, searching each face. "Doesn't anybody here have any doubts about this gang?"

Before anyone could answer, Luke announced, "We've got company."

As Katie and her neighbors watched from the cabin door, Simon Fry and his five remaining outlaws rode into the front yard. He dismounted after directing his men to remain in the saddle. Jack Pitt guided his horse over beside Horace Spratte's wagon, where he could watch the front and one side of the cabin. The other four men spaced themselves so that they covered the front of the cabin.

Fry had been uncertain about the reception they might receive upon arrival at the secret meeting, so he had instructed the men to be alert. It was going to be a long winter, and he preferred to keep things peaceful until he was ready to loot the valley in the spring. He wasn't sure what the purpose of the meeting was, but the fact that Whitey Branch had told him that he was not supposed to tell anyone about it had piqued his curiosity. He could assume that it had to do with Monk Grissom's demise.

Unlike Fry, Pitt was becoming more and more in favor of making their move right away. He was no longer concerned with keeping things peaceful until spring. The first winter snows that would close the passes into this valley would be coming any day now. If they went ahead and killed the residents, then the gang could just loot every cabin as they pleased and not worry about any interference from outside the valley. This was an opportunity that shouldn't be missed, as far as he was concerned. The greatest proportion of the valley's population was gathered in Rufus Colefield's tiny cabin. It would be quick work to take care of the lot of them. Fry had to be mighty persuasive to talk Pitt into holding off a little longer.

"Afternoon," Fry said cheerfully as Rufus and his daughter walked out to meet the intruders. Behind them, the other families filed out slowly, looking for all the world as if they had been caught doing something illegal. Fry affixed a wide smile to his face. "Days are getting a mite chilly, aren't they?" When his greeting was met with no more than a nod, he continued. "Well, looks like everybody in the valley is here. When I heard about the meeting, I thought it might be a good idea to have the military represented. After all, we're vitally interested in everything that happens in the valley."

Katie shot a quick glance in Whitey Branch's direction. She had a pretty good notion who might have leaked the news of the meeting to Fry. Whitey immediately looked away, reluctant to meet her gaze.

As the self-appointed leader of the community, Reverend Lindstrom decided it was his duty to broach the subject. "Well, Captain, maybe we were negligent in not notifying you, but seeing as how you're here anyway, we might as well hear your side of it." When Fry's expression indicated that he didn't know what issue the reverend was referring to, Lindstrom went on. "We've just found out that Monk Grissom was killed between here and the west ridge, and there's been some discussion as to who the guilty party or parties might be."

Fry nodded his head thoughtfully. "Yes, that's a terrible tragedy. In fact, that was one of the things I was going to tell you. I didn't know you had already heard the news. It hit us kind of hard, too. I lost one of my men as well— young Hicks. He was shaping up to be a first-rate trooper. Looks like they were jumped by Indians. Grissom will be a loss to my unit. He had agreed to do some scouting for us. He and Hicks were on a special scout when they were jumped." He shook his head sadly. "I'm afraid the Shoshonis are doing a lot of raiding, but we'll keep our eyes open. My men and I will be on constant patrols, watching the passes to make sure nobody gets in the valley."

Or gets out, Katie thought. She glanced around her and was immediately dismayed by the gullible expressions she witnessed. *Lock, stock, and barrel. They're all so damn frightened that they'll hear just what they want to hear.* She realized then the folly of her hastily called meeting. There was no one here, outside of a fourteen-year-old boy and herself, who had the courage to stand up to these outlaws, and the two of them were not enough to drive them out. Seeing the looks on their faces, she was dismayed to find that the little congregation even swallowed the story that Monk had been working with the outlaws. Confirming her thoughts, she heard Lindstrom reply.

"Injuns. That's what we figured." His statement was endorsed with nods and comments of agreement from some of the other settlers. Katie knew then that she was going to have to scrap her plans to organize her neighbors into a vigilante group to rid the valley of this plague. She was going to have to play along as if she accepted Fry's version of the murder and think of some other way to seek help.

Confident that things were going his way, Fry fashioned a broad paternal smile for the benefit of the souls huddled there. "You can all rest assured that my men and I will be on constant guard. I'll be sending out patrols to find the ones responsible for the murders of Grissom and Hicks. I don't think the Indians will risk coming into the valley as long as we're here. They're waiting outside the passes to jump on poor unfortunates like the two good men we lost. You're all safe as long as you stay close to home and don't go wandering outside the valley."

Katie, because she knew the boy so well, was the only one who noticed the fiery glint in

Luke's eye as he listened to the lie Simon Fry
concocted. Luke knew what the sign had told
him, and he had little patience for liars in any
form, especially those of Fry's ilk. With a slight
movement of her head, her eyes locked on his,
she motioned for him to remain calm. Fearful
that he might challenge Fry's tale and get himself in trouble, she frowned at him until he acknowledged her with one brief nod of his head.
Although his face remained expressionless, she
knew there was a fire burning inside.

The gathering of families relaxed as first one
and then another of the men agreed that Indians
were the most likely suspects in the murder of
Monk Grissom. But Fry and his gang remained
there until the settlers began saying their good-
byes. Katie, with Luke close beside her, stood
watching the departing families as they filed out
of the yard, anxious to return to their own
homes before darkness set in.

"Thank you for the refreshments," Effie
Spratte called out as Horace reined his horses
back to permit Whitey to precede him. Katie responded with a wave. She could well imagine
what her neighbors thought about what they
perceived as a senseless meeting. Most of them
regarded her as a rather strange woman, anyway—with her pistol on her hip and her re-
served attitude. Receiving the polite nods and
waves of the others as they followed the Spratte
wagon out of the yard, Katie couldn't help but
picture the lot of them as sheep, blissfully

awaiting their slaughter. And she was convinced that a total slaughter was exactly what it would be, because she could not imagine Simon Fry willing to risk word of the rape of Canyon Creek leaking out.

Simon Fry waited until all of the families had turned at the corner of Rufus's garden and headed for their respective homesteads before he stepped up in the saddle. Guiding his horse over to stand before Katie and Luke, he flashed another benevolent smile and gave them a piece of advice. "It might be a good idea if you let me know if you're thinking about calling for any more meetings. You know, I was sent here to keep the peace. I somehow get the idea that you're set on working against my mission."

Katie could not help but bristle in response to the undisguised reprimand, but she did her best not to show the sudden anger that threatened to choke her. "Well, now, Captain, I don't know what gave you that idea. But to be honest with you, I guess I'll invite my neighbors over any time I damn well please. And I don't reckon I'll feel like I have to notify anyone."

If her sharp response angered him, he didn't show it. Instead, his smile widened just a bit as he glanced from her to the young boy beside her and back again. "I expect it might be a mite dangerous to be moving about the valley now, what with the Indians on the prowl. I'd advise you and the boy to stay pretty close to the cabin." Not waiting for her reaction to his veiled threat, he wheeled his horse around. "Come on, boys," he said as he rode past the line of men silently sitting their horses before the cabin. "Mr. Colefield," he acknowledged as he rode by Rufus at the corner of the garden.

Like a pack of surly wolves, the other five filed out behind him, leering contemptuously at the old man, his daughter, and the half-breed boy. *They're already dividing up our possessions*, Katie thought as she stared back defiantly at the sullen faces. One in particular, the one called Wiley, caused an involuntary shiver to course along her spine. There was no mistaking the lewd gaze in those hungry eyes, and she felt a strong desire to cover herself to escape his visual fondling.

When they had disappeared beyond the rise that ran down to the river bluffs, Katie turned to the boy and shook her head in dismay. "It's an evil wind that blew that bunch into our valley."

"Oh, I don't think you appreciate how lucky we are to have Captain Fry and his men here," Rufus said, having overhead his daughter's comment to Luke. "I just hope we ain't stirred up a lot of trouble for ourselves with this meeting. The militia's the best bet we've got for protection. I'm just worried that they ain't enough, what with all the Injun trouble."

Exasperated, Katie complained, "What Injun trouble? Pa, sometimes I think you're a little touched in the head. Luke has already told you it wasn't Injuns that murdured Monk. Can't you see we're at the mercy of those coyotes? They can do what they want in this valley. And who's to stop them?" As an afterthought, she added, "I'd bet my soul that Monk's mare is grazing with Fry's horses behind Jed Springer's old cabin." She shot an accusing glance in her father's direction. "Probably just wandered in all by herself," she said sarcastically.

Chapter 8

"**D**ammit, Wiley, you're gonna git both of us an ass-kickin' if Fry finds out about this," Trask whined.

"Why don't you stop worryin' so damn much," Wiley replied without turning his head to look at his partner. Keeping his gaze focused upon Rufus Colefield's cabin, hoping to get a glimpse of Rufus's daughter, he said, "What are you worried about, anyway? Hell, we're doin' what Fry told us to do, ain't we?"

Trask looked around him nervously, afraid they might be spotted so close to the cabin. "Fry said we was supposed to keep an eye on 'em, make sure they didn't try to send for help from some of their Injun friends. He didn't say to slip right up to the back of the cabin." He glanced behind him again. "Ain't no tellin' where that half-breed boy is."

Tearing his eyes away from the cabin no more than thirty feet from the old wagon bed they were hidden behind, Wiley looked at his fearful companion and grinned. "Me and you both saw that boy go inside with an armload of firewood no more than ten minutes ago, and he ain't come out. They's all three of 'em in there, all warm and cozy. Me and that young lady are gonna have us a little dance before we pull outta this valley. I just wanna git me another look at her right now so's I can think about how good it's gonna be." He gave Trask a wink. "Hell, I might even save a little for you, Trask. That'd be all right, wouldn't it?"

Inside the cabin, Rufus's dog, Bacon, suddenly pricked up his ears and listened. After a moment, he got up from his place next to the fireplace and moved over to the door. Luke, having just put new wood on the fire, turned to watch the dog. "What is it, boy?" he asked, almost in a whisper. "You hear something?"

"Probably that old coon is trying to get in the corn crib again," Rufus speculated. "I'll let him out." He got up from the table, still holding the bridle he was mending, and lifted the latch on the door. The dog pushed through and was outside before Rufus opened the door more than halfway. In a few moments, they heard him barking at something.

"There's something out there," Katie said, wiping her hands on a dish towel, "but it seems to me to be a bit early for it to be that coon. He usually comes around here later in the evening."

"That's what I was thinking," Luke said. "I'd best go out and see what he's barking at."

"Bacon'll chase it off, whatever it is," Rufus decided and returned to his chair at the table.

"Take a look outside, Luke," Katie said. Like her father, she was not especially concerned.

The dog barked at a lot of noises. Still, she reminded herself, his barking had once turned up two of Simon Fry's riffraff skulking around the place. "Wouldn't hurt to see. You know, the Sprattes said they spotted a mountain lion sneaking around their place. He might have come nosing around over to this side of the river."

Outside, huddled behind the broken wagon bed, Wiley and Trask were in the middle of an argument when the dog suddenly appeared at the corner of the cabin and started barking. "Uh-oh," Trask whispered. "We'd better hightail it before somebody comes out to see what that damn dog is barking at." He started to back away toward the horses.

Wiley reached out and caught his arm. "Hold on a minute, Trask. That damn dog don't know what he's barkin' at hisself. He'll shut up directly. Then I'll just slip up to that back window and have a look."

"I'll be damned," Trask shot back. "I ain't hanging around here for that crazy woman to take a shot at me." He pulled his arm away from Wiley. "You know what Fry told us." He got to his feet, remaining in a stooped posture to avoid being seen above the wagon bed. "You coming?"

"Hell, Trask, you spook too easy."

"Suit yourself," Trask replied. Not wishing to hesitate a moment longer, he started toward the horses, running as fast as he could without slipping and falling on the thin layer of snow that had fallen the night before.

Wiley smiled to himself as he turned to watch his partner retreat. Just as he had figured, the dog saw the fleeing man and immediately gave chase, raising enough fuss to alert those in the cabin. The door opened at once, and a figure Wiley recognized as that of the half-breed boy came out to see what the disturbance was.

The light of day was fading fast, but Luke could still see the hazy form of Trask, with Bacon right on his heels, as the intruder leaped on his horse and galloped through the cornfield to reach the wagon track.

"It was one of those militia skunks," Luke yelled back to Katie and Rufus. "Bacon's chasing him back down the trail."

Hidden behind the wagon box, Wiley almost chuckled, tickled to think they weren't aware that he was no more than thirty yards from them as they spoke. Easing his head above the rim of the wagon box, he could clearly see Luke standing before the open door. A moment later, Katie walked out to stand beside the boy. Wiley involuntarily sucked his breath in at the sight of the slender young woman. *There you are, you little honey. I knew I'd get a look at you if I waited long enough. That's right, just stand there with your hand on your hip. Ol' Wiley's gonna be seeing you before long.* The longer he gazed at Katie, the more his lustful desire for the young woman increased. He could already imagine how it would be when he held her helpless before him. Wiley tore his eyes away from the woman long enough to glance back at the open cabin door, wondering where her father might be. *Maybe the old man ain't here after all,* he thought. At the sound of the boy's voice, he jerked his attention back to the two standing outside in the light snow.

"Maybe I ought to follow him down the trail a ways," Luke suggested, "to make sure he doesn't circle around and come back."

"Maybe," Katie replied. "But you be careful, Luke. There might be more of them out there nosing around."

This caught Wiley's attention immediately, causing him to risk his entire head above the edge of the wagon bed. *That's right, boy, why don't you go follow ol' Trask.* He felt an uncontrollable wave of excitement sweep over him as he watched Luke quickly throw a bridle on his pony and leap upon its back. In a matter of minutes, the boy was galloping off after Trask. With still no sign of Rufus Colefield, Wiley assumed that the girl was now alone.

Wiley's simple brain was reeling as the implication of that possibility struck him. *She was alone!* He allowed his mind to picture her as she probably stood by the fireplace, warming herself after being outside in the cold. The thought of it was enough to drive Wiley crazy. *I can't wait until spring,* he thought, desperate to take her. It wouldn't take long. He reasoned that he could be in the cabin, do his business, and be gone before the half-breed kid got back. Even if he wasn't finished with the woman by then, the half-breed was just a boy, and Wiley could damn sure take care of him. He gave no more than a few seconds' thought to Fry's instructions to keep away from the woman. *What's it gonna hurt? We're gonna end up killing all of 'em before we leave here, anyway. To hell with Fry and his instructions. I've got serious needs.*

With no concern for Simon Fry's plans for the valley—or any other thought beyond his overwhelming lust—Wiley got to his feet and looked around him while he dusted the snow from his trousers. Everything was quiet. There was no sign of the boy. Wiley decided that the Indian in the boy would make him want to scout Trask for some time yet. There was little thought wasted on other possibilities that might hamper his desire for Katie. Briefly, he considered the chance that her father might be inside after all. Maybe he just hadn't come outside when his daughter had come out to see what the noise was about. Already walking briskly toward the cabin door, he discarded the thought, for the fountain of his lust was past the point of overflowing. He decided that it didn't matter if the old man was inside. In the short time he had been in the valley, he knew what everyone else knew. Rufus Colefield offered no threat. Even Wiley and his companions knew that Rufus had turned tail and run while a war party of Utes had killed his son-in-law.

Inside the cabin, Katie paused to listen a moment. "Bacon's back," she commented to her father. It was an unnecessary remark because the dog was still barking, even after Luke had sent it back to the cabin.

"He's still riled up after chasing that fellow off," Rufus said. "I reckon he wants back in so he can lay by the fire. I expect I'd better let him in, or he won't ever shut up."

No sooner had Rufus gotten to his feet than the dog's shrill bark changed to a menacing growl of warning. Katie, always alert to the possibility of danger, immediately recognized the difference. "Wait a minute, Pa," she cautioned. "He's found something else out there."

Rufus hesitated but a moment, accustomed to his daughter's tendency to be overly concerned about the possibility of hostile attacks. "Probably that ol' coon again. I'll take a look."

"You be careful. Bacon doesn't growl like that unless he's fixing to jump on something." She was a little more cautious than usual due to the uninvited visit that night from Simon Fry's man. At the moment, she had a feeling that maybe she should not have allowed Luke to trail after the man. She felt more comfortable when the boy was close by. *The boy can take care of himself,* she told herself. Still, there was a nagging sense of concern that would trouble her until she heard his pony return.

"Bacon, what's the matter with you?" Rufus called as he stepped outside into the chill air. Puzzled to find the dog standing like a sentry in the fading light with his hackles raised and his teeth bared, Rufus turned to see what had caused the dog's aggressive behavior. "What is it, boy?" were the last words he spoke before he fell in the snow, rendered unconscious by a sharp blow from Wiley's pistol across the back of his head.

Upon seeing his master assaulted, Bacon immediately launched his body in attack. Bacon was a sizable dog, and the force of his attack was enough to almost knock Wiley off his feet. Shocked and fearful for his safety, Wiley had no choice but to shoot the angry animal. His pistol shot cracked the frigid night air, ripping the silence of the growing darkness. Knowing he no longer enjoyed an element of surprise, Wiley frantically kicked the dog's carcass aside and lunged toward the cabin door. Shoving the door open, he found himself staring at the barrel of Katie's Colt Peacemaker. His reactions quick for a heavyset man, especially when looking down the business end of a pistol, Wiley dodged behind the doorjamb barely in time to avoid the bullet that sent splinters of wood flying by his face. "Goddamn!" he yelped and flattened himself against the outside wall of the cabin.

I forgot about that damn gun she wears, Wiley thought as he frantically pondered his next move. Rufus Colefield was lying motionless at his feet. *I reckon I cracked his skull good and proper. He ain't gonna cause no trouble*. The thought crossed his mind that maybe he should just retreat, but he discarded the idea immediately. Fry was already bound to raise hell, so he might as well have his pleasure while he had the opportunity. Fry would get over it.

"Hold on there a minute, lady," Wiley yelled. "There ain't no call to take a shot at me."

Katie answered immediately. "You stick your nose in that door again, and I'll blow it off."

"I just come to pay a friendly visit, and that fool dog come at me. I had to defend myself. All I wanna do is talk to you. Swear to God, that's all."

"Pa?" Katie called. "Are you all right?" There was no answer from Rufus.

"He's all right," Wiley answered. "Just bumped his head. I reckon he musta slipped on the ice. I was fixin' to bring him in when you took a shot at me." As he said it, he noticed some signs of movement from the fallen man. "Yeah, he's all right, but he needs a little lookin' after. Put that pistol down so's I can bring him inside." He was beginning to get edgy. It was taking too long, and he couldn't be certain no one had heard the gunshots.

"Pa?" There was still no answer from her father. Uncertain about what had happened to him, knowing in her heart that Wiley had come to do them harm, Katie didn't know what to do. What if Wiley wasn't lying, and he really only wanted to bring her father inside so she could tend to him? *He's bluffing*, she told herself. *There's only one reason he wants to come in here*. Still, she couldn't take the chance. "All right," she finally consented, "bring him inside."

Outside the door, a slow grin spread across Wiley's face. "Yes, ma'am, I'll bring him right in." He looked down at Rufus, who was now struggling to get up on his hands and knees. Another sharp rap across the back of his head sent the wounded man back down on his face. "You might have to give me a hand. He might be hurt more than I figured."

Anxious for her father yet unwilling to trust Wiley completely, Katie hesitated. She could not see the man through the doorway, nor could she see any sign of her father. With her pistol aimed at the open door, she said, "Step out where I can see you."

Wiley moved closer to the doorway, hugging the wall of the cabin. "Lady," he said, affecting an exaggerated hint of impatience, "I got my hands full right now trying to hold your pa up out of the snow." He grunted as if straining. "Are you gonna help me with him? Or are you just gonna let him bleed to death?"

"I'm coming, I'm coming," Katie cried out, fearful now that her caution might be jeopardizing her father's fate. Not willing to throw all caution to the wind, however, she moved very deliberately to the door, her pistol in front of her, cocked and ready. She inched her way slowly toward the open doorway, her every nerve on edge as she tensed herself to be ready for any sign of treachery. Squinting her eyes, straining to see into the darkness outside, she suddenly stepped out, her pistol before her. For one brief instant, she saw her father's prone figure lying face down in the snow with no sign of Wiley near him. In that instant, she knew she had been tricked. Before she could turn, Wiley's hand clamped down hard on her wrist, rendering it helpless to turn the pistol on him.

"Well, now," Wiley gloated, grinning from ear to ear. He jerked her all the way outside and slammed her hard up against the wall of the cabin. "I believe you'da really used that pistol on me. Wouldn't you, missy?" He dodged the knee that she aimed at his crotch and beat her wrist against the wall until she was forced to release the pistol.

Still defiant, though helpless against his superior strength, she spat in his face as he leaned in close to her. "Yes, I'd use it on you, you slimy dog," she hissed and continued to struggle to get free.

"Goddamn you!" he swore. Then, almost immediately, the grin reappeared, and he pressed against her, wiping the spittle from his face on her breast. "You're a little hellcat, ain't you? That's gonna make it even better. I like it best when they struggle a little bit—but not too much, or I might have to knock you in the head, too."

The horror of what was happening swept over her like a frigid wave, freezing her thoughts inside her brain. She found herself helpless to resist as she fought in vain to keep Wiley from forcing her to the ground. As he gradually pulled her down, his foul breath bathed her face with the stench of rotting teeth and strong tobacco. She could not bear for this to happen—*would not* let it happen. But her defiance was suddenly lost in the face of her helplessness, and, without realizing the depth of her despair, she heard herself cry, "Please . . . please, don't."

Her cries only served to intensify his lust, and, with one final thrust of effort, he wrestled her to the ground, pinning her flat with his body. "I knew you'd be sayin' please before I was through," he mocked.

"Get your filthy body off of her," a voice demanded behind him, and he turned to see Rufus Colefield struggling in an effort to get to his feet.

"Old man," Wiley warned, "you want some more trouble?" He snatched his knife from his belt and pressed it against Katie's throat. "If you don't drag your ass away from here, I swear I'll open her gizzard right now."

Rufus staggered drunkenly when he finally managed to get to his feet, a trickle of blood seeping down the back of his neck to soak his shirt collar. Still, he was determined to come to the aid of his daughter. The sight of Wiley's knife pressing against Katie's throat was enough to give him pause, but he was bound to defend his daughter. He was not going to run this time. "Turn her loose, or, so help me, I'll kill you," he threatened.

The feeble threat made Wiley laugh. "I might just give you that chance, old man."

"Pa, don't," Katie gasped. She knew why her father was determined to make a fight of it even though he didn't stand a chance against the solid bulk of Wiley Johnson. It was to make up for the Ute raid when he had failed to show the courage to fight. "Do like he says, Pa," she calmly urged. Resigned to her fate now, she was no longer terrified.

"You better do like she says," Wiley warned, watching Rufus as he fought to stay on his feet. Following the line of Rufus's gaze, Wiley smiled when he saw Katie's pistol lying near the wall of the cabin. "Maybe you wanna make a try for that pistol layin' there." Keeping his knife tight against her throat, he suddenly sat up and pulled his own pistol from his belt with his other hand. Katie tried to escape, but his weight, settled firmly upon her hips, kept her pinned to the ground. His lust intensified by the prospect of killing the old man, he forced her back down with the knife, pressing hard enough to draw blood. "Now, now, sweetheart, you and me ain't even started yet." Katie was helpless. The beast was crazed by his desire to spill blood. His eyes were glazed, his nostrils flared, and tiny rivulets of drool ran down into his filthy beard.

Turning his attention back to Rufus, he taunted, "All right, old man, let's see just how quick you are." He cocked the hammer back on his pistol. "Bein' a sportin' man, I'm gonna give you a chance to grab that there pistol. You can go for it, or stand there and let me shoot you down where you stand—your choice. Whaddaya say, old man?"

"Leave him alone," Katie pleaded. "You've got me. That's all you came for, ain't it? Let him go."

Rufus just stood there, trying to make a decision that might mean the end of his life. Wiley, thoroughly enjoying the old man's dilemma, continued to toy with his victims. "You're right, honey, your little tail is what I came for. But this old man ain't got sense enough to die. I stove his head in pretty good, and here he is tryin' to ruin our little party. When we git to goin' hot and heavy, I don't wanna have to worry about him sneakin' up behind me. What about it, old man? You gonna try for that pistol or just stand there and take it like a coward?"

Katie was horrified. She realized then that Wiley intended to kill them both whether her father backed down or not. His plans stretched far beyond his lustful desires. He had no intention of leaving witnesses after his needs had been satisfied. Seeing her father literally quaking as he made up his mind to act, she was suddenly overcome with a feeling of compassion for him, and she knew she must somehow do something to save him. In a move of desperation, she tried to grab Wiley's gun barrel. Alert for a move on her part, Wiley responded to Katie's attempt with a shallow gash across her throat, causing her to fall back in pain.

Rufus panicked, infuriated by the sight of the blood running down his daughter's throat. Before there was time to consider the consequences, he lunged for the pistol next to the cabin wall. Lost in the sound of Katie's scream and the discharge of his pistol, Wiley's shocked grunt of pain went unnoticed. Feeling Wiley's knife drop from his hand, falling to the ground beside her shoulder, Katie was locked in a chaotic moment of confusion. Looking frantically for her father, she was shocked to see him unhurt, crawling for the pistol she had dropped. Looking up then, she realized what had happened to cause Wiley's shot to miss. No longer concerned with her or her father, Wiley was clutching at his throat and the arrow that protruded from both sides. *Luke!* She knew at once.

Though still pinned to the ground by the bulky Wiley as he sat straddling her hips, she could see that the outlaw had no thoughts beyond his own agony. His pistol and knife lay forgotten where he had dropped them, and he clawed desperately at the cruel wooden shaft that pierced his throat, reducing his attempts to yell to a bloody gurgle as he choked on his own blood.

In a matter of seconds, Luke suddenly appeared. Running up to the heavy man, he aimed a kick at Wiley's shoulder, but Wiley's bulk was too much to knock over with one kick from the slender youth. It took the efforts of Luke and Katie, he shoving and she straining, to finally roll the desperate man away.

Wiley fell to the ground, rolling in agony, each turn jarring the arrow and causing him to blubber nonsensical syllables as the blood began to strangle him. Concerned for Katie, Luke rushed to help her, leaving the mortally wounded man to writhe in pain.

"I'm all right," she assured him when his face registered concern at the blood covering her throat. "See about Pa," she said. At that moment, they were both startled by the explosion of a gunshot directly behind them. Turning at once toward the source, they saw Rufus Colefield seated with his back against the cabin wall and Katie's pistol in his hand. Immediately turning to look back at Wiley, they discovered him sitting upright on the ground, vainly reaching for his pistol, which lay only inches from his fingertips. There was a small black hole in his coat just above his belly button.

Moving quickly, Luke kicked the gun away from the outlaw's outstretched hand and stood back to watch him die. But the big man refused to die. Unable to speak, he cursed them with bloody growls as he painfully tried to push himself to his feet. Katie and Luke looked at each other in alarm. Then Katie went to her father's side and took the pistol from his hand. He simply sat there dazed as she fired two more shots into Wiley's body, aiming at his chest. He sat down again, heavily, his eyes glazed like those of a butchered cow. Then he tried to get up again.

"Die, damn you!" she screamed in frustration, firing once more before her pistol misfired. Throwing it aside, she looked all about her in the snow until she spotted Wiley's knife. But before she could pick it up, Luke snatched up Wiley's pistol and fired a bullet into the huge man's brain. Like a wounded buffalo, Wiley finally keeled over onto his side, blubbering once with his final breath.

Exhausted from their efforts, Luke and Katie stared blankly at each other for a long moment before Katie was calm enough to think about her father. "Help me get him in the house," she said to Luke.

Tending to her father's wounds before she permitted Luke to clean the knife wound on her neck, Katie heated some water over the fireplace to soak the matted blood from Rufus's hair. Luke watched in silence, moving occasionally to the door to look at the dark, lifeless mound that was Wiley's body. The man had been so hard to kill that Luke halfway expected the body to move. He had not hesitated to release the arrow that was still lodged in Wiley's throat—the man had been about to shoot Rufus—yet he could not explain the feeling that had now come over him. Somehow he knew that his life would never be the same. He could no longer say he had never killed a man. As a child, raised by his Shoshoni mother, he had seen violence in his young life. And like all Shoshoni boys, he dreamed of becoming a great warrior. But his boyhood dreams had all been in imagined scenes of battle against the Sioux or Cheyenne. This killing of Wiley had been desperate and personal. He would always remember this feeling.

It was almost an hour before Rufus seemed to regain his faculties and was able to sit up in a chair. "How do you feel?" Katie asked, watching her father closely. She had feared that Wiley's blows might have left him permanently addle-brained.

"Well," he sighed, "I reckon I'll live, but I ain't never had a headache like this before."

"I was afraid he killed you."

"I reckon I got a pretty hard head," he replied, wincing as he tried to smile. Then his face was serious for a moment. "I was trying to save you, honey."

She smiled. "I know you were, Papa. You did a brave thing, and no telling what might have happened if you hadn't shot him. I'm proud of you."

He smiled then, knowing that he had stood up in the face of disaster and done what any man of courage would have done. "I'm feelin' kinda dizzy. I think maybe I'd best lay down for a little while."

Katie knew it was time to confront the problem that loomed before them. If it was discovered that they had killed a member of the militia, they would be severely dealt with—no matter that it had been a case of self-defense. "We've got to get that body away from here before his friends find out he's missing," Katie said. "That so-called captain ain't going to take the killing of one of his men lightly."

Leaving her father in the cabin to rest, Katie

began to rake new snow over some of the blood-stains before the cabin door while Luke went to find Wiley's horse. When he returned, Katie was waiting for his help in removing the body. "I hope the two of us can get him up on that horse," she said. "He's as big as a mountain." As she had predicted, it was with a great deal of difficulty that the task was done. When the huge man's corpse was finally draped across the saddle, Katie shook her head and breathed a sigh of relief.

"I'd best cut my arrow out of his neck," Luke said.

"No, leave it. They'll know he was here as soon as that other man gets back. Maybe they'll think this one was killed by Indians on his way back."

"What if they think Chief Washakie's warriors did this?" Luke asked. "I don't want to cause trouble for my people."

"I wouldn't worry about it," Katie replied. "I don't think Simon Fry and his handful of scoundrels want to go after a village as big as Washakie's." She smiled slyly. "Besides, he's been trying to tell everybody in the valley that the Shoshonis have been raiding. This might make him believe his own lies."

"Maybe I oughta scalp him, then."

Though usually never squeamish about such things, Katie made a face. "Maybe. But wait till I go in the house."

After completing the grisly ritual, Luke led Wi-

ley's horse back down the wagon trace toward
the northern end of the valley. He left the horse,
with the corpse draped across the saddle, in a
thicket of young pines. When the sun came up
in the morning, he would ride his horse around
the old wagon bed, leaving plenty of tracks. No
use, he figured, in leaving only the tracks of the
two intruders, in case someone tried to piece the
puzzle together. Maybe Fry's men would not
know that Wiley had actually approached the
cabin after the other man rode away.

Katie was waiting for him when he returned.
"Luke, I can't ask you to stay here any longer.
There's gonna be hell to pay for this. That mur-
dering bunch is gonna come down on us hard.
They're not gonna rest before they've killed us
all."

Luke looked unblinking into Katie's eyes, steel-
like determination in his gaze. "I'm not gonna
leave you to fight Fry by yourself," he stated.

"Listen to me, Luke," she insisted. "I want you
to leave this place as soon as it's daylight. Go to
your mother's people. You'll be safe there.
You've got all your life ahead of you. You'll die
for sure if you stay here."

"What you say is probably true. Why don't
you go to Washakie's camp with me?"

"I can't. I have to take care of Pa, and I don't
think he can travel. He looks pretty stove up, but
he'd tell you the same thing I did. You go—as
fast as you can."

"I reckon I'll stay," he stated in a tone that left

no room for argument. "That bunch of trash might overrun us, but it'll damn sure cost 'em."

The issue settled, they returned to the cabin to prepare for the assault they knew would come. It wasn't likely to come before daybreak, but, unwilling to bet on it, Katie and Luke loaded their rifles and prepared to sit up all night.

Both Katie and Luke were unwilling to chance another visit from Fry's men that might not find them alert and ready to defend themselves. With the lamps extinguished and only the light of the fire, they each sat by a window with a rifle propped up close at hand. After several hours had passed with nothing outside but the silent snow, Katie got up and made a pot of coffee. While it was heating over the coals, she pulled the blanket that served as a partition aside and looked in on her father. Rufus was sleeping peacefully. She stood over him for a few moments, watching his steady breathing. She shook her head slowly in a brief moment of compassion as she noticed dried bloodstains on the pillow. *You done good, Pa*, she thought and smiled down at him before replacing the blanket and returning to her post by the window.

The long night finally faded into shades of gray, and the dark, solemn line of trees along the river rapidly began to acquire definition. Young Luke Kendall glanced back at Katie, now sleeping peacefully at her post by the small window in the front of the cabin. Finally overcome with fatigue, she had drifted off some two hours before sunup.

Reluctant to wake her, Luke had taken on the responsibility of keeping an eye out for Fry's men. Moving almost constantly from the front window to the smaller window at the back, he had waited out the night for the attack that never came. He knew Katie would scold him for allowing her to sleep, but he felt she needed the rest.

In a matter of mere minutes, the light crept across the yard from the edge of the corral, announcing the official end of the long night. With no sign of unwanted visitors in front or back, Luke laid his rifle aside and walked to the door. Stepping outside onto the frozen snow, he scanned the horizon from the white peaks beyond the northern end of the valley, along the low ridges to the east, and finally to the southern foothills. There was no one in sight.

"Luke?" He turned to glance back at the cabin when he heard Katie call from inside.

"I'm out here," he answered. In a few moments, she appeared in the open doorway. "Looks like we sat up for nothing," he offered in hopes of defusing the scolding he knew he was about to receive. As he had anticipated, he got it, anyway. But it was short and not too severe. When she had finished, she stepped back inside long enough to grab a coat to throw over her shoulders while she hurried along the frozen path to the outhouse behind the cabin.

"If you'll go ahead and build up the fire," she called back over her shoulder, "I'll fix us some breakfast."

"Yessum," he replied and started toward the stack of firewood at the side of the cabin. From the size of the stack, it looked to be about time for him and Rufus to take the wagon over beyond the ridge to cut some more wood. The thought brought his mind to Katie's father and the realization that the old man was sleeping later than usual. *He got a pretty hard blow to the head*, Luke thought. *Little wonder he might be in bed for a spell.*

When Katie came tiptoeing back from her toilet, shivering with the cold as she clutched the coat around her shoulders, Luke had already thrown a couple of chunks of firewood on the glowing coals and stirred up a fresh flame. Seeing him start for the door to look after the livestock, she said, "I'll look in on Pa. Then I'll start breakfast." When he nodded in response, she added, "Take your rifle with you." He nodded again, paused to pick up the weapon, then went outside.

Stopping behind the barn to take care of his own morning toilet, Luke thought about the events of the night just passed. It was a dead certainty that the so-called militia would pay them a visit. He and Katie had both expected it to come before daylight. The fact that it hadn't was no guarantee that the outlaws had been fooled by Luke's attempt to make it seem that Wiley had been attacked by Indians on his way back from the cabin last night.

Standing inside the small open-ended structure

that passed for a barn, Luke measured out a small amount of grain for each of the mules and horses. Ordinarily, he would have let them out to scratch around in the snow for grass, saving the grain for those long months when the snow would be too deep for them to graze. On this morning, he deemed it best to keep the horses close at hand. Replacing the grain bucket, he hesitated a second, thinking he had heard something from the cabin—a low cry or exclamation. Keeping very still, he listened, but there was nothing more. He figured it had just been his imagination. All his senses were acutely alert this morning, and his nerves were a little jumpy from lack of sleep.

When he started to return to the cabin, the black-and-white paint gently pushed its muzzle against his chest to be petted, and Luke paused to give it some affection. "I'm afraid I've spoiled you rotten," he said as he stroked the animal's forelock.

As soon as he walked in the cabin door, he knew something was wrong. Katie was standing by her father's bedside. She turned when she heard Luke come in. "Pa's gone," she said softly, as if trying not to wake him. She did not cry, but her eyes were wide and moist as she looked at Luke, revealing a sorrow that ran too deep for tears.

Rufus Colefield had passed on peacefully during the night, the blows that Wiley Johnson had administered to his skull having done fatal damage. Katie stood looking at him for a long time, thinking back to the start of their trek across the continent, which now seemed a hundred years past. The frightened little man was now at rest. Always remorseful for his failure to properly stand and fight beside his son-in-law, he had died while trying to fight in his daughter's defense. Then the condemning reality struck her that she was responsible for his brutal murder. She had pushed him to make the trip west, convinced him that there was no future in the rocky soil of his tiny farm in southern Ohio. She was the reason he had worked long hours scratching a living out of the soil, looking all the while over his shoulder for the Indian raid he feared might come again. At once her heart was filled with sorrow, and she silently begged for his forgiveness. Turning once again to Luke, she tried to speak but found she could not.

"It ain't your fault." The boy had stood silently by while she gazed down at her father. When she turned to face him again, he could read the guilt in her eyes and knew that she blamed herself. "Things happen the way they're supposed to."

She managed a smile for him. "I suppose so," she admitted quietly, knowing that he was repeating words that she had said to him when his mother and father had been killed. Calling on the strength and resolve that had carried her through so many hard times, she marshaled her will to face this new tragedy. "I don't know how much time we've got before we can expect a visit from the militia, but I'd like to bury Pa before they get here."

"Yessum," Luke replied softly and turned to leave.

She stopped him before he went out the door. "Luke, I reckon there's no longer any reason to stay here and wait to get killed. We might as well make a run for the Shoshoni camp."

Luke nodded, then said, "We can stay with my uncle."

Katie looked around her as if second-guessing her decision. This was her home, but was it worth standing to fight for? She gave a brief thought to the possibility of seeking help from one of the other families in the valley. But then the image of their faces when she had called them all to the meeting came back to her, and she remembered how blindly they believed in Simon Fry. She decided that she and Luke would be better off in the Indian village. "Then I guess we'd better bury Pa and get ready to ride."

Katie picked a gravesite under a towering cottonwood that stood by a narrow stream feeding into the river. It was a favorite spot of hers, where sagebrush buttercups signaled the first signs of spring each year. The ground was already hard from the snow and cold, but Luke attacked it with pick and shovel until he had a fair-sized grave. When it was ready, they went back to the cabin to get her father. "Help me put his coat on," Katie said as they started to move the stiffening body. "It's awful cold out there."

After they lowered Rufus Colefield's body into his grave, Katie covered his head and shoulders with an old tablecloth. "I don't want dirt in his face," she explained as she took one last look at her father before covering him. Then she got to her feet and turned abruptly toward the cabin, leaving Luke to shovel the dirt over him. "I'll get some food together. As soon as you're finished, get the horses. I don't know how much time we've got before they show up." Unable to prevent the tears any longer, she ran for the cabin, her rifle in her hand, her teary eyes searching the horizon for the sudden appearance of Simon Fry and his men.

Packing all the essential items they could on the horses, Katie and Luke rushed to get ready to run. There was no time to fret over the many things that would be left behind. They had to travel fast, and they couldn't be slowed down by a wagon. Consequently, Katie had to leave treasured family keepsakes and personal items that she had accumulated over the years. Luke dropped the bars in the feed room so the cow could help herself to the hay that was balled there. On Katie's suggestion, he left the barn door open. She figured the cow might wander down in the willow thickets by the river when she needed water. It saddened Katie to leave her, but they couldn't afford to be hampered by a cow if Simon Fry was on their trail.

A light snow began to fall as they climbed into the saddle and, each leading a couple of pack horses, rode out back of the barn and down by the river. Crossing over, they nudged the horses into an easy canter until they had left the cabin a couple of miles behind them. Reining their mounts back to a fast walk, they skirted Monk Grissom's cabin and crossed over the low ridge that ran the width of Horace Spratte's place. Katie was concerned that Horace might see them. They would just have to trust to luck that he was sitting by the fire on this cold winter morning. Once past Spratte's place, they hightailed it for the pass at the northern end of the valley. Katie did not voice it, but she made a solemn vow to herself that she would be back. Simon Fry might have the advantage now, but she had no intention of being chased out of her home for good.

Simon Fry was furious. "That rutty son of a bitch," he fumed. "I knew he was going to keep sniffing around some female until he fouled up my plans." He felt no remorse at Wiley's demise. Fry was angry because their number had been reduced by one. Now he had lost three men since his small gang had descended upon this valley and its settlement of peaceful farmers who should have offered no threat to his band of outlaws. To further irritate him, he had to send Caldwell out to find Clell, who, he suspected, was asleep somewhere instead of watching the trails out of the valley like he had been told.

Trask had returned the night before and told Fry what Wiley was up to. At the time, Fry was mad enough to go after Wiley, but Pitt had talked him out of it. "Let him have at that woman and get it outta his system," Pitt had advised. "He ain't gonna be worth a damn until he does."

"And then what?" Fry had wanted to know. "Explain to the rest of these folks why one of my men raped that Mashburn bitch? Then they'll probably expect me to discipline him some way."

Pitt had remained unperturbed. "If I know that crazy son of a bitch, I reckon Wiley won't leave nobody alive to complain."

"He better have killed the lot of them, the old man and that damn half-breed kid, too," Fry had stated. "We'd better ride over there first thing in the morning and see what kind of mess he left. We can burn the place and tell the rest of them that it was another Injun raid."

The light of day had revealed a worrisome twist to the situation, however: one that further fired Fry's anger. For Pitt spotted Wiley's horse leisurely making its way back to the cabin with Wiley's stiff and frozen corpse draped across the saddle. Trask had grabbed the horse's bridle when it came up to the cabin while Pitt walked around to its side. Taking hold of Wiley's boots and heaving up on them, he dumped the body unceremoniously onto the hard-packed snow.

They now stood staring at their former partner, his frozen body still half-bent from the saddle. "Injuns," Trask surmised, looking at the arrow protruding from Wiley's neck and the black blood-crusted dome where his scalp had been.

Pitt was not so eager to jump to that conclusion. "Injuns, my ass. You ever see an Injun kill a man and leave his horse—and his rifle in the saddle sling?" He glanced at Fry for his answer. "Well, I ain't," he concluded.

"That damn half-breed kid," Fry said, his mind in the same groove as Pitt's. "He's pretty handy with that damn bow of his."

"That arrow's just for show," Pitt concluded. "He's shot plumb full of holes. I reckon they wanted to make damn sure he was dead."

"You dumb whore-hound," Fry fumed now, directing his anger at the corpse. He drew his foot back and kicked the body hard, planting the toe of his boot in the dead man's ribs. It made a dull thud, as if he had kicked a rotten log.

Pitt grunted, amused by Fry's reaction. It always amused him to see Fry lose his temper. It sometimes made him wonder how he lasted as long as he did in that St. Louis bank before he had busted that senior vice president over the head. *The upright and proper Mr. Finch*, he thought.

"I told him he oughtn't to hang around that place," Trask reminded them. "But he wouldn't pay me no mind."

Ignoring Trask's remarks, Fry and Pitt were already looking ahead to the possible effect this latest incident might have on the rest of the people in the valley. "We've got no choice on one thing," Fry said. "We've got to get over to the Colefield place and silence the three of them. If they think they can get away with something like this, they might get the rest of these damn sheep thinking they can buck us, too. Let's get saddled up."

"You wanna wait for Clell and Caldwell to get back?" Pitt asked.

Fry hesitated for a second. "No," he decided. "No tellin' how long it'll take Caldwell to find that lazy bastard."

"What about Wiley?" Trask interjected.

Fry glanced down at the late Wiley Johnson as if annoyed to be reminded of him. "Drag him off in the woods yonder," he said, gesturing toward the river. "I don't wanna have to step over him every time I walk in the door."

Chapter 9

Lettie Henderson had made a big mistake. She knew it, and she was willing to admit it to herself. Things had not turned out as she had planned since leaving St. Louis to search for her father's murderer, Steadman Finch. But how could she have known that Harvey would contract cholera? He had been frail and sickly since he was a baby, and most of her friends in St. Louis had tried to convince her that her older brother could not stand up to the rugged land beyond the Missouri. It turned out they were right. Harvey had only made it about twenty miles past Fort Kearny before coming down with the debilitating sickness so many feared. That didn't mean she had been wrong to start out on the journey—just unlucky. They had actually been doing just fine. The weather had been good, and they had made good time ever since leaving Westport Landing.

She had done the best she could for Harvey when he became ill, but she was forced to watch helplessly as he retched his fragile life away until there was nothing left of him but a sheet of thin skin stretched over some bones.

Poor, sweet Harvey. He had been as zealous as

she to pack up and head out across the country in search of the man who had murdered their father. The mistake she had made, and now feared she was in danger of paying for, was in the hiring of Henry Bingham to guide them. Unwilling to spend the time to check Mr. Bingham's references because of the approaching winter, they had hired him wholly upon his word. Bingham had run off as soon as it was suspected that Harvey's sudden illness was cholera. He had heard the many tales of cholera epidemics and was not willing to expose himself to the possibility of catching it. Lettie suspected he had not run very far and had been keeping his eye on them from a distance, for as soon as poor Harvey was safely in the ground, Bingham had come slinking back, claiming his conscience wouldn't permit him to leave her all alone after contracting to take her to find Steadman Finch. He had showed up a little before dark, as contrite as could be, talking about how much he had worried about her.

There was little doubt in Lettie's mind that Bingham had returned solely because of the money he suspected was hidden in the wagon. What Bingham didn't know was that the money was not in any of the bags or satchels packed in the wagon. It was sewn inside her flannel drawers, and she vowed that if he or any other man found it, it would be on her cold, dead body. Wearing Harvey's revolver on her slender hip, she made it obvious to Bingham that she was not to be considered easy pickings.

The decision to terminate his contract had been made the instant he set foot back in camp. She hadn't told him of it yet, but she was of the opinion that she would not be safe alone in his company. Since Fort Kearny was only one day's ride back east, she felt now was the time to notify him of the change in plans.

After waiting for him to place new limbs on the fire and settle himself, she said, "I won't be needing your services any longer, Mr. Bingham. Since my brother is dead, I think I'll turn back to Fort Kearny." Her statement caused him to jerk his head up quickly, but, before he could respond, she went on. "Of course, I'll pay you for taking me this far."

His eyes dull as slate, he stared at her for a few moments before speaking. "Well, now, that sure is a right sad piece of news at this late date. I had to make a lot of changes in my plans to guide you out to Montana. Your sudden decision to turn back is gonna cause me some hardship. It's a long way back to St. Louis. Yes, ma'am, no doubt about that. But I reckon it'll be all right if you just pay me the whole fee we agreed on."

Lettie was firm in her response. "I think the advance you were paid in St. Louis should be sufficient to compensate you for your trouble to this point. I believe your desertion in the face of my brother's tragic illness would more than justify the cancellation of the agreement we made. I'll need what money I've got left—I've decided to take the train to Ogden in Utah territory. It's getting too late in the season to continue with a wagon. I see now that we were too optimistic in starting out, even before my brother fell ill."

"You're gonna take the train," Bingham repeated with a hint of contempt in his voice. "What about Steadman Finch? Who's gonna help you find him?"

"I'll hire someone in Ogden to guide me." She strove to maintain a firm posture.

"What about the wagon and the horses?" He continued to press her.

"I'll sell them at Fort Kearny."

He didn't say anything more for a long moment while he stood staring at her with eyes as lifeless as coal. His mind already made up, he glanced around him briefly, although there was no one in sight for miles.

Lettie's instincts told her that he was contemplating some evil deed, so she backed away a step and let her hand rest on the handle of her pistol. "I think it would be best if you take your leave now, Mr. Bingham," she said, striving to keep her voice from quavering.

Bingham watched her intently, considering his possibilities. A slight smile began to form at the corners of his mouth as he took a step toward her. "Well, all right, missy, if that's the way you want it." His smile broadened. "No harm done, I reckon. I'll just git my stuff together and be on my way."

Lettie relaxed a little, relieved that he seemed

to be agreeable to the parting—she should not have. He turned as if starting toward his horse. Then, before she could draw the pistol from its holster, he was upon her, knocking her to the ground. She tried to roll over so she could free her weapon, but he pounced upon her, pinning her arms against her sides. She fought to maintain possession of the weapon, but he easily overpowered her. Tearing away with her revolver now in his hand, he got to his feet and stood back a few steps, the pistol aimed at her.

"Now, I reckon I'll be the one what says what's gonna happen. First off, you owe me some money. You can save me some time by tellin' me where you got it hid." When she didn't reply, he grinned playfully. "Come on, now, it ain't gonna do you no good. I'm bound to find it. Might as well make this as easy as we can."

"I'm not going to tell you anything," Lettie replied defiantly. "I'm very disappointed in you, Mr. Bingham. I should have suspected you were a dishonest person. And you've had a surly attitude ever since we left St. Louis."

Bingham grinned again, unable to hide his amusement at her scolding. "My, my," he clucked. "I do apologize for being so rude." He moved to stand directly over her. Placing the pistol in his belt and extending a hand toward her, he said, "Here, give me your hand." She would not take it, watching him warily. "Come on," he coaxed, as if trying to calm a horse. "Come on, take my hand. I'll help you up."

Still she did not move, continuing to sit there in the dust while his hand remained extended toward her. After several minutes had passed with no motion by either party, she finally succumbed, grasped his hand, and started to pull herself up.

"That's better," he said, grabbing her hand and pulling her up toward him. When she was almost on her feet, he suddenly slugged her with his free hand, driving her back down upon the ground. The force of his fist against her jaw rattled her brain to the point where she was almost unconscious. "Now, let's git one thing straight," he advised. "If you sit there like a good little girl, I might not hurt you. But it's gonna be hell to pay for you if you make me any trouble, 'cause I'll hurt you bad." She lay there in a painful stupor while he turned and proceeded to start rummaging through the wagon.

After a few minutes, her head started to clear. She managed to get up on her hands and knees. Still groggy, she stared at her assailant through glazed eyes. She had never known personal violence in her young life, and the shock of her first experience with such brutal behavior was almost enough to totally incapacitate her. Bingham paid her very little attention, glancing in her direction from time to time as he pulled personal possessions from the packs and left them strewn upon the ground. Unsuccessful in finding what he searched for in the packs, he paused to give her a hard look before turning his attention to her late brother's gear. Though he spoke not a word, that look promised more violence to come if he didn't find the money soon. She almost cried out as she felt the warm tears of terror well in her eyes, and the throbbing of her jaw seemed to intensify with every beat of her heart.

Now she heard him cursing to himself as each compartment and each sack yielded nothing more than clothing and various dried foods and cooking utensils, his anger increasing by the second. Finding nothing in the wagon, he rifled the contents of her brother's saddlebags. Finally, when his search was completed with nothing to show for his efforts, he spun around to face her, but she was no longer there.

"I shoulda looked there in the first place," he muttered, realizing that she must have hidden the money somewhere on her person. It did not concern him that she was gone when he turned around. It would do her no good to run. There were very few places to hide along the creek bank where they had made their camp, and there were miles of open prairie beyond that.

Feeling no need for urgency, he untied his horse and stepped up into the saddle. In her haste to escape, Lettie had left an obvious trail through the sandy loam beside the creek. It was no trouble for Bingham to follow even in the failing evening light. The tracks led him down along the water, weaving around the thin line of cottonwoods that lined the bank, and into the shallow creek. He smiled to himself when he saw the imprint on the other side where she had fallen as she tried to run up the bank after leaving the water. He prodded his horse with his heels and crossed over. Once clear of the brambles that competed with the cottonwoods for the stream's nourishment, he looked out across the prairie. Espying her right away, he paused to watch her for a moment. Over a hundred yards away by then, she staggered drunkenly as she tried to run, her wind obviously having just about played out. Knowing he had all the time in the world, he held his horse to a walk.

When he was within twenty yards of overtaking her, Lettie heard the sound of his horse over the labored gasps of her breathing. She looked back at him and tried to scream, her face a desperate mask of terror. But she had no wind left to scream for help. Bingham could scarcely hear her thin cry. He chuckled to himself, amused by her helplessness.

Guiding his horse up against her, he took one foot from the stirrup and planted it between her shoulder blades, sending her crashing headfirst to the ground. Seeing the girl was spent, he took his time dismounting. "Well, now," he said, standing over her, "are we gonna do this the easy way or the hard way?"

Still gasping for breath, she tried to crawl away from him. "Get away from me," she pleaded, pushing herself through the dust as he paced her step for step.

"Have it your way," he said with a shrug. "Makes no never mind to me one way or the other." He placed his foot in her side and kicked her over onto her back. Before she could recover, he was on top of her, straddling her. When she tried to fight him, he slapped her hard across her face with the back of his hand. Although the blow made her head spin, she still struggled to resist him, but her efforts were becoming more and more feeble. His face a picture of pointed determination, he grabbed a handful of the heavy shirt she wore and, with one violent move, ripped it down the middle, revealing her long flannel underwear. "Huh," he grunted, surprised to find her wearing long johns. She made a desperate attempt to resist, but he easily overcame her efforts, ripping the buttons down the front.

Halted momentarily by the sight of her exposed chest, he stared stupidly at finely sculptured breasts that lay like perfect mounds of alabaster. "Damn," he exclaimed. "You ain't as young as you look. If I'da knowed what you been hiding under that shirt, I mighta made my move before we got to Westport." Stunned for only a moment, and driven by his lust for her money, he recovered to continue his search of her body. The money first, he decided, then the girl, knowing that he would kill her afterward.

"Come on, honey, I know you got it on you somewhere." Running his hand under the gun belt she wore and down inside her underwear, his fingers touched a pocket sewn inside the garment. "Hot damn!" he exclaimed. "I think I found something here."

She tried to claw at him with her nails, but he was too quick, grabbing her wrist before she could strike him. Feeling satisfied with himself now, he didn't bother to retaliate. His face lit up with an evil grin as his hand groped farther down into her long johns. If she heard the sharp crack that ripped the evening air, it didn't register in her terrified brain. She wasn't even aware of her own screaming until Bingham's grin froze briefly on his face and then melted away, replaced by a look of horrified disbelief. Then suddenly he was gone, snatched from her body in the wink of an eye, the fingernails of his groping hand leaving raw marks across her belly.

Unable to believe her eyes, Lettie sat up to discover a man on horseback dragging Bingham behind him. Bound by the end of a whip lashed tightly around his throat, the hapless man clawed frantically to free his windpipe as his body bumped unceremoniously over the rough ground. She gazed in wonder at the man who had appeared from nowhere to dispatch Mr. Bingham in such rude fashion. Still unsteady, she managed to get to her feet, not sure if she should try to run or not.

The stranger pulled his horse to a stop about fifty yards away from her and turned to face Bingham, who was now on his feet, still trying to free his throat of the rawhide coil. The stranger sat silently watching Bingham, a rifle lying across his saddle. Shaken and bruised, Bingham finally flung the end of the whip from him. Almost in the same instant, he pulled the pistol from his belt and fired. In his haste to vent his anger, he didn't take time to aim the weapon, and his shot went wide of the mark. He did not have the luxury of a second shot. Before he could pull the trigger again, he was struck in the chest with a .45 slug from the stranger's Winchester.

Jim Culver held his rifle trained on the wounded man, ready to put another bullet in him if necessary. But the pistol dropped from Henry Bingham's hand, falling harmlessly in the prairie dust. Bingham stared at Jim, unseeing, for what seemed to Lettie to be minutes before he finally crumpled to the ground. Only then did the stranger take his eyes off him and dismount.

"Are you all right, miss?" Jim asked as Lettie hurriedly pulled her torn shirt together in an effort to cover her exposed bosom. He reached down and picked up the pistol that had fallen from Bingham's hand.

"Yes," she stammered, not really sure. "I think so." She watched the stranger with a wary eye, not certain at this point if she had been rescued from one peril only to be subjected to another.

"My name's Jim Culver," he said. "I hope that man was not your husband." There had been no way he could have known if he was interrupting a family fight or not. If it was, he knew that it was no way for a husband to treat his wife, so he felt he had been left with little choice but to interfere. As far as the shooting was concerned, that had been Bingham's choice and not his. His intention had been simply to stop the lady's obvious distress.

"Heavens, no," Lettie replied at once. "He was my guide. No, I think you have just saved my life, sir."

"Then I guess it's good I came along when I did," Jim said. He had an opportunity now to take a closer look at the second damsel in distress he had rescued. He realized that she looked a bit younger than he had first imagined. He dismounted and dropped Toby's reins. Although he had scouted the camp and found no one before riding in, he looked around him now, half-expecting other members of the party to appear out of the growing darkness. But no one showed, which brought to mind the obvious question: What was a young lady doing out here on the prairie with no one but a guide? *A rather frail young lady at that,* he thought as he studied the thin white face, now slightly lopsided with a red welt and a lump on one cheek. He couldn't help but blink when his gaze lifted to find two dark doelike eyes locked on his, and he realized that he was being evaluated with even more intensity. He attempted to put her mind at ease.

"My name's Jim Culver," he repeated. "I came across your camp back yonder by the creek. I wondered where everybody was. Then I heard you scream, and I decided I'd better come have a look." He endeavored to form a friendly expression on his face. The girl still seemed a little nervous. "Are you sure you're all right?"

Gradually, she began to relax her guard, sensing the honesty in his voice. "Yes," she answered after a furtive glance in the direction of Bingham's body. "I'm all right now."

"Here, maybe you better hang on to this." He handed her the pistol, noticing she wore an empty holster. "I'm wondering what in the world you're doing out here and how you happened to be with that fellow. You say he was a guide?"

"He said he was," she answered, calm again now that she sensed this stranger intended no harm. "Although I'm afraid it was poor judgment on our part. I'm not sure he had the slightest idea where he was leading my brother and me."

"I doubt he intended to lead you anywhere except maybe the middle of nowhere," Jim said. "Why don't we go on back to your camp. I could use a cup of coffee." He tossed a glance toward the late Henry Bingham. "He ain't going nowhere. I'll take care of him in the morning."

Taking Toby's reins, he walked back to camp with her. When he started rummaging in his saddlebags for some coffee, she stopped him, insisting that she would furnish the coffee beans. "It's the least I can do," she said. So he rekindled the fire, then took care of his horse while she ground the beans and fetched water from the creek. Soon coffee was boiling, and he sat across from her while she told him how she happened to be in such a forsaken place with the evil Mr. Bingham.

It was a little over seven years ago when her father had been murdered. Lettie had been just a child of nine when a man who worked with her father had brutally murdered him by crushing his skull with a poker. Jonah Henderson, a senior vice president of the Midland Bank, had provided a handsome living for his family. Lettie and her older brother, Harvey, had adored their father and were devastated by his death. Their mother had never really recovered, seeming to wither away a little more with each year that passed after her husband was so cruelly taken.

Steadman Finch was the man who had so wantonly struck her father down, killing a man who been a mentor to him—even after the ungrateful Finch was promoted to a vice presidency himself. It had been her father's misfortune that Steadman Finch's integrity had failed to match his ambition. Lettie's mother had told her in later years that her father had begun to suspect some of Finch's dealings some time before he actually caught him in the act of transferring funds to his personal account. When confronted with the deed, Finch had taken the course that men of low moral values and evil intentions often take. He had struck her father down and run.

"I think the fact that Finch escaped punishment for taking my father from us greatly contributed to my mother's failing health," Lettie said. "I don't believe a day passed that she didn't dwell upon it. I think she just didn't care to live anymore. A year ago, she developed pneumonia, and the doctor said it was like she didn't even try to fight it. In less than a month, she was gone." Lettie paused a moment to compose herself before continuing.

"Last fall, a friend of the family returned from Montana territory, where he had spent the summer hauling freight from the mining towns. He was certain that he had seen Steadman Finch in a saloon in Virginia City." Her eyes opened wide with emotion at the thought. "My brother and I decided to go to Virginia City and bring my father's murderer to justice."

Jim listened to Lettie's story without comment. Gazing at the slip of a girl on the opposite side of the fire from him, he marveled at the audacity of the undertaking. "Where is your brother now?"

"I buried him yesterday," she answered softly, her chin dropping slightly.

"Oh. I'm sorry. Bingham?"

"No," she quickly replied, shaking her head. "Harvey was ill. I think it was cholera."

"Damn, excuse me, you've had your share of

bad luck." Seeking to change the subject, he asked, "How did you hook up with Bingham?"

"We placed an advertisement in the paper," she replied, dropping her head again to hide her embarrassment at having to admit to such naivete.

Jim was kind enough to keep his opinion of that to himself. He was sure she had already paid dearly enough for that mistake. "Well," he remarked, "a lot of things don't work out the way we plan 'em. I reckon I can escort you back to Fort Kearny in the morning. Can you get back to St. Louis all right from there?"

"I'm sure I can, Mr. Culver, but I hate to delay you any further. I'm sure you were on your way somewhere when you happened upon us."

"No trouble, miss. I'm heading out Montana-way myself, but it's already a little late to be starting out. It took me over a month to get this far from Virginia. A day or so longer won't make much difference. I expect I'll be able to get to Fort Laramie in a week or ten days, maybe Montana territory, before hard winter hits."

"Very well, then. Once again, I find myself in your debt."

Lettie insisted upon fixing a late supper for them even though it would have to be pretty skimpy. It consisted primarily of some side meat and more coffee. What with the activities of the past couple of days, there had been little thought toward planning meals. There were not even any dried beans soaking in the crock. She apologized for her lack of preparation, but Jim assured her that he was not really hungry, anyway.

After their meager supper, Jim helped Lettie recover the strewn items that Bingham had pulled from the wagon during his frantic search for her money. When that was done, she retired to the wagon while Jim rolled out his bedroll by the fire. In spite of her first impression of Jim Culver, she had every intention of staying awake during the night in case her knight had a blacker side that he had kept hidden.

Despite her intentions, she found it difficult to remain awake, dozing off several times through the night only to awaken with a start and peer under the edge of the cotton wagon cover—each time to observe a man peacefully asleep. In the deep hours before daybreak, she unwittingly surrendered to her growing state of exhaustion and settled into a sound sleep. Sunup found her still warm in her blankets, finally stirring to the sound of a frying pan bumping against stones set in the campfire. Remembering where she was, she bolted upright and grabbed the edge of the wagon cover to look out.

At last seeing some sign of life from the wagon, Jim stood up and called out, "Good morning, miss. I hope you don't mind. I borrowed your skillet. Thought we could use a little bacon and coffee before we get started."

Embarrassed at having slept so late, she quickly scrambled out of the wagon. "If you'll give me a minute to freshen myself, I'll see if I can't fix something to add to that." She hurried down to the creek, glancing back at him frequently until she was hidden by the trees that lined the bank.

The morning was chilly, with a light dusting of frost on the willow branches where Lettie performed her toilet. Washing her face and hands in the shallow current, she could not help but shiver. As she dried her face, she thought about her decision to go to Omaha to catch the train. Now that Harvey was no longer with her, it would be easy to lose her resolve and go back to St. Louis. Her uncle was probably right. It was utter foolishness for a girl of sixteen to cross the continent with no more than a boy of eighteen to look after her. He would think it absolutely insane for her to continue if he knew that Harvey was dead. And yet it galled her to her very soul to know that Steadman Finch was roaming free as you please after slaying her father.

She walked back a short way along the creek bank until she had a clear view of the camp again. Shielding herself behind a large cottonwood, she peered around the trunk to study the tall young man who had appeared the night before. His back to her, he busied himself by the fire, seeming to display no interest in her private goings-on. She had made a mistake by accepting

Henry Bingham at face value. Was she now making a similar mistake? What did she know about this man? He might be a cold-blooded murderer or highwayman. After all, he had dispatched Bingham handily. *If he were going to murder me and take my money, he would most likely have done it last night while I was sleeping so soundly.* She knew she had no desire to return to St. Louis. There was nothing there for her now that her family was gone. And she couldn't bear the thought of going to live with her aunt Mattie. *No.* She made her decision. *I'm going to find Steadman Finch, and I need someone I can depend on to help me.* The matter settled in her mind, she walked back to the campfire.

"I've changed my mind," she announced as she approached. "I'm not going back to Fort Kearny. I'm taking my wagon on to Montana as I had planned."

Jim sat back on his heels and gave her a long appraising look. "That don't sound like a real good idea," he said. "There's a lot of wild country between here and Montana territory—no trip for a young girl to take alone. It might be a whole lot better if you go on up to take the train like you said before."

"I guess you're right, but I'm not planning to go alone. I'm going with you."

"Whoa! Hold on a minute," Jim uttered in surprise. The determined look in the young lady's eyes told him that she was deadly serious. "I don't know if that's a good idea or not." Momentarily flustered by the audacity of the young woman, he tried to collect his thoughts. "You can't go with me," he blurted.

"Why not?"

"W-well," he stammered, "you just can't. I mean, I'm traveling alone. I can't . . ." He struggled to find reasons, but none leaped to mind. "Why, you're not much more than a kid. How old are you, anyway?"

"It doesn't matter how old I am. I'm old enough to drive that team of mules, and I'm going to drive them to Montana with or without you." She watched him closely, waiting for his reaction. "I've got some money. I can pay you to guide me." She paused, raised an eyebrow, and smiled. "Since you killed my guide . . ."

He shook his head in wonder, finding it difficult to believe he had ridden into such a situation and not really knowing what to tell this precocious girl. "Hell, I don't want your money. I'm not a guide, anyway. Right where I'm sittin' is as far west as I've ever been. I'm not even sure where I'm heading. I'm just heading west."

"You mentioned that you hoped to make Fort Laramie in a week or so. Do you know how to find Fort Laramie?"

"Well, yeah. Any fool can find Fort Laramie. I ain't worried about getting there. I just don't know where I'm going after I get there. I was aiming to look for my brother Clay. He's out in the territory somewhere. But it's an awful big territory. I don't know if I'll ever find him."

"All right, then," she replied with dogged determination. "You can take me as far as Fort Laramie, and I'll make other arrangements there."

Lost for an answer, and not really sure why he was against the proposition, he remained silent while Lettie gazed impatiently into his eyes. He returned her gaze for a few moments before having to avert his eyes to escape the girl's penetrating stare. Having made up her mind, she was not to be put off. "I could not help but notice that you seem to be traveling extremely light to be contemplating a trip of such length," she said.

He shrugged indifferently. "I don't need much. I can hunt for my food."

"What about your horse?" Lettie insisted. "I notice that he is looking a bit poorly. So much of the grass has been fairly well grazed off."

Again, he shrugged. "Toby's pretty tough. He'll manage."

She continued. "I've got an ample supply of grain in my wagon, enough for my animals and your horse. I've also got two hundred pounds of flour, almost one hundred and fifty pounds of bacon, and a twenty-five-pound bag of coffee, sugar, salt, and a great many other things one needs to cross the continent." She paused to see if he appreciated the significance of her words. "It would seem that I'm better equipped to undertake the journey than you are, Mr. Culver. It would make sense to join forces."

He shook his head, defeated. "It does seem that way, doesn't it?" Convinced that she was probably truthful when she threatened to go it alone if he declined, he relented. He decided someone as precocious and stubborn as Lettie Henderson shouldn't be allowed to wander off across the prairie by herself. The next fellow she bumped into might be another Henry Bingham—or a hostile Indian. And she did have all those provisions. He scratched his head, hesitating to close the deal. Then, extending his hand, he said, "All right, you've got a partner."

Beaming with delight, she eagerly took his hand. "Good," she pronounced. "Let's get started to Fort Laramie."

"Let me go take care of Mr. Bingham first. I don't wanna take a chance on poisoning the buzzards."

Not waiting for—or asking for—his help, Lettie immediately went about hitching her team while Jim saddled Toby and rode back across the stream. When he arrived at the site of the prior night's fatal confrontation, there was already a ring of buzzards circling high overhead. Holding a pick he had taken from Lettie's wagon, he dismounted and stood looking at the stiffened corpse gazing wide-eyed up at him. It registered with him that he was looking at the second man he had killed. It was not something that overly disturbed him. Each man had made the first move. And as far as he could judge, each man had left the world a better place without him. After relieving Bingham of his gun belt and a pocketknife, he looked at the hard-baked prairie upon which the late Henry Bingham lay. To test the ground, he took a half-hearted swing with his pick. It penetrated no more than three inches before meeting solid resistance. He glanced back up in the sky to watch the buzzards circling. "Buzzards gotta eat, too," he said. He picked up the pick and climbed back on Toby. Turning his horse toward camp, he tossed back over his shoulder, "Clean up after you finish, boys."

Chapter 10

Remaining on the south side of the river, Jim and Lettie set out for Fort Laramie, following the Platte and the obvious trails left by the thousands of settlers who had made the journey before them. Jim learned right away that he had teamed up with an exceptionally capable young lady. As frail as a splinter, Lettie nonetheless commanded her mules with a firm hand on the reins. He had suspected that he would have to do most of the driving but soon found out that she had not been exaggerating when she boasted that she had driven them all the way from St. Louis.

Lettie had been correct in her assessment of Jim's horse. Toby was showing signs of fatigue after carrying Jim and his provisions all the way from Virginia without rest periods of any length. Jim felt a genuine sense of guilt for not taking better care of his horse. Until Lettie had to draw his attention to it with her casual remark, it had always been fixed in his mind that Toby was indestructible and could stand up under any task. He now reminded himself that he was not the only one setting out on a journey of this length for the first time. It was Toby's first time, too. And the gentle Morgan had been raised on a portion of oats at regular intervals throughout his lifetime. Ever since Kentucky, Toby had survived on grass alone. It was taking him some time to adjust to it even though it should have been his natural way of feeding. Jim promised his horse that he would take better care of him from that day forward.

They now had two extra horses tied on behind the wagon, a solid black with a white star on its face—the late Mr. Bingham's horse—and a handsome bay that Lettie's brother, Harvey, had ridden. Given the opportunity to rest Toby, Jim elected to ride the bay while scouting along their route of travel. The horse's name was Samson, after the biblical strongman. But the name was immediately shortened to Sam after Jim got more acquainted with the spirited stallion. Lettie said it had been her brother's favorite horse, purchased from a breeder in Jim's home state of Virginia. It didn't take long for Jim to appreciate the horse's qualities. After spending one day in the saddle, he was properly impressed with the quickness and agility of the horse. Its massive quarters and heavily muscled thighs and gaskins enabled the even-tempered mount to spin on a notion and start quicker than a thought. Sam was about the same size as Toby, a little over fifteen hands high, and Toby seemed not to resent the competition. The two horses took to each other right away, blowing in each other's nostrils to introduce themselves. In fact, Jim figured his horse appreciated the vacation.

For almost the first full week of travel, there was very little conversation between the two in the newly formed partnership. Jim, as a rule, was not inclined to make idle conversation. And Lettie, in spite of her secure feelings about the man she traveled with, was still cautious about her situation. As a result, conversation tended to consist mostly of polite communication regarding trail decisions and camp chores. After a few weeks of monotonous grinding across a never-changing Nebraska plain, however, a more casual atmosphere naturally developed. By the time they reached Scott's Bluff, they had become quite easy in each other's company.

For much of the journey, Jim tied the horses on behind the wagon and walked along beside it. Always, when the terrain up ahead threatened to take on different characteristics from the gently rolling plain, Jim rode out ahead to find the best route around hills or gullies. He was also mindful of the possibility that the closer to Fort Laramie they came, the more likely there might be signs of Indians. In their entire trek together, all the way since Plum Creek, they had seen no sign of Indians of any kind. This flew in the face of what Henry Bingham had told Lettie to expect. Jim suspected that Bingham had probably been trying to justify the fee he had charged Lettie by planting some seeds of danger in her mind.

Several miles past the point where the river forked, creating the South Platte and the North Platte, they saw their first Indians. Jim spotted them first. Off in the distance, three mounted Indians sat motionless at the top of a rise to the north of the trail Jim and Lettie followed. They showed no signs of interest in the two white people in the wagon.

A blacksmith at Fort Kearny had told Jim that there had been no reports of Indian trouble for some time along the old immigrant trail. But he had also advised the young man that it was always prudent to keep your eyes open anyway. Indians were like most folks: there were good ones, and there were bad ones. The blacksmith's comments were in the back of Jim's mind now as he guided Toby up a bluff to look for the best route for the wagon to skirt a line of cutbacks and gullies that ran down to the river. The favored route, verified by the multitude of wagon tracks Jim could see from his position on the bluff, was obviously through a short draw some one hundred yards from the banks of the river. He turned to take another look at the three Indians. They had not moved, seeming content to merely watch from a distance. Deciding that was the extent of their interest, Jim wheeled Toby and made his way back down the bluff to intercept Lettie.

"The best way seems to be up that draw yonder," he said, turning in the saddle to point the way. "Our three friends out there are still sitting in the same place, but I think we'd best get on through as soon as we can and get out on that flat beyond, where we can keep an eye on 'em."

"Do you think they see us?" Lettie asked, not at all comfortable in her first encounter with Indians. As if in answer to her question, one of the mounted warriors raised his hand and held it high in the air.

"Well, I reckon there ain't any doubt about that now." Jim raised his hand in response to what he assumed was a polite greeting. "I don't claim to know a blame thing about Injuns, so I don't know what they've got in mind. Looks like they're just watching so far." He nudged Toby with his heels. "Let's get this wagon to the other side of these gullies." Whipping up her mules, she drove her wagon after him.

Knowing they could get the wagon past the narrow draw long before the three Indians would have time to catch them, Jim figured he'd rather meet them on the open flat if, in fact, the Indians had it in mind to pay them a visit. Looking back frequently to hurry Lettie along, he led her along old wagon tracks cut deep in the sand of the narrow passage. Even with the four mules pulling, the wagon mired deep, coming almost to a stop near the middle of the draw. Just as Jim was turning back to help, he heard the first shot and saw one of the lead mules drop in its traces.

Cursing himself for a greenhorn, he knew then that the three Indians they had seen were but a part of a larger raiding party. And the gesture he had assumed to be a friendly greeting was, in fact, a signal to the ambush waiting ahead. With no time to lament and precious little to get back to the wagon, he kicked Toby hard, as he could now hear more shots ringing out. The other lead mule dropped, kicking and screaming in agony as it rolled over onto its mate in the traces. "Get down!" he yelled to Lettie.

She was on the ground beside the wagon, her pistol in hand, when he slid to a stop and came immediately out of the saddle. Her eyes wide in alarm, she waited for his instructions.

"Get down under the wagon," he commanded. "Stay behind the wheel and dig into that sand as much as you can." He looked around him, quickly assessing their position and trying to spot the origin of the rifle fire while Lettie did as he directed. "Damn," he muttered, "this ain't good." The raiders had effectively stopped the wagon by shooting the mules. And now they had the two of them pinned down under the wagon.

After a few more random shots, there was a lull in the rifle fire. Jim continued to scan the sides of the draw, looking for a target. He came to the quick conclusion that there was only one rifle, but he still could not find the source. He glanced over at Lettie in time to see an arrow jam into the sand behind her feet. A moment later, he heard dull thuds above them as more arrows struck the sides of the wagon box.

"Keep watching that side over there," he said and shifted his body around to face the opposite direction. He had been unable to spot the one with the rifle, but he figured that a man had to expose himself to use a bow. His rifle ready, his eyes darted back and forth along the crest of the draw, searching for movement. Suddenly, he spotted a warrior coming quickly to his knee to take aim. Before he had time to release his arrow, Jim cut him down and immediately shifted his eyes back along the ridge of the draw, searching again. As an arrow embedded itself in the side of the wagon just above his head, Jim spotted a slight movement in a large clump of bushes to his right. He fired at the clump, but there was no sound to indicate whether or not he had hit anything. Out of the corner of his eye, he caught movement to his left, and he quickly shifted his rifle back to cut down a second warrior who had raised himself up to shoot.

"What about the horses?" Lettie yelled, still keeping her eyes pasted on the other side of the draw.

"There ain't much we can do for 'em," Jim replied. "They probably want the horses. I doubt they'll try to shoot 'em." At that moment, he spotted more movement in the leaves of the clump of bushes, followed by another arrow in the sand before him. This time the arrow had come from another part of the bushes. He fired at the bushes again but hit nothing. *You son of a bitch*, he thought. *I'll fix your ass.* Moving with all the hustle he could muster, he crawled out from under the wagon, jumped up on the front wheel hub, and jerked a double-barreled 12-gauge shotgun from under the seat. His sudden action brought the Indian with the rifle back into the attack, and a bullet sent splinters flying only inches from his behind. He heard Lettie's pistol answering.

"I see where he is," Lettie said, her voice trembling with excitement as Jim scrambled back under the wagon.

"Good," Jim said, " 'cause that last one was a little too close for comfort." He wriggled around to see where she was pointing. "Keep your eye on that spot. I've got to take care of this one in the bushes." After checking to make sure the shotgun was loaded, he crawled back close to the front wheel and watched the clump of bushes closely. In a few seconds, he caught the slight movement of a couple of leaves move. Almost instantly, another arrow struck the wagon box. The shotgun roared as Jim sent a hail of lead where he had seen the leaves move. Not waiting, he shifted his aim a few feet to the right and fired the other barrel into the clump. This time he was rewarded with a sharp yelp of pain. Putting the shotgun aside, he picked up his rifle again and reloaded while keeping a sharp eye on the rim of the draw behind them. For a little while, the rain of arrows on Lettie's side increased. But there were no more from Jim's side.

After a few minutes with still no shots from that side, Jim decided that there had been no more than three on that side of the draw—no doubt the same three they had seen on the hill before the ambush.

Turning his attention back to the Indian with the rifle, Jim crawled up beside Lettie. "You all right?"

"I'm all right," she replied. "I just can't hit anything with this pistol."

"You shoulda grabbed this shotgun when you jumped down. Too bad I didn't have time to get some shells with it. Maybe I can get a shot at this son of a gun that's got the rifle. You still got him spotted?"

She nodded and pointed to a low mound near the mouth of the draw. "He stays behind that hump with just the barrel sticking out when he shoots. I shot at him twice, but I didn't hit anything but dirt."

"What about the others?" he asked.

"As best I can determine, there are several others spread out to the right of him. I can't tell how many."

Feeling reasonably confident that their assailants were all on one side of them now, Jim studied the mound that Lettie had pointed out. "I figure they ain't got but one rifle. And I'm betting he ain't got a lot of ammunition for it, 'cause he sure ain't shooting very much. I'm gonna see if I can get a better angle on him." He started to back away from her.

"What do you want me to do?" Lettie asked, sensing he was preparing to make a major move.

"Just keep your eyes open, honey, and shoot at anything you think you can hit." He pulled back on his hands and knees, then paused again. "Shoot at it even if you don't think you can hit it."

Crouching low behind the wagon, Jim moved quickly past the front wheel before dropping to one knee to take another look at the mound. Lettie was right. He could see the barrel of a rifle laying in a scooped-out groove to the left of the mound. He still had no clear shot. The angle was not right. Rising to a crouch again, he moved quickly forward to take cover behind the frightened mules. Already frantic from the shooting and the two carcasses that prevented them from bolting, they spooked when he suddenly appeared beside them. Their movement was spotted at once by the Indian behind the dirt mound, and he rose up and fired. Jim's reaction was immediate. He returned fire, nailing the Indian in the center of his breastbone, then jumped quickly aside to avoid being buried beneath the mule that had caught the warrior's bullet.

Certain that the rifle was the only one among the raiding party, he knew he had no time to lose. It was a race between him and the rest of the warriors to get to the rifle. With reckless abandon, he ran across the draw and charged up the other side. Seeing his charge, warriors popped up from the edge of the rim to take shots at him. Ignoring the arrows that flew all around him, Jim scrambled up the steep side of the mound to confront a startled Indian in the process of reloading the single-shot Springfield rifle. The unfortunate warrior never had a chance, instantly doubling over with a slug in his belly. Before the man hit the ground, Jim turned his Winchester on the brave's comrades, firing as fast as he could cock the lever and pull the trigger. There were seven of them along the rim. Jim dropped three of them in rapid succession before the other four fled in the face of certain death.

Jim stood there for a few minutes, watching as the four surviving warriors leaped upon their ponies and disappeared over the rise to the north. He remained there until they were out of sight before turning back to see about Lettie. Just as he turned, he was startled by a gunshot right behind him. On reflex, he dropped to one knee and brought his rifle up to shoot, only to discover the warrior he had shot in the breastbone crumpling to the ground, a war ax in his hand. Behind the Indian, Lettie stood, still pointing her Colt Peacemaker at the warrior's back.

"Godamighty," he said softly. The look on the young girl's face told him that she was more startled than he. Seemingly dazed, she stared at the body of the warrior for a long moment before looking up at Jim with eyes wide open.

"I'm much obliged," he said. Realizing that the act of killing a man could be quite a shock to anyone, and likely even more so for a girl of her age, he walked over and took the pistol from her hand. Then he gently dropped it in her holster. "Looks like he was about to settle my hash with that ax," he said. She blinked several times as if waking up from a dream, and then the color began to return to her face.

"I thought he was going to kill you," she uttered, barely above a whisper.

"He would have," he said with quiet conviction. "Now, we'd best get ourselves out of this place. We've got some work to do before we can get started."

With Jim directing her, Lettie soon recovered from the shock of killing a man. He didn't let her take the time to think about it. Wasting as little time as possible, he cut Lettie's one surviving mule from the traces and set about rigging a couple of pack harnesses. They had no choice but to leave the wagon, as well as much of the provisions Lettie had hauled all the way from St. Louis. Using the mule and Bingham's black horse as pack animals, Jim loaded as much of the supplies as he thought they could carry. When they were ready to get under way again, Jim took a last look at the bodies of the dead Indians. Then they started out for Fort Laramie. Lettie didn't look back at her wagon as she sat on Sam's back, following Jim's lead.

* * *

As near as Lettie could figure, it was the end of October when the buildings of Fort Laramie first appeared on the horizon. They were a welcome sight. She stood up in the stirrups to acknowledge Jim's signal as he circled Toby a few hundred yards ahead, waving and pointing toward an assembly of buildings on an almost treeless expanse. To Jim, gazing at the wooden structures as he waited for Lettie to catch up to him, the buildings looked more like a town than a fort. Nevertheless, it was a military installation and that fact gave him pause to think about the reason he had left Virginia.

Maybe he should be concerned that the army might be looking for him. But he reasoned that there were several witnesses to the incident on the banks of the Rapidan River, one of them a civilian, Sheriff Thompkins. Thompkins would surely testify that it had been a simple case of self-defense when Jim shot Lieutenant Ebersole. It seemed unlikely that the army would pursue the issue, especially in light of the fact that their numbers had been so drastically reduced since the war. They were already spread too thin on the western frontier to worry about little more than protecting settlers on their way to Oregon and California. The vast country west of the Missouri was still a world apart from Virginia. It didn't figure that the army had the time or the manpower to chase after the hundreds of outlaws who had fled to the west to lose their former identities. If he had remained in Virginia,

however, he felt that there most likely would
have been some investigation. He had long before decided that he was going to head west.
Shooting the arrogant lieutenant had just presented him with the opportune time to leave.
After thinking it over, he decided he had no
reason for concern as he entered Fort Laramie.

Arriving at Fort Laramie caused a bewildering
mixture of emotions for Lettie. As she guided
Sam along the sandy banks of the Laramie
River, she suddenly experienced a feeling of
dread at the realization that her journey with
Jim Culver had reached its end. Fort Laramie
was the agreed-upon destination for their partnership. Confident and independent, defiant
even, when their journey had begun, she now
realized how much she had come to depend
upon the broad-shouldered young man riding
easily in the saddle, the two pack animals on
lead ropes behind him.

The damning thought kept returning to her
mind: *What would she had done without his
blazing-fast rifle when the Indians had ambushed
them?* Yet she admitted to herself that there was
more to her feelings than that. She would simply
flat-out miss having him around. He was a
friend. They had fought off an Indian attack together. It didn't seem right that they should just
say, *So long, maybe I'll bump into you again somewhere.* She wondered if he was having similar
thoughts. *If he did, he would never say so.* She
remembered little things that had stuck in her

mind. When they were pinned down under the wagon, and he told her to shoot at anything she thought she could hit, he had called her "honey." Did that have special meaning? Or was it just a casual slip of the lip? She suddenly shook her head as if to clear it of such useless meandering and reminded herself that she had come west to find Steadman Finch. She forced herself to concentrate upon that objective and not let girlish emotions interfere.

The object of her emotional contemplation led the horses toward the parade ground, past a long building that looked to be a barracks. A group of several soldiers lounging on the end of the porch stopped talking to gaze at the young woman riding the bay. Jim asked directions to the sutler's store. He was directed to a building a little way beyond the barracks.

Jim pulled Toby up at the rail and dismounted. "Well, I reckon we made it to Fort Laramie," he said with a broad grin on his face, waiting for Lettie to hand him Sam's reins.

"Yes, I reckon we did," she replied, reflecting his smile. She stepped down, stiff from riding and the chilly afternoon air. It felt good to be on her feet again, and she took a few steps back and forth to give her blood a chance to flow, warming her legs.

There was now the question of what to do, a subject that neither party broached at this time, simply because neither Jim nor Lettie had the slightest idea. Jim wasn't quite sure where he

was heading from here. He had a vague determination to look for his brother Clay, but he
had no idea where to look and sense enough to
realize the vastness of the country beyond Fort
Laramie. He hoped that someone here might
know of Clay and possibly his whereabouts.
Lettie likewise was possessed only of purpose
and nothing more as far as direction was concerned. Montana territory could just as well be
on the moon. And though her resolve was still
there, she was almost ready to admit that there
was little hope of finding Steadman Finch in the
great expanse of the high plains and the Rocky
Mountains. It was with these separate but
equally discouraging realizations that the two
travelers entered the sutler's store.

"Clay Culver?" echoed Alton Broom, the clerk
in the Post Trader's Store. "Sure, I know Clay.
I mean, I know him about as well as anybody
does. He keeps pretty much to hisself. It warn't
more'n a month ago he was here, though—rode
scout some for the army this past summer. I
couldn't say where he is now. He didn't say
where he was goin'—just that he was goin'. Clay
seldom does. What was you lookin' for him
for?"

"He's my brother," Jim replied. "I was hoping
to join up with him for a while."

"Your brother?" Broom was genuinely surprised. The statement equated to someone saying they were brother to a timber wolf. "Well,

I'll be . . ." He extended his hand. "Alton Broom's my name."

"I'm Jim Culver."

"Well, pleased to meet you, Jim. Did Clay know you was coming? He didn't let on, if he did. 'Course, Clay Culver never says much, anyway. Oh, he might whisper 'fire' if your pants was a'blazin'." He paused to laugh at his joke. When Jim said that Clay had no idea he was coming, Broom scratched his chin thoughtfully. "That's a shame. If you'da just been here a month ago . . . But when he ain't ridin' for the army, hardly nobody knows where he goes— just loses hisself up in the mountains somewhere." He turned to look at Lettie, who was examining some bolts of cloth at the far end of the store. "And you and the missus came all the way out here just to see Clay, and he's gone."

"That ain't my missus," Jim quickly replied. "Her name's Lettie Henderson. I met her on the trail just past Fort Kearny. Her brother and their guide were killed, so she came on with me."

"Well, forevermore," Broom said. "That's a real shame. Has she got kin out here?"

"No. She's looking for a man named Steadman Finch, out in Virginia City, Montana territory."

Broom rubbed his chin again, trying to prime his memory. "Steadman Finch—I ain't ever heard that name before. But you said he's out in Virginia City." He took another look at the young girl now fingering some ribbon. "Is she

thinking about goin' up in Montana territory
this time of year? It's too late to head up there
now. Why, folks coming through from up that
way last week said it's already come a good
snow not more'n fifty miles north of here. She'd
best wait till spring."

As Jim was about to confess that neither he
nor Lettie had made up their minds about what
they were going to do, he was interrupted by a
man who had been busy loading a wagon with
supplies. Standing at the end of the counter listening to Jim and Alton Broom talk, the man
had become interested in the conversation.
"Couldn't help overhearing what you were saying, young fellow. I know your brother. He
shows up now and again in the little valley
where I live. He comes to see a friend of his, an
old trapper named Monk Grissom." He glanced
at Broom. "You know Monk, Alton."

"Oh, hell, who don't?" Broom replied.

The man turned back to Jim. "My name's
Nate Wysong." They shook hands. "I run a little
store in a place we call Canyon Creek. Alton's
right. It's too late in the year to start out to Virginia City. I expect if I had waited another two
or three weeks, I might not have had time to
get back to Canyon Creek with my wagon—and
that ain't but four weeks from here."

"I expect you're probably right," Jim said, not
sure what to do at this point. He looked over at
Lettie, who was close enough now to have heard
Wysong's comments. "I suppose we'll both have

to find some accommodations around here somewhere to ride out the winter. I can't speak for her, though." He smiled. "She might look young, but she's sure got a mind of her own."

"Well, I'm not asking what the arrangement is that you and the young lady has," Broom said. "But there are some places here where you could stay."

Jim was quick to set him straight. "Me and the young lady ain't got no kind of arrangement. We just joined up when she was in trouble and traveled from Plum Creek to here—all fit and proper."

"All right, then," Broom replied. "Like I said, I didn't mean to insinuate nothin'. There's a couple of places where a single girl can get a room."

Nate Wysong had been studying the two young strangers carefully while Broom had been talking. "I've got a better idea," he said. "Why don't you two come with me to Canyon Creek? We've got room in my cabin for the young lady. My wife would enjoy having another woman to talk to. And there's an empty cabin not too far from my place. An old trapper named Jed Springer built it. He's long gone now, but Jed built a right stout cabin—got a dandy fireplace. You could spend the winter there, Jim. You never know—you both might decide you wanna stay. It's a right friendly community. We've got a church and a general store and a blacksmith."

It was a neighborly gesture that Nate had made, but he had ulterior motives as well. When

he had first walked into the store, he had heard
Jim and Lettie explaining to Alton that they had
lost a wagon and mules to an Indian raiding
party. More than likely, that raiding party had
been Pawnee. There had been reports of some
scattered bands of Pawnees preying on isolated
settlers and freighters. But that was east of Fort
Laramie. No one had seen any such activity out
toward South Pass, but that didn't mean there
couldn't be other young bucks looking to cause
a little trouble. With a month's drive ahead of
him, it wouldn't hurt to have this young fellow
and his Winchester along if he was even half
the man his brother was reported to be. As for
the young lady, the Colt she wore on her hip,
aside from reminding him of Katie Mashburn,
made Nate think that she might be handy to
have around as well if there was trouble. Apart
from these considerations, Canyon Creek desperately needed fresh blood. After Reverend
Lindstrom worked on them for a whole winter,
he might sell them both on settling in Canyon
Creek.

Lettie didn't have to think about the proposition twice to know that she couldn't have asked
for a better arrangement. Feeling lost only minutes before, she now regained some of her old
confidence. With a whole winter to work on
him, she was confident she could persuade Jim
Culver to help her search for Steadman Finch in
the spring. "Why, thank you, sir," she gushed
at Nate. "That's most generous of you. I'm sure

I can earn my keep." She turned to Jim. "That would put you one month closer to Montana territory in the spring."

"Yeah, I reckon," Jim said, not sure what he should do.

Nate sought to aid her cause. "That's a fact, and, like I said, your brother shows up in Canyon Creek occasionally. Matter of fact, that might be your best chance of seeing him this winter. I can't say I really know him, but he's been in my store a couple of times. Monk Grissom says he's half mountain lion—spent a couple of years living with the Lakota Injuns—said he was close friends with an old trapper named Badger. When Badger died, Clay moved up into Shoshoni country. But you might see him this winter if he comes to see Monk."

It was settled, then. The next morning, Jim, Lettie, and Nate Wysong set out for Canyon Creek—Nate driving a heavily loaded wagon, Jim and Lettie following, each leading a packhorse loaded with Lettie's provisions.

Chapter 11

Caldwell raked the snow away from the base of a large boulder and proceeded to break up some dead pine branches that he had pulled out of the stand of trees below them on the slope. "You know, it wouldn't hurt you none to help me find some more wood."

Trask sat huddled against the boulder, seeking protection from the frigid breezes that swept constantly across the high ridge. With his blanket wrapped around his shoulders, he reluctantly moved away from the huge rock. Showing no enthusiasm for the task, he poked around the edge of the trees until he uncovered a sizable limb, which he dragged over to the spot where Caldwell was in the process of starting a fire. "That damn pine's gonna smoke like hell," he said as he dropped the limb at Caldwell's feet. "I don't know if Fry would like it too much if we build a fire. No telling how far a body can see the smoke."

Caldwell didn't bother to look at Trask when replying. "Fry, or Pitt, either, ain't setting up here freezing their asses off."

Trask shrugged, then looked around him as if afraid Fry or Pitt might overhear. "Fry's still mad 'cause we couldn't catch them two that killed Wiley." He hesitated for a moment, thinking about the circumstances that had dictated the need for him and Caldwell to be sitting lookout on a frozen mountain ridge. "Fry thinks the woman and the half-breed hightailed it for the Injun reservation. Do you think that's where they went?"

"Hell, who knows? Maybe—I don't really give a shit." Foremost in Caldwell's mind was coaxing the tender flame he had created into a warming fire. "Hot damn," he exclaimed triumphantly as the flame blossomed into a bona fide blaze. "Now we got somethin'." He sat back on his heels, carefully feeding sticks and branches to the fire. When he was certain it was established, he turned to look at Trask. He said nothing for a couple of minutes, watching Trask frown as the fearful little man worried about the thin column of smoke drifting straight up until it cleared the top of the boulder, where the wind swept it away.

"I don't like bein' in no damn militia," Trask finally blurted. "Settin' up here watching that pass below. What if them two did make it to that Snake camp? That don't mean them Injuns is gonna come riding over here lookin' for us, does it?" It irritated him that Caldwell didn't appear to be as agitated over the task assigned to them. "Why the hell ain't Clell out here freezing his ass off?"

Caldwell laughed. "Fry told Clell to ride out

to the other side of the north ridge and keep a lookout. Clell probably dug him a hole somewhere and crawled in it." He backed away from the fire a little when it began to throw out some heat. "Why don't you quit peeping around that rock and come over here and get warm? Ain't none of them Injuns gonna come riding over here. It keeps snowing like this, that pass'll be closed in the morning." He laughed again. "If I see a whole passel of Injuns come riding through that pass before then, I ain't sure I'll even bother goin' to tell Fry. I just might light out down the other side of this mountain."

Trask didn't respond right away. In fact, he wasn't even listening to Caldwell's rambling. He had spotted something on the far side of the narrow pass that guarded the entrance to Canyon Creek. It captured his complete attention until it took identifiable form through the veil of falling snow. Without taking his eyes from the gap in the mountains, he called to his partner. "Caldwell, come look at this! Somebody's coming."

"Damn, you're right. Who in the world . . ." He paused while the party approached the valley. "It's somebody driving a wagon."

"There's two more on horses coming up behind him," Trask said. "Who in the world would be driving a wagon in here this time of year? It ain't the Mashburn woman and the boy. Maybe they're lost. Whaddaya think we oughta do? Fry didn't say nothin' about this."

"Fry'll think we've been sleeping up here if we just let 'em drive on in without saying nothin'. So I guess we'd best just ride on down there and play soldier." After thinking about the unlikely appearance of the wagon in the valley, something triggered Caldwell's memory as he stepped up in the saddle. "I reckon I know who that is. What's the feller's name that runs the store?"

"Wysong?"

"Yeah, Wysong. That's who that is. He's been gone to Fort Laramie for supplies. That's who it is, all right. Let's go down and welcome him back, 'specially since he's bringing us that wagonload of provisions."

Jim Culver caught sight of them first—two riders working their way down through the timber to cut them off. He nudged Toby and pulled up beside the wagon. When Nate looked over at him, Jim said nothing but pointed toward the slope on the left. Nate squinted up at the snowy hillside, trying to identify the riders.

"You know them?" Jim asked.

Nate hesitated before answering, still straining to make out the faces. Finally, he decided. "No, can't say as I do. Don't look like anybody I know."

Jim reached down and pulled his rifle from its sling. "You might wanna keep your rifle handy," he told Wysong. Calling back to Lettie, he advised, "Pull your horse around the other side of the wagon till we see what these two have on their minds."

They pushed on through the narrow pass, where the snow was already beginning to accumulate to over a foot in the low places. Jim scanned the slopes on either side, looking for signs of anything out of the ordinary. It appeared the two riders were alone. They rode at a leisurely pace toward a point in the trail where they would intercept the wagon and waited there for Nate to approach.

"How do," Caldwell called out when they were within thirty yards.

"Howdy," Nate responded, keeping a wary eye on the strangers.

Caldwell flashed a wide smile. "I reckon you might be Mr. Wysong. Is that right?"

"Yes, I'm Wysong," Nate replied, surprised that the stranger knew his name.

Caldwell, confident that he could play the game as well as Simon Fry, glanced up at the sky. "Well, Mr. Wysong, looks like you mighta just beat the snow here by the look of that sky. We knew you was coming back from Fort Laramie, and the captain was getting ready to send some of us out to look for you."

"Is that a fact?" Nate could only wonder what the smiling young stranger was talking about. He glanced at Jim, baffled.

"Yessir, that's our job. I'm Corporal Caldwell, and this here's Private Trask. We're in the Montana Militia." Trask said nothing but glowered darkly upon hearing his assigned rank. Caldwell went on to relate the story Fry and his men had told everyone else, about their assignment to Canyon Creek to protect the citizens there.

"Oh my Lord in Heaven," Nate Wysong exclaimed, shocked by the news that the Shoshonis had been raiding in the valley. They had always been friendly and peaceful ever since he had built his cabin and store there. He was now more anxious than ever to get home to his wife and children. Caldwell assured him that his family was safe, but he told him that there had been others who had not been so fortunate. The Cochrans and Monk Grissom had been killed by the Indians. And just two days before, the Colefield place had been burned to the ground. Rufus, his daughter, and the boy were missing. "It's been a bad streak of Injun meanness," he said. "We've lost four of our men, but we're staying right here to protect you folks."

Jim had no reason to suspect Caldwell's story. With no knowledge of the Shoshoni people, he could imagine that they were as hostile as the Pawnees who had ambushed Lettie and him east of Fort Laramie. He did, however, wonder about the quality of the Montana Militia if these two were any examples, especially Private Trask. They certainly bore no resemblance to the soldiers he had seen at Fort Laramie. Both soldiers seemed extremely curious about him and Lettie when Nate introduced them.

Caldwell explained that he and Trask were on

patrol, watching for Indian raiding parties that might try to enter the valley, but he'd be glad to escort them to Nate's store if the storekeeper wished. Nate declined, figuring it unnecessary since they had said there were no Indians in the valley. So they hurried on, leaving the two scruffy-looking soldiers by the side of the trail. Nate apologized to Jim after having been told that the soldiers had taken over Jed Springer's old cabin for their headquarters. "Won't be no trouble finding you a place to stay," he promised him. Jim assured him that he wasn't concerned about it.

While Caldwell and Trask watched the three latest arrivals to Canyon Creek, Clell Adams sat himself down before a blazing fire in the fireplace Monk Grissom had built of stones from the river's edge. It was better than the fireplace in the cabin Fry and the gang had taken over. But the cabin itself was smaller than the one built by Jed Springer. Clell looked around him as he made himself comfortable on Monk's bed of buffalo robes, searching the tiny interior of the cabin in case he had missed anything of value when they had ransacked the place before. *The old fart sure didn't have much plunder to show for living as long as he did.* A few packs of skins, some salt, dried venison and flour, and one gray mare. That was about all they had found at the cabin—anything of value he had owned had been carried on his body. And those few items had been split up among the gang after they had killed him. Fry and Pitt had naturally taken the weapons, leaving precious little for the rest of them. About all Clell had gotten out of it was Monk's pistol and a foxskin cap with the head of the fox intact. He reached up to touch it. *It's a sight warmer than that old hat of mine,* he thought.

He reached in his pocket, pulled out a piece of jerky, and began to work it around in his mouth to soften it. He could only chew on one side of his mouth since he had no bottom teeth on the other side, but that hampered him very little. He still managed to keep a well-rounded belly in front of him. Feeling cozy and comfortable, he reached over to push a stick of wood farther into the fire. He figured that by the time the fire started to burn out, it would be time for him to get back on his horse and return to headquarters, as Fry liked to call Jed Springer's old cabin.

Headquarters, he thought and snorted. Fry and Pitt were beginning to act like they really were soldiers. *Sending the rest of us out on patrols to keep an eye out for the Mashburn bitch and that boy—well, this ol' coon ain't built for riding around in the snow while everybody else is setting in front of the fire.* He almost chuckled with the thought. *I wonder if ol' Caldwell and Trask are sitting up on that mountain freezing their butts off—more likely holed up somewhere like me.* Then he did chuckle. *Problem is, they ain't got no cabin to lay up in like I have.* Giving more thought to the idea, he speculated that Trask, scared to death of Pitt, was probably plodding back and forth up in the north end of the valley, his fingers and toes about to fall off with the cold. *Foolishness*, he thought. *These people in Canyon Creek don't suspect nothing. Even if they did, they're too damned scared to do anything about it.*

The solitary, buckskin-clad figure sitting motionless on his horse on the bluff overlooking the river hesitated before descending to the cabin below him. His paint pony stamped its right front hoof several times, impatient to get moving again. "Easy, boy," Clay Culver said softly and patted the Indian pony on the neck. Something looked awry. There was smoke coming from the chimney of Monk's cabin, but there was a strange horse tied to the front corner post, saddled and standing in the snow. Glancing over at the corral and the lean-to Monk had built for his horses, Clay could see no sign of Monk's mare or the buckskin. "Maybe we'd best go on down and see who Monk's visitor is," he said as he pressed his heels gently against the paint's belly.

The blue roan tied at the corner of the cabin whinnied a greeting as Clay approached, leading his packhorse. But the man taking his ease inside on Monk's soft buffalo robes paid it no mind as he dozed before the warm fire. Still half-asleep, Clell wasn't aware that he had company until he felt the surge of cold air that rushed over him when the cabin door was suddenly opened.

"Damn! Close that damned door," he yelped. Thinking he had been found out by one of the other members of the gang, he scrambled to his hands and knees, trying to extricate himself from the buffalo robe. When the door was not closed at once, he looked up, about to curse again. The oath was choked off in his throat by the sight of the formidable figure filling the doorway. "W-who the hell are you?" he stammered.

Ignoring the question, Clay demanded, "Where's Monk?"

Recovering somewhat from the initial shock of having been suddenly doused with frigid air, Clell got to his feet only to find the figure that had towered over him was still a head taller. "Monk ain't here," he blurted. "He's gone under—kilt by Injuns."

The man's statement hit Clay like the kick of a mule right in his chest, but there was no change of expression on his face as he continued to glower down at the nervous intruder in his old friend's cabin. Clay did not want to believe what he had just heard. Still, as was his nature, he remained calm as he asked, "And just who might you be?"

Clell strained to stand taller, attempting to affect a posture of authority. "I'm a soldier in the Montana army," he blustered, unable at the moment to remember exactly what Simon Fry called the sham military unit.

"I've never heard of any Montana army," Clay said, his eyes measuring the grimy-looking man before him, "and you don't look much like a soldier to me." He glanced quickly around at the disheveled state of Monk's cabin. It had obviously been plundered, and the thought of this riffraff going through Monk's belongings was enough to cause his blood to simmer. In particular, the foxskin cap pulled down snugly on the man's head looked a hell of a lot like the one Monk wore.

Even a man of Clell's limited intelligence could see that the buckskin-clad stranger was not one to fall for a bluff. Still, he attempted to bluster his way through. "Militia," he suddenly remembered. "That's what I am—and we was sent to protect the folks in this here valley."

Clay stood glaring at the man for several long seconds, silently thinking that this man was no soldier, militia or regular. Of that, Clay was certain. He knew a skunk when he saw one, and this one was beginning to give off an odor. Although his anger was threatening to surface, he continued to maintain a calm exterior until he got some definite answers to the questions in his mind. "Protect them from what? You say Monk was killed by Indians? What Indians?"

"Why, Snakes, they was," Clell replied confidently.

Clay was certain now that the man was lying. He knew without doubt that the Shoshonis— or Snakes, as some called them—had not been responsible for Monk's death. Less than six days before, Clay had visited Washakie in the Shoshoni camp. The old chief had related the conversation he had had with Monk about rumored raids in Canyon Creek. What part this dingy-looking scoundrel now standing before him had played in the actual murder of Monk, Clay could only speculate. His first inclination was to execute the man right then and there, but he knew there was still the possibility that Clell really was in some form of hastily organized militia. After all, Clay had been away from Canyon Creek for some time now. A lot could have happened that he wasn't aware of. Yet he could not ignore his gut feeling about this scruffy-looking individual. With great reluctance, he suppressed the impulse to simply strangle the man and be done with it. He felt Monk's soul crying out for vengeance, but he resisted the urge to strike prematurely.

"Suppose you tell me just what the hell you're doing in Monk's cabin," Clay said, his voice low and devoid of emotion.

"Why, I . . ." Clell sputtered, indignant but intimidated by the stranger's appearance to the point where he was not sure how much bluff he should hazard. "I'm supposed to be here," he said after a moment, "taking care of things for the militia."

"This ain't the militia's cabin," Clay calmly replied.

"Well, I was just fixin' to leave, anyway. Got to report back to headquarters."

"Is that a fact? Just where is headquarters?" Clay asked.

"We set up in an old abandoned cabin on the other side of the river."

Clay thought for a moment, trying to recall. Then, remembering, he said, "Jed Springer's cabin?"

"I don't know. I reckon." Clell was beginning to tire of the questioning. "I've got to git on back now."

"Jed didn't have a very big cabin—not much bigger than this one. How big is your outfit?" Clell didn't answer. "There must not be very many of you unless you're sleeping in tents."

"Mister, you ask a helluva lot of questions." Clell's hand dropped to rest on the handle of the pistol in his belt. "Now, I expect you'd better get on with your business, whatever it is."

Clay's eye never wavered as he took notice of Clell's hand tightening around the handle of the pistol. "I wouldn't advise you to pull that weapon out of your belt unless you're prepared to answer to God right now."

Clell hesitated. He could see no firearm on the mountain man's person. Still, there was something in the tall scout's eyes that told him it was not an idle threat. Since back-shooting was more to Clell's calling, he decided it prudent to back down. The thought also flashed through his mind that Monk's pistol had misfired once before, when he had attempted to put Hicks out of his misery. Something told him that could be fatal for him if it happened at this instant.

"Why, hell, mister, you've got the wrong idea. I got no reason to pull a weapon on you." He immediately held both hands up before him, palms out. "But I got to go now. The captain will be looking for me."

"I expect I'll be calling on your captain myself," Clay said and turned his back on Clell, preceding him out the door. Fully anticipating what was to follow, he eased the war ax out of his belt, shielding it from view with his body as he started in the direction of his horses. Just as he expected, he heard the sound of a hammer cocking before he had taken three steps past the door. He didn't wait to react.

It happened so fast that Clell was still preparing to aim his pistol when the war ax slammed into his chest with such force that the blade embedded itself almost to the handle. Having dropped to his knee when he whirled around to throw the ax, Clay was able to avoid the bullet that whistled harmlessly over his head.

The pistol clattered noisily on the flat stone sill Monk had set in his cabin doorway. Clell staggered backward, horrified by the sight of the ax buried deep in his chest. He grabbed the handle in both hands, screaming in pain as he struggled to extract the blade, knowing he was mortally wounded.

While the stricken man fell back against the cabin wall, Clay moved unhurriedly toward him, his long skinning knife in his hand. He felt no remorse in taking the man's life. By deliberately

offering Clell his back, Clay had confirmed what
he had almost been certain of—that the man was
a murderer, and his execution was justified.

His eyes wide with fright, Clell Adams looked
into the face of death's messenger. Paralyzed by
fear, he was unable to resist when Clay slapped
the foxskin cap from his head and grabbed a
handful of hair. Jerking Clell's head back, he
growled, "You better hope Monk Grissom ain't
waiting for you in hell." The sound of blood
gurgling, followed by the whisper of Clell's last
breath from the clean gash across his windpipe,
was the foul man's last utterance before Clay
sent him on his way to whatever awaited men
of his kind.

Washakie had been justified in his concern for
Monk. *I should have come straight over here when
I left Washakie*, Clay thought, *instead of going
hunting for elk*. Something evil had descended
upon the peaceful valley of Canyon Creek. The
question that bothered Clay's mind now was
how many others had been murdered by this
band of outlaws calling themselves militia? Before leaving the Shoshoni reservation to find
Monk, Clay had promised Angry Bear that he
would look in on his nephew, the half-breed
Luke Kendall. He was living with Rufus Colefield and his daughter. Clay had met them
briefly once when visiting Monk. He would go
there next, but he decided to wait until darkness, when he would be less likely to be spotted
by this so-called militia.

Chapter 12

Mary Wysong was standing in the door of the little general store that fronted her cabin when she spotted her husband's wagon round the crook in the trail just past the church. She didn't wait for him to make his way up to the store. Without taking the time to throw a shawl over her shoulders, she ran to meet him. He pulled his mules to a stop so his wife could climb up to the seat.

"Hey, darlin'," he said as she threw her arms around his neck.

"I feared something terrible had happened to you," she whispered breathlessly, "with the Indians raiding all over the territory." With a great sigh of relief, she released him and reared her head back to look at him. "You let your beard grow," she noted. "I'm just thankful to the Lord you didn't lose your hair. Captain Fry and his men have been trying to protect us from the Indians. I just thank the Lord that you got through."

Nate still found the news difficult to believe. "I didn't see anything between here and Fort Laramie."

This, in turn, surprised Mary. "Captain Fry

said the Shoshonis were raiding all over the territory. I know they've sure hit here." Her face took on a worried frown. "Nate, they hit Rufus Colefield day before yesterday. We saw smoke from the cabin in the morning. Reverend Lindstrom rode over there with Whitey Branch and Horace Spratte. They didn't find any trace of Katie or Rufus—the boy, either. They said the Indians must have carried them off." She wrung her hands nervously. "I'm so glad you're back. Nate, what are we gonna do? I heard a gunshot a little while ago. It sounded like it came from over near Monk Grissom's cabin." She interrupted herself. "Nate, Monk's dead."

"I know. I heard," Nate said. "A couple of those militia fellows told me." Having been distracted by his wife's nervous chatter, Nate just then remembered Jim and Lettie, seated on their horses, quietly watching the reunion. Remembering his manners then, he introduced them. "This here is Miss Lettie Henderson. I told her she could stay with us till spring."

Lettie was quick to respond. "I hope I won't be putting you out, Mrs. Wysong. Your husband said you wouldn't mind, but I can find someplace else if it's a bother."

After apologizing for her rudeness in ignoring Lettie at first, Mary managed to smile. "Call me Mary. Why, it's no bother at all. It'll be a treat to have some female company for a spell. I'm just sorry you had to come when we're having all this Indian trouble."

Wysong waited for the women to finish their greetings. "And this is Jim Culver. I told him about Jed Springer's cabin, but those soldiers told us they're using it. I reckon he could bunk in the storeroom till he finds a better place."

"You're welcome, Jim, but it might get a mite chilly in that storeroom. We'll have to find you plenty of blankets." Mary was always hospitable to visitors, and, in these troubled times, she was especially glad to see the broad-shouldered young man and one more rifle.

"You don't need to go to any trouble, ma'am. I've got all I need to stay warm. I'm just grateful to get out of the snow."

Nate smiled approvingly. "Jim here is looking for his brother, Clay Culver. Has he been here yet this winter?" When Mary looked puzzled, he realized that she probably didn't recognize the name. "Big fellow," he said. "Always wore buckskins. He came in the store with Monk last spring, looking to buy some coffee."

Then she remembered. "Oh, him," she replied. "I know who you're talking about now." She laughed. "I remember I thought Monk had brought a grizzly bear into the store." She looked at Jim with an expression of amazement, as if finding it surprising that the man who had frightened her children just by his appearance could actually have a family. "Is he your brother?" When Jim nodded, she said, "No. He hasn't been here so far this winter."

Before Jim had an opportunity to take care of

his and Lettie's horses, Reverend Lindstrom rode up, having seen them when they passed the church a few minutes earlier. Nate introduced the two visitors to the preacher, and, while the men talked, Mary took Lettie inside to show her where to put her things. Mary immediately filled the coffeepot and placed it on the stove. "It won't be long before Whitey Branch shows up," she confided to Lettie. "Any time more than two folks get together, Whitey will be there before you finish saying 'Howdy-do'. That man has a nose for coffee."

Lettie glanced out the window to discover another man had joined the group of men. "I guess Whitey must have already smelled the coffee," she remarked.

Mary glanced up from the table, where she had already started rolling out dough for biscuits. "No," she said. "That's Horace Spratte. He probably saw you from his place across the river. His cabin is up near the pass where you came in." She returned her attention to the dough. "Now set yourself down here, young lady, and tell me how you happen to find yourself in a little out-of-the-way place like Canyon Creek." There was a twinkle in her eye when she added, "And tell me about that young man with you."

Flushing visibly, Lettie was quick to inform her new friend that there was nothing to tell about Jim Culver aside from the fact that he had come along at the right time and had been gentleman enough to come to her aid. Without being asked, she then pitched in to help Mary with the biscuit dough while relating the events that had brought Jim and her to this valley. Before the biscuits went in the oven, the woman and the girl were fast friends. And before the biscuits came out of the oven, Whitey Branch rode up to join the other men. "Nate," Mary called out the door. "I've got hot biscuits and coffee ready." She smiled at Lettie. "Now, don't get in the way of the stampede, honey."

The conversation around the Wysongs' kitchen table soon turned to the concern shared by all those who had staked their future on Canyon Creek. Reverend Lindstrom was perhaps the most concerned of all, for it was the reverend who had persuaded most of the others to settle here, and his dreams of a town and a large congregation were rapidly fading away as each year passed. He had pressed Captain Fry more and more lately about when they could expect to see a full regiment of militia. Fry's answers were becoming increasingly curt and irritable. When the soldiers had first arrived in Canyon Creek, Fry had intimated that there might be plans to actually build a fort here. Now, the reverend confessed, he was beginning to wonder if maybe Monk Grissom might have been right in saying that such talk was nonsense.

Nate Wysong spoke up. "I know one thing for sure. We keep losing folks like we have lately, none of us will be left." He held his cup out when Lettie passed by with the coffeepot. "I can't run a store unless there's folks to buy things. I may have to close it up and just stick to farming."

Then Horace Spratte voiced what more than one of them had on their minds. "This business over at Rufus Colefield's place worries me. Katie and that half-breed boy of John Kendall's spoke out against Captain Fry and his men. And then they got burnt out, and there's no trace of 'em. They tried to tell us that it wasn't Injuns that kilt Monk." He shook his head slowly, as if perplexed. "I don't know—don't it strike anybody else that it's a mite peculiar that, if the Shoshonis are really on the warpath, they don't just come on through and kill us all at once instead of one here, one there, and the rest of us don't even see 'em?" He paused a moment before confessing, "I fear we owe Katie Mashburn an apology. I only hope we see her again."

A few minutes of dead silence followed Horace's words. Gradually, the others expressed some of the same feelings. Jim found it hard to understand their reluctance to express their doubts. Even from the little he had heard about the events that had occurred since the militia's arrival, he knew something was strange. He had only met two of these so-called soldiers, and they hadn't looked to be the kind of men that he would feel comfortable having at his back. The discussion continued for almost an hour, until finally someone suggested that Nate

should ride over and take a look at the ruins of
Rufus Colefield's place.

"If we're going, we'd better go now. We've
only got about two hours of daylight left," Nate
said. He turned to Jim. "How 'bout it, Jim? Are
you interested in taking a look?"

"Yeah, I'll ride along." The discussion had
generated a strong curiosity in Jim. "It wouldn't
hurt to take a look."

Jack Pitt walked his horse slowly around the
blackened timbers that had once been Rufus
Colefield's home. If the snow kept falling, it
wouldn't be long before the last little pockets
of smoldering flames were extinguished. He
grunted his satisfaction when he noticed that the
snow had already covered the hoofprints, hiding
the fact that the horses had all been shod and
not Indian ponies. When he had left Fry back at
the cabin, he told him he was going to check
on the lookouts. Trask and Caldwell were right
where he had told them to be. He had been unable to find any sign of Clell, so he was on his
way to Grissom's old cabin. He had a hunch he
would find the lazy slacker there. And he had
already decided he was going to take it out of
his hide if Clell was laying up by a fire in that
cabin.

Hearing a noise, Pitt turned to look back
toward the wagon road that ran by the front of
the property. *Well, now, lookee here,* he thought.
Some of the town's leading citizens. Wonder what in

hell they want. Recognizing Horace, Lindstrom, and the half-wit, Whitey, he couldn't identify the other two—one, a young fellow sitting tall in the saddle. *Who the hell is that?* Pitt wondered as he guided his horse over to the front of the cabin to wait for them.

Riding up from the corner of the cornfield and past the garden patch, Reverend Lindstrom led the delegation of Canyon Creek's citizens up to meet Pitt. Always uneasy in the presence of Captain Fry's second-in-command, the reverend's companions hung back a little to let Lindstrom do the talking. Jim couldn't help but notice.

"Good afternoon, Lieutenant. Or is it sergeant?" Reverend Lindstrom called out, still somewhat confused as to Pitt's rank.

"Just Pitt," the huge man replied with more than a hint of annoyance in his tone. "What are you doing up here, Preacher?"

Lindstrom could never understand why Pitt always seemed so belligerent. He was the opposite of his captain. Fry was always willing to engage anyone in conversation, while Jack Pitt was almost noncommunicative. When he did talk, it always came out curt and unfriendly. Nevertheless, the reverend, in good Christian fashion, always strove to ignore the man's rudeness. In answer to Pitt's blunt greeting, he replied cheerfully, "We just decided to come take a look at Rufus's cabin."

"There ain't much to see," Pitt said. Then,

nodding his head toward Jim, he asked, "Who's this here?"

Since the question wasn't aimed directly at him, Jim didn't reply. He didn't particularly care for the way the big man was eyeballing him, so he guided Toby around the other horses and pulled up beside Lindstrom. *You might as well get a good look,* he thought and proceeded to do some eyeballing of his own. He could readily understand why the others tended to hang back in Pitt's presence. He was a surly son of a bitch and big, with hands the size of small hams. Jim decided the man was a bully and bad trouble in a large size.

"This is Jim Culver," Lindstrom said. "He came in with Nate, here, from Fort Laramie."

Pitt grunted, then demanded, "What's he doing in Canyon Creek?"

Before the reverend could answer, Jim spoke up. "Mister, I reckon I can talk for myself. If you wanna know something, you can ask me." He didn't care for the huge man's attitude. There was no call for it. "And as far as what I'm doing in Canyon Creek, I reckon what I'm doing is minding my own business, which is a good idea for anybody."

Pitt was surprised by the stranger's spunk, but he didn't let on. His face remained a dull mask as he glared at Jim. Then a faint smile tugged at the corners of his mouth. It developed into a smirk before he finally remarked, "Now, that's good advice for all of you." He locked his gaze on Jim's eyes for a few more moments before turning back to Lindstrom. "Like I said, there ain't much to see."

"We was just curious and thought we'd take a look," Nate Wysong offered, hoping to relieve some of the tension.

"Go ahead and look," Pitt said. "I ain't stopping you." He gave his horse a kick and rode around them, keeping his eyes trained on Jim. *You're gonna be just enough trouble to get your ass killed*, he thought, *and I'm gonna enjoy doing it.*

After Simon Fry's sullen enforcer rounded the corner by the cornfield and disappeared down the trail, the rest of the group found their voices once again. The relationship between the townsmen and one who was supposedly there to protect them was very puzzling to Jim. They were obviously ill at ease around him. Lindstrom assured him and Nate that the captain was a different sort altogether and was in definite control of his men.

Getting back to the reason they had ridden over to the Colefield place, Lindstrom and the others dismounted and walked around the burnt-out cabin, now almost completely covered with snow. Jim remained in the saddle and walked Toby around the outer perimeter of the homestead to get a picture of the farm.

Nate could only shake his head in sympathy for Rufus and his daughter. It was difficult for him to believe that Katie and Rufus were gone— Luke, too. Katie and her husband, Robert, had come into the valley with Rufus in the original wagon train Reverend Lindstrom had organized. There was hope, Horace had told him, that they might still be alive. Like Whitey and Lindstrom, Horace had come running when he saw the smoke from the burning cabin. Captain Fry and a couple of his men were already there, but there was no trace of Rufus or Katie or the boy. There was no sign of blood, and there would have been some sign had they been killed—even in spite of the snow, because the heavier snowfall hadn't begun until that evening.

The four friends had paused to look down toward the river when they were suddenly summoned by Jim. "There's a milk cow down in the willows by the river," he called to them.

"Well, that's Rufus's cow, all right," Whitey said, stating the obvious as the four of them rode over to join Jim.

"Sure is," Horace agreed. "Throw a rope on her, Whitey."

Jim moved up the bank a few yards while the four of them debated the question of what to do with the cow. They all came to agree that Horace Spratte should take her with him since he didn't have a cow. Whitey didn't own a cow, either, but they all decided—Whitey included—that he wouldn't milk her regularly.

"Wonder why them Injuns didn't take the cow?" Nate questioned. "They took the horses. It's a wonder they didn't at least shoot the cow.

That's generally what Injuns do when they raid—what they don't take, they kill."

Before anyone could speculate, Jim gave them something else to consider. "There's a fresh grave over here under this cottonwood. Anybody know who's in it?"

He didn't have to hear an answer. The surprise in all four faces told him that the grave was news to them. They quickly gathered around the mound of freshly overturned sod, and the speculation began in earnest. Whitey immediately suggested they should dig it up and see who was buried there. There was some hesitation, primarily by Reverend Lindstrom, who was reluctant to desecrate the grave.

"You reckon all three of 'em is in there?" Whitey wondered.

While they were still discussing it, Jim gave them something else to think about. "I don't know a helluva lot about Indians, but it seems strange to me that a raiding party would bother to bury their victims."

"They wouldn't," Nate Wysong stated emphatically.

"I expect we'd better see who's buried here," Reverend Lindstrom said solemnly. "There's probably a shovel in the barn somewhere."

In less than thirty minutes, Whitey's shovel struck something yielding in the shallow grave. "Go easy now, Whitey," Reverend Lindstrom implored, and Whitey began to carefully remove the remaining dirt from what could now be determined to be a body. It was obvious that there was only one person buried there, and everyone crowded around the grave as Whitey brushed away the final soil with his hands.

"It's Rufus," Horace said even before Reverend Lindstrom reached down to remove the cloth covering the body's face.

"Sweet Jesus in Heaven," Lindstrom uttered as he removed the cloth. "Poor Rufus. I don't see any bullet holes or other wounds besides those places on his head, and they don't look like much."

"Looks to me like he musta got clubbed on the head," Nate said. "Musta broke something in his skull."

Lindstrom stood up and looked around at the faces gathered around the rude grave. "That means the Injuns run off with Katie and the boy."

"This ain't the work of Injuns," Horace pronounced solemnly. "And there ain't no use hiding from it any longer. Katie and Luke—and Monk Grissom—were right about that bunch. They ain't no more soldiers than I am. Looks to me like Fry and his gang done this. There ain't no Injun sign about it. The question we've got to decide right now is what are we going to do about it?" He looked into the faces of his friends and read the reluctance to face the truth. "What else could it be?" he implored. "Why else would that mean-looking brute, Pitt, be snooping around here, acting like we got no business coming here?"

"Horace is right," Lindstrom said. "Them soldiers ain't done nothing but leech offen us, and they sure ain't protecting nobody." He paused for emphasis. "And since they showed up in our town, we've lost John and Ruth Cochran, Monk, Grissom, and now Rufus Colefield. And no telling what happened to Katie Mashburn and Luke."

"Yeah, but some of Captain Fry's men has been kilt, too," Whitey said, still not convinced the militia was responsible for the deaths.

"I hate to say it, Whitey," Nate said, "but it looks to me like the reverend and Horace might be right. And I'm afraid our little community is in great danger. We've got to do something before they kill someone else. I ain't been away but a little over two months, and I come back to find half my neighbors dead."

Jim stood back, leaning against the tall cottonwood that sheltered Rufus Colefield's grave, and listened to the fretful discussion taking place. These men were farmers, hardly fighters, and there was a conspicuous absence of enthusiasm for physically confronting Simon Fry's gang of hardened outlaws. It wasn't his fight, but he could see that they desperately needed his rifle. He'd already decided he didn't like Jack Pitt, anyway. He might as well give them a hand, whatever they decided to do.

"They've lost men, too," Whitey insisted again. "It musta been Injuns."

Reverend Lindstrom gazed patiently at his simple-minded neighbor. "I don't think so,

Whitey. When you think about it, any time they lost somebody, someone of our folks ended up dead, too. We just have to realize that we've been bamboozled by a gang of cutthroats, and we've got to chase them out of our valley." He hitched up his trousers and stood squarely at the foot of Rufus's grave, taking his customary attitude of responsibility. "We'll have a meeting at the church tomorrow night right after prayer meeting to decide what we're gonna do." They all nodded agreement. "In the meantime, we'd better not let on to them what we're planning to do." He looked directly at Whitey. "Don't say nothing to any of the soldiers." The issue decided for the time being, they covered the grave, and after Reverend Lindstrom said a prayer, left for home before darkness overtook them.

At approximately the same time the group of Canyon Creek neighbors left the Colefield place, Jack Pitt stood before Monk Grissom's cabin, looking down at the body of Clell Adams. He looked around him cautiously in the growing twilight lest Clell's killer might still be near. Feeling reasonably sure that there was no one else around, he then knelt down to take a closer look at the body. He felt no compassion for his fallen comrade. His only feelings were anger and disgust—anger that someone had depleted the gang's ranks by one more, and disgust with Clell for obviously having been careless enough to get himself killed.

It struck him as especially curious that Clell wasn't shot. His throat was cut, and there was also a deep wound in his chest—the kind of wound an ax might make. *Injun?* He wondered. *Maybe that half-breed boy slipped back into the valley.* He immediately discarded that idea. It took a powerful arm to sink an ax deep enough to leave a wound like that. The boy looked strong, but not that strong. *Ain't Fry gonna love to hear about this,* he thought as he got to his feet again. Untying Clell's horse, he led the blue roan away from the cabin, leaving Clell's body where he had found it. There was something strange going on in the quiet little valley, something that was going to require Fry and him to make some decisions. Fry's little plan to lay up in Canyon Creek for the winter hadn't turned out to be successful. Eight men when they first discovered the isolated valley, they were now down to four. He would hear Fry's ideas as to what action to take now, but Pitt was of the opinion that it was time to slaughter the rest of these farmers and be done with it.

The paint pony stepped lightly down the snow-covered bluff, picking its path carefully and sure-footedly in the falling snow, guided only by a slight nudge of one knee and then the other. They were so in tune with each other, rider and horse, they almost functioned as a single unit. "Whoa," Clay said softly, and the paint came immediately to a stop. Clay looked up into

the heavy, dark clouds and wondered if this little valley would be sealed off before morning.
Bringing his gaze back to the clearing below him
and the stark white ruins of the cabin he had
once visited with his friend Monk Grissom, he
figured there would be no good news for Angry
Bear regarding his nephew.

A gentle pressure from his heels signaled the
paint to continue, and Clay guided the pony in
a circle around the ruins of Rufus Colefield's
cabin. There were many tracks. Soon they, too,
would be covered, but they were still fresh
enough to tell Clay that several horses had recently been here. It was hard to say what had
happened here—accidental fire or deliberate—
but Clay had a feeling it had to do with the
militia of which the man at Monk's cabin had
claimed to be a member. He saw the grave and
knew that it had been opened recently. *More killing,* he thought. *It's beginning to look like a pack
of wolves has hit the valley.*

He paused to recall the people who had lived
in the cabin. *Nice folks,* he remembered. *Monk
thought a lot of them.* Something was going to
have to be done about this wolf pack for reasons
beyond avenging Monk's death. They were in
the process of killing the community. Never one
to rush headlong into any situation before he
knew what the stakes were, he decided to keep
out of sight until he could see what he might
be up against.

It was late now, and he had to find feed for

his horse. So he guided the paint past the grave and along the riverbank, looking for a suitable spot to camp. About a quarter of a mile from the remains of the cabin, he found what he was looking for, a dry pocket where the spring floods had washed away part of the bank. Branches from the line of cottonwoods would provide sweet bark to feed his horse. Tomorrow he would scout Jed Springer's cabin and try to find out how many outlaws he might have to deal with.

Chapter 13

"I'm tired of pussyfooting around with these damn farmers," Simon Fry uttered between clenched teeth, his anger fired by the news of Clell's death the night before. "I was willing to go easy on these people if they behaved. But, by God, if they want to play rough, then we'll show 'em what rough really is."

"There ain't but four of us left," Trask reminded him.

"Four's enough to handle this bunch of farmers," Fry fired back. "And the best way to keep any more of us from getting bushwhacked like Clell and Wiley is to make sure there ain't nobody left to do the bushwhacking."

There was a long moment of silence following Fry's angry outburst. Then Pitt calmly asked, "Women and children, too?" Pitt had no qualms about killing anyone, but, if they were to take Fry at his word, it meant the total slaughter of an entire community.

"Hell," Fry replied, somewhat mollified, "we could make it look like another Injun massacre." He read the reluctance in Trask's and Caldwell's faces, however. He glanced at Pitt. "What do you think, Pitt?"

Pitt shrugged indifferently. "I wouldn't give a shit if we cleaned out the whole valley, but there ain't enough of us now to hit everybody at once. And if we didn't, some of 'em's sure as hell gonna get away, and then we'd have a damn patrol from Fort Laramie looking for us. We'd be better off just taking what we need and cutting outta here before this weather gets any worse and closes the pass."

Fry considered Pitt's advice for a moment before nodding approval, his mind already working again. "Maybe you're right. We could tell 'em we're declaring martial law because of Clell's murder and confiscate their weapons." The more he thought about it, the more he liked the plan. "Who's gonna stop us from taking what we want? The preacher? The storekeeper? Old man Bowen?" He looked around at them and grinned. "Or maybe ol' big-belly Horace Spratte . . ."

"What about that new feller?" Caldwell asked. "He looks like he might be a little trouble."

"He might be at that," Pitt answered. "I expect he's gonna have to have an accident. I ain't worried about him, though. I know where I can find him." He looked at Fry and raised an eyebrow. "There's another cat in the woods around here, and this'un might be a mountain lion. He drove an ax so deep in Clell's chest you could stick your hand in it up to your wrist."

It was a mystery none of the four could explain. Pitt felt reasonably sure that Clell hadn't been killed by any of the settlers in Canyon Creek. Jim Culver was the likeliest suspect, but both Trask and Caldwell could testify that they had watched him come through the pass with Nate Wysong. He would hardly have had the opportunity to settle with Clell. "All right, then," Fry concluded. "We've got some other son of a bitch sneaking around in the valley. We'll just make sure we don't go anywhere by ourselves from now on. He'll have to show his face sometime. In the meantime, we'll have a little talk with the good people of Canyon Creek and let 'em know how things are gonna be around here." His mind still working on it, he paused for a few seconds. "If they put up any fight, we're gonna have to clean 'em all out. We can't leave any witnesses. The army's got to think it was an Injun massacre." He looked around him for signs of hesitation. There was no dissent. "What day is it?" he asked. Nobody knew. He thought a moment longer. "If I'm not mistaken, today's Wednesday." He grinned. "Boys, I think it's time we went to prayer meeting."

From a low hillock on the far side of the river, Clay Culver watched the activity around Jed Springer's old cabin. He had kept an eye on this headquarters of the Montana Militia for a good part of the afternoon. And although they had accumulated quite a few horses, some of which were Indian ponies from the looks of them, he could only account for four men. A little before the dingy gray sky began to fade into twilight, all four men came out of the cabin, mounted up, and rode off toward the settlement. Clay left his vantage point, crossed over the river, and took a look around the cabin before he rode after them.

Jim Culver looked up when he heard Lettie approaching, her footsteps crunching in the freezing snow. She wore a heavy coat draped over her slender shoulders. "You're gonna freeze to death sitting out here," she said and motioned for him to make room for her on the step of Nate's store. "Scoot over," she ordered, "before I spill this on you." She settled herself beside him, taking care not to spill the hot black coffee she carried. "Here, I brought you some coffee."

He was hoping she would say that. "Ahh, thank you, ma'am. I could sure use it. You sure this is for me?"

"Yes. I've already had mine." She sat quietly beside him for a few minutes, watching evening approach the silent valley. "Mary said Nate and the others were worried about the soldiers, and they're gonna talk about it tonight after prayer meeting."

Jim took a long sip of coffee, which was already losing its heat to the cool night air. "Yeah, that's what they said." He didn't continue for a long moment, wondering how much he should tell Lettie. He didn't want to alarm her, but he didn't want her to be unaware of the seriousness of the situation, either. He decided she deserved to know what they had ridden into. "Lettie, I'm afraid this peaceful, friendly little town Nate sold us on when we were at Fort Laramie is fixing to have a whole passel of trouble. Don't blame Nate, though. He didn't know any more about this gang of riffraff than we did."

Her expression reflected her concern as she asked, "What do you think's going to happen?"

"I can't say for sure. I guess it'll depend on what Nate and the others tell those militia fellows. It could get ugly. I haven't seen the one who's supposed to be the leader of the bunch, but the one called Pitt looks like he'd just as soon shoot you as look at you. They're gonna decide what they're gonna do after church tonight."

"Maybe I'd better start wearing my gun again," Lettie said.

Jim couldn't resist a chuckle. "I noticed you haven't been wearing it lately."

"I didn't think it looked proper, a lady wearing a pistol around the house, especially in front of Mary's children." Changing the subject abruptly, she asked, "Are you going to prayer meeting tonight?"

"Reckon not. Me and churches don't mix too good."

She registered mild surprise, having grown up in a God-fearing family. "Don't you believe in God?" she asked. "Don't you ever pray?"

"I didn't say that. But if I'm gonna pray, I'd rather do it outside where I'm sure the Lord is gonna hear me. To my way of thinking, prayers get bottled up inside a little log building like that, especially when you've got a bunch of people praying at the same time. It's a wonder the Lord don't get confused with the jumbled-up noise that leaks out." He shifted around to change his position on the hard oak step. "I guess I'll just wait till the praying is done. Then I'll slip in to hear what's said at the meeting."

Looking a bit exasperated, she said, "I'm going to pray for you." She got up from the step then and announced that she had to get ready for church. She took his coffee cup and, leaving him sitting where she had found him, returned to the house. He watched her as she walked away. For some reason, it made him smile just to watch her—heavy coat around her shoulders, boots almost up to her knees and baggy pants tucked inside them, pants so large they looked like they might have belonged to her late brother. *Little ol' spindly thing. It's a wonder she can tote all those clothes.*

Noticing the cold a little more now, Jim got up and stretched, pulling some of the stiffness out of his joints from sitting too long. He decided to saddle his horse in order to be ready to ride over to the church later. That done, he went into the house and sat down at the kitchen table to be out of the way of the family getting ready for church. Nate's two sons, ages nine and eleven, came out first, all ready to go. They sat down at the table with Jim. Always nervous around young children, Jim tried to affect a friendly smile while the two stared at him.

He was rescued a few minutes later when Nate came out dressed in his church clothes. "Come on, boys. Let's go hitch up the wagon." Both boys dutifully got up from the table to follow their father out the door. Jim started to get up to help, but Nate insisted that the boys knew how to do it. "You might as well stay in here where it's warm."

Seeing his coffee cup on the end of the long plank table, he glanced at the stove to discover the pot still sitting on the edge. He had just started to get out of his chair when the blanket that partitioned off a corner of the room was pulled aside, and Lettie walked out. Jim froze halfway up from the table. Startled at first, he thought she was a stranger. He had never seen Lettie in a dress before, with her hair undone and lightly resting on her slender shoulders. Somehow the sassy facade that had always tended to characterize her disposition was transformed into the face of an angel, innocent and sweet. And Jim was obviously caught off guard by the transformation. Lettie was aware of it and was visibly pleased. From the bedroom, Mary Wysong entered the room, witnessed the reaction, and smiled. "Sure you don't want to come with us?" she asked.

"What?" Her question didn't register at once.

"Ah, no." He stumbled over his words. "No, I reckon not. I'll be at the meeting after." He sank back down in the chair, his eyes still on Lettie.

Lettie favored him with a warm smile as she draped her heavy coat over her shoulders and followed Mary out the door. She was very much aware of the effect her appearance had upon Jim. And with a new feeling of confidence, she joined the Wysong family waiting in the wagon.

In Reverend Linstrom's mind, it was always proper to put God and God's business before other worldly considerations, so he proceeded to conduct the weekly prayer meeting in the usual fashion. However, in the sense of urgency, and the concerned faces looking up at him, he started the meeting early and cut it considerably short—much to the delight of the children. After releasing them to play outside in the snow, Lindstrom called the town meeting to order.

Lettie sat in the back of the log building with the wives and listened to the intense discussion taking place among the men, who numbered five in total. They spoke about the neighbors who had gone under since the militia had ridden uninvited into their little community, all killed by the Shoshonis, according to Captain Fry. "And yet not one of us here in this room ever saw hide nor hair of the first Injun," Horace Spratte reminded them. The question to be decided was what action they should take. Or, more accurately put, what action *could* they take? Spratte suggested that it might be time to notify Captain Fry that Canyon Creek no longer desired militia protection. "Maybe they'll just ride on out of here and leave us in peace," Horace said.

"I kinda doubt that," Nate Wysong replied. "Why should they? We can't stand up to those gunmen. They'll just stay right here till they bleed us dry. Some of you may not have been hit as hard as I have. I came back after being gone for two months and found a stack of vouchers signed by Captain Fry. He told Mary that the territorial governor would send me the money for them in the spring." He turned to glance at his wife in the back of the room. "I ain't blaming you, honey. I don't know that I could have refused him the supplies. They'd have probably just took 'em, anyway."

"Fry seems like a reasonable man," Reverend Lindstrom said. "I think we should try to negotiate with him for the peaceful departure of him and his men."

Horace Spratte made a point then that had somehow been overlooked. "He ain't going nowhere in this weather. We've got that bunch till the weather breaks, and that's all there is to it."

At that point, everybody tried to talk at once, causing Lindstrom to raise his voice, calling for order. It was becoming quite clear that the people of Canyon Creek were helpless to do anything against Fry and his men even though they had been reduced to four in number. The reverend's little flock was about to receive confirmation of that truth. For, at that moment, one of Nate Wysong's sons ran in from outside and announced excitedly, "Pa, the soldiers are coming!"

A stony silence fell over the small congregation as Simon Fry strode in, followed by his three men. Fry proceeded straight to the front platform that served as a pulpit, while Pitt stationed himself and the other two at the back corners of the building. Fry carried no weapon except for the pistol strapped on his hip, but the other three held rifles conspicuously cradled in their arms. Affecting a wide smile for Lindstrom, Fry directed the dumbstruck reverend to take a seat with the other men in his group. At a loss for words, Lindstrom did as he was told. Fry turned to address the gathering, all of whom were seated and wide-eyed with apprehension.

As soon as Fry turned to face them, Lettie suddenly gripped Mary Wysong's arm and gasped. "Steadman Finch!"

Startled, Mary looked at the girl, alarmed by the force of the fingers gripping her arm. "What is it?" she whispered, confused by the young girl's outburst.

Lettie didn't answer. She didn't even hear Mary's question. Her eyes were locked on the man standing at the pulpit. Her heart racing, she could scarcely believe what her eyes were telling her. "Steadman Finch," she repeated, this time above a whisper.

Simon Fry cocked his head toward her immediately upon hearing his name. His eyes narrowed beneath heavy black brows as he tried to identify the young lady staring so accusingly at him from the back bench. The room was sunk in confused silence for a few moments as Fry glared at Lettie. Other than these two, only Jack Pitt knew Fry's real name. An amused smirk on his face, Pitt took a step closer to get a better look at Lettie.

After a prolonged pause, during which Fry could not recall ever having seen the girl before, he started to address the gathering. "There are going to be some new rules around here for a while." That was as far as he got before being interrupted again.

"Steadman Finch," Lettie blurted, getting to her feet. "You're a low-down, murdering coward, Steadman Finch."

Fry's eyes flashed with anger for only a brief second before he relaxed his expression to the point where a wry smile appeared. "I do believe you've mistaken me for someone else, young lady," he replied with exaggerated politeness. "My name is Simon Fry. And what, may I ask, is your name?"

"I'm Lettie Henderson, *Mr.* Finch," she retorted accusingly. "And you murdered my father!" She stood there, defiantly staring him down, thinking that if only she had brought her pistol, he would now be a dead man.

Stunned for a moment, Fry quickly recovered,

smiling in the face of the accusation. "As I said, you've obviously confused me with someone else. I've never even been to St. Louis."

"Ha!" She shouted triumphantly, pointing her finger at him. "I never said I was from St. Louis! You tripped on your own lying tongue, you murderer."

Fry smiled almost sheepishly for making such a stupid blunder. "So I did, didn't I?" The smile froze on his face, replaced by an annoyed scowl. "Pitt," he directed, "set her down."

Pitt took no more than three steps toward Lettie before he was stopped by the distinctive sound of a rifle cocking. "I wouldn't, Pitt." In the tension that filled the small church building, no one had noticed when Jim Culver silently moved inside the door. Now, when all heads turned at the sound of his warning, Pitt discovered a Winchester leveled at his belly. It served to give him pause before making another move. For a few frozen moments, there was not a sound in the room beyond that of an occasional popping of the fire in the fireplace. The faint laughter of the children playing outside seemed miles away.

From their positions in opposite corners at the back of the room, Trask and Caldwell brought their rifles to bear on Jim but, unsure of themselves, did not fire. Jim breathed a silent sigh of relief, thankful that they had hesitated to think about it. If they hadn't, he'd be dead now. He gazed steadily into Pitt's snarling face. "I know what you're thinking. You're wondering if you can get your rifle up and cock it before I cut you down. Or maybe you're wondering if your captain there can pull that pistol in time. I can guarantee you that I'll get you and your captain even if one of those jokers in the corner puts a bullet in me. I'm the only one who knows how fast I am, and I'm willing to bet on it. You can decide if it's worth the gamble. No matter what happens, I'm taking you two with me. You two behind me—you'll be outnumbered after your friends are dead. You'll be next." Jim knew he was bluffing when he intimated the men in the congregation would fight. He didn't know if they would or not, but neither did Trask and Caldwell.

Simon Fry rapidly evaluated the situation. The young stranger looked very capable of backing up his threat to take him and Pitt out. Never one to risk his neck in any situation, he decided it best to back down now and call it a stalemate. "Folks," he pleaded. "Let's just calm down here. You've got the wrong idea, young fellow. It was never our intention to harm the young lady or anyone else here. You've got no call to pull a gun on us. We're just trying to do right by you folks and protect you. Why, one of my men was killed just today, murdered while he was watching out for Indians. I just came to your meeting tonight to see if I could ask for your help in finding the guilty party."

Since no one else appeared willing to speak

up, Jim took it upon himself to deliver the message. "The folks here figure they can't afford your protection anymore, so I reckon it's time for you boys to move on."

Fry struggled to hold his anger in check. "Well, now, I don't think that's up to you to decide."

Reverend Lindstrom found his voice at last. "He's right, Captain Fry. We all decided at this meeting that it would be best if you and your men left us in peace."

"Oh, you did, did you?" Fry's eyes flashed angrily for a second. He glanced at Pitt, who had not moved but was still glaring menacingly at Jim. Then he glanced at Trask and Caldwell. The two men wore confused expressions and were looking to him for instructions. *Stupid jackasses,* he thought. *If they had just cut down on him at first, he'd have been dead before he could even think about pulling the trigger.* Now it was too great a risk. "All right, then," he said at last. "We certainly don't want any trouble with you folks. We'll just leave you, and we'll discontinue our patrols. There won't be anybody protecting you from any more Indian raids, but if you're all sure that's what you want . . ." He paused, waiting for a response.

At first there was none. Then Reverend Lindstrom spoke for his neighbors. "We've made a final decision. We were getting along just fine with the Injuns before you came. I reckon we'll get along just fine after you leave."

"All right, then." Fry stepped down from the pulpit and signaled Pitt with a nod of his head. Pitt moved toward the door, his eyes still smoldering as he continued to stare at Jim. As he neared the door, he turned to look at Caldwell, still stationed in the back corner of the room. With a slight nod and a shifting of his eyes, he signaled, and Caldwell understood his meaning.

Trask followed Pitt out the door while Fry walked up the aisle. He paused at the last row of benches, where Lettie was still standing, staring at him. "So you're Jonah Henderson's little girl." He favored her with a crooked smile. "Last time I saw you, you weren't much more than a pup." The smile abruptly faded. "Too bad about Jonah, but if you go getting any crazy ideas, the same might happen to you."

"Just drag your sorry ass on outta here," Jim said, his rifle now aimed at Fry.

Fry turned to faced Jim. Deliberately looking him up and down, he grinned contemptuously. "I guess you've got the high hand right now, but this game ain't over yet. You'd better watch your step from now on."

"Thanks for the advice," Jim said, matching the grin with one of his own. When Fry turned and headed for the door, Jim said softly but firmly, "Sit down, Lettie." Pitt's slight nod to Caldwell had not escaped his notice. Recognizing his tone to be that of a command, Lettie did as she was told.

Caldwell waited for Fry to pass him. Then,

using Fry's body to shield his movements, he
raised his rifle. As soon as Fry passed, Caldwell
opened fire. Anticipating the obvious move, Jim
dropped to one knee, using the end of the pine
bench as cover. His reactions were so quick that
the two shots sounded as one. Caldwell's .45
slug cut a chunk of pine from the bench beside
Jim's head. The young outlaw crumpled to the
floor, Jim's bullet buried deep in his chest.
Oblivious to the sudden commotion behind him
of women screaming amid the confusion of
overturning benches as everyone sought cover,
Jim moved quickly to the church door. Lying
flat on his belly, he took a position to shoot,
using the doorjamb as cover.

Outside in the churchyard, the children stood
stunned by the sudden outburst of gunfire from
inside the church. The three outlaws, their
weapons ready, paused for a few moments to
wait for Caldwell. When their companion failed
to emerge, they wasted little time thinking about
it. Pitt knew Caldwell had lost the gunfight.
"Grab a young'un!" Pitt roared and swept up
one of the children. Fry and Trask were not
quick enough, and the rest of the children scattered. Pitt had sized Jim Culver up, and he figured the tall young stranger knew how to use
his rifle.

Using the terrified youngster as a shield, Pitt
backed toward the horses. "Get behind me, unless you wanna get your ass shot off," he ordered the others and handed his rifle to Fry in

order to free his gun hand. Eagerly taking cover behind the huge man, Fry and Trask backed up until reaching the horses. Pitt, meanwhile, emptied his six-shooter, blasting away at the church door, pistol in one hand and the child in the other.

Lying on his stomach, Jim watched as the three outlaws moved to a safe position behind a low mound, their backs to the river. He was forced to helplessly watch the retreat as Pitt's bullets ripped chunks from the heavy church door, unable to risk a shot himself for fear of hitting the child. He figured there was little chance they would simply ride away, leaving them in peace. He had anticipated Caldwell's move. So now the odds were even better in favor of the men of Canyon Creek. He had been right about Caldwell, but he soon found he had misjudged the people of Canyon Creek.

"Looks like they're gonna spread out behind that mound and try to smoke us outta here," he called back over his shoulder while keeping a constant eye on the outlaws. "If a couple of you set up on either side of that window, we might be able to get an angle on them."

"The children!" Mary Wysong wailed. "We've got to save the children." Her cries were echoed by the other women.

Once Pitt reached the safety of the mound, he flung the child from his arm. The child, a boy of ten, wasted no time in hightailing it down the riverbank to catch up with his playmates.

Seeing this, Jim reported, "The young'uns are all safe. They've run off down the river a piece. Now, a couple of you men set up on that window."

"We didn't bring no guns to church," Horace Spratte answered from his position behind an overturned bench. "The reverend don't think it's fittin'."

"Damn," Jim uttered. He hadn't counted on that. "Not one of you brought a gun? Hell, with the trouble you folks got here, you shouldn't go to the outhouse without a gun."

"The house of the Lord is no place for weapons," Reverend Lindstrom inserted weakly from his place behind another bench.

"I've got a pistol." This reluctant confession came from Nate Wysong.

More than a little perplexed, Jim said, "Well, get up to that window and get ready to use it."

Nate had barely time to position himself beside the window before the shooting started. Their rifles placed several yards apart, the outlaws laid a steady volley across the front of the log building. Chips and splinters flew as their slugs tore into the timbers, making loud smacks on the partially opened door. Jim returned the fire as rapidly as he could shoot, peppering the sandy mound with lead. As soon as the first volley of bullets plastered the front of the church, Nate lost his nerve and scurried back to seek cover behind the benches again. "Gimme that," Jim heard Lettie demand. Taking the pistol from Nate, she ran to the window and emptied it in the general direction of the mound.

Jim glanced over and nodded approvingly. Lettie smiled at him, then shrugged helplessly, showing him the empty pistol. Nate hadn't brought any additional bullets.

Soon after the siege began, there was a lull in the shooting as both sides paused to reload and evaluate the situation. Jim motioned for her to pick up Caldwell's rifle.

"We ain't doing nothing but wasting lead," Fry said as he crawled over closer to Pitt. "It don't do no good to keep filling up those logs with bullets. And we can't get a clean shot at that son of a bitch with the rifle without rising up to shoot—and he's too good a shot to risk that."

"We gotta get them outta that cabin," Pitt said. "We need to smoke 'em out. We've just gotta get that one man. The rest of 'em ain't got no fight in 'em." He motioned for Trask to come closer. "Trask, go on back down the riverbank a ways. Then work your way around behind 'em. If that back window ain't shuttered, you might be able to get a shot at him."

Trask was not enthusiastic about the plan. "I don't know, Pitt. That feller was too quick for Caldwell."

"He can't watch both sides at the same time," Fry said. "Do like Pitt says."

"Get your slicker off your horse and take it with you," Pitt instructed. "If they've got that window closed, maybe you can climb up on the roof and cover the chimney. Smoke 'em out, and we'll nail 'em when they come out the door."

It didn't sound like much of a plan to Trask, but he reluctantly went along with it—primarily because he hesitated to argue with Pitt. Crawling on all fours until he reached the riverbank, he scrambled to his feet and, crouching for fear of attracting a bullet, started out along the water's edge. Abruptly halting, he returned to his horse and untied his slicker. "Stupid idea," he mumbled to himself before resuming his flight down the river.

With the lull in the shooting, Jim looked around behind him at the huddled bodies. Mary Wysong was crying. He glanced from her to Effie Spratte, who was seated on the floor, rocking back and forth behind her husband and wailing, "They're gonna kill us all." His gaze darted back to the front window and found Lettie gazing expectantly at him. He smiled and shook his head. She understood and smiled back at him.

"Maybe they've gone," Lindstrom ventured hopefully.

"They're still there," Jim replied. "More than likely they're trying to figure how to smoke us out of here."

"Well, what are we gonna do?" Lindstrom asked in anguish. "We can't just sit here while they decide how to kill us."

"Nothing we can do but sit here," Jim replied,

impatient with the preacher's questions, "unless you want to walk out there and ask them to leave again." His reply brought a new intensity to the crying of Mary Wysong, so he tried to assuage their fears. "Maybe they'll get tired of waiting us out by morning."

Slipping and sliding as he made his way up the snowy riverbank, cursing every time he lost his balance, Trask finally decided he was out of range of Jim's rifle. His rifle in one hand and his slicker in the other, he crossed over the clearing where he and the others had first met the preacher. There had been eight of them on that day—and him with an arrow in his shoulder. *It was bad luck the day we found this damn valley. Three of us left—if I had any sense, I'd jump on my horse and leave this place behind me.* He would have given the notion serious consideration had it not been for his great fear of Pitt.

Working his way through the pines that covered the ridge behind the church, Trask struggled through the brush in the darkness, cursing each branch that surprised him with a sudden slap across the face. Back toward the river, he heard rifle shots ring out as Fry and Pitt let those inside the church know they were still under siege. When he reached a point directly behind the building, he came out to the edge of the trees and knelt on one knee to take a long look at his objective. The back window was shuttered and latched. *Stupid idea! Pitt thinks he's so smart. Of course the damn window is shut. The man ain't gonna lay in there with a window open behind his back.* Glancing down at his slicker, he then looked back at the cabin to consider the second option. The roof was low in the back, the eaves no more than six feet off the ground. He figured that if he could find something to stand on, he should be able to climb it.

Moving with great caution, half-expecting the back window to fly open suddenly and present him with the business end of a Winchester 73, he inched his way up to the cabin wall. Spying a chopping block over by the woodpile, he thought, *That's just about the right height.* He pushed it over on its side, rolled it over to the edge of the roof, and stood it up again. *Stupid idea. What if they hear me and start shooting through the roof?* Thoughts of Fry and Pitt sitting safely behind a dirt mound while he risked his neck on a rooftop served to irritate him further as he prepared to mount the roof. With his rifle slung on his back, he grabbed the underside of the eave and started to throw one leg up. Suddenly he was in midair, his arms and legs flailing to find purchase. In another second, he realized that he had not simply slipped, for something had him by the back of his collar. In the next instant, he was slammed down in the snow, flat on his back. The impact made his head spin. When it was clear again, he found himself staring up at a towering figure dressed in animal skins. Trask had made bad decisions

all his life. This would be his last. He reached
for his pistol. The big man in buckskins buried
his war ax in Trask's skull before he had a
chance to aim and pull the trigger.

After making sure that Trask was no longer
a threat, Clay Culver stood up and softly said,
"There's another one, Monk." He listened for a
few moments to the murmur of voices inside
the church. He heard a couple of shots from the
riverbank and answering fire from inside. Then,
moving with the grace of a great cat, he pulled
himself up on the roof and crawled up to the
ridge, taking cover beside the stone chimney. He
lay there for a while, waiting for the next shots
to come from the river, watching the bank intently. In a few seconds, he spotted two muzzle
flashes in the darkness as shots rang out. Bringing his own rifle to bear on the dirt mound near
the water's edge, he began to lay down a blanket of fire, cocking and shooting without pause.

Stunned by the sudden attack from the church
roof, both Fry and Pitt dived for cover at the
base of the mound. With bullets snapping angrily over their heads, kicking up dirt and snow
around them, Fry yelled, "That damn fool! What
the hell's wrong with him?"

Pitt was already crawling toward the horses.
"That ain't Trask. They got some help from
somewhere, and whoever it is has got the angle
on us." When Fry just lay there, still confused,
Pitt commanded, "Come on, dammit! We can't
stay here. He's bound to hit one of us sooner or

later." As he struggled along on hands and knees, he pictured Clell's corpse, and he had a pretty good idea that this was the work of the same man.

Riding low on the necks of their horses, Fry and Pitt galloped down the riverbank, whipping their mounts unmercifully. The hail of bullets—from the roof as well as from inside the church—continued to speed them on their way. Fry yelped involuntarily when he felt a slug smack against the cantle of his saddle. Pitt, hearing his partner's cry, didn't bother to look around to see if Fry had been hit. He just tried to lie lower on his horse's neck and urge it to go faster.

Back at the church, Jim got to his feet and walked outside to glimpse the two outlaws galloping out of sight around the bend in the river. Satisfied that there was no further threat from them for the time being, he called back to those inside to let them know they could come out. Then he looked up at the roof to see who his unexpected ally might be. There was no longer anyone there. He turned to walk around the building just as his benefactor came around the corner, and the two met face-to-face.

The man he faced was big—not wide and bulky like Pitt but towering like a solid oak tree. Dressed from head to toe in animal skins, with long sandy hair to his shoulders, he carried a rifle in each hand and wore a belt that held a long skinning knife and a hand ax. Jim didn't doubt that he was facing a genuine mountain man.

As the shaken settlers of Canyon Creek filed out of the church, thankful to again breathe the cold night air, the two riflemen shook hands. "Looks like you folks were having a right lively prayer meeting," the mountain man commented dryly.

Jim laughed. "You could say that. Glad you could make it."

"My pleasure. Clay Culver's the name," he said, then puzzled over Jim's sudden expression of surprised amusement.

"Jim Culver," Jim returned, a wide grin spreading across his face.

Clay was startled for a moment. Before he could reply, however, Reverend Lindstrom and Nate Wysong rushed up to greet him. "Clay Culver!" the reverend exclaimed. "You're a welcome sight. You came along at a most opportune time. Jim here sure needed the help."

"Reverend," Clay acknowledged. Then, glancing back at Jim, he commented, "Yeah, looks like he wasn't getting much from inside."

"Well, we better go help the women round up the children," Lindstrom replied sheepishly. He and Nate turned to leave.

"Reverend," Clay stopped him. "There's a dead man round at the back of the church you might want to take care of. If the weather turns warm, he might start to stink." Turning back to Jim, he squinted slightly, as if trying to see him better. "Culver, you say? I've got a brother James back in Virginia."

Jim couldn't stifle a chuckle. "Have you, now? Are you sure he's still in Virginia? He might be standing right in front of his big ol' dumb brother right now."

"Well, I'll be go-to-hell," Clay uttered, flabbergasted. "James? Is that really you?" He grabbed Jim by the shoulders and looked him over at arm's length. "Well, I'll be go to . . . Last time I saw you, you were just a skinny kid. I would have never known it was you." He laughed delightedly.

"Well, I'd have never known it was you, either. The last time I saw you, you'd just come back from the war." He smiled. "And you didn't look like something that lives in a cave."

They hugged then and pounded each other on the back in joyous reunion until finally interrupted by Lettie Henderson's insistent tugging at Jim's sleeve. "I see you found your brother," she said, "but Steadman Finch is getting away."

"Who's this?" Clay asked.

"This is Lettie Henderson. She came out here looking for one of the men who just rode off down the river. Lettie, this is my brother Clay."

She favored Clay with a brief smile, then turned abruptly back to Jim. "He's getting away," she insisted.

Clay glanced at his brother, a question in his eyes. The young lady seemed to presume responsibility on Jim's part. He looked back at Lettie. "Young lady, don't worry your head about those two. I've got a debt to settle up with them for murdering Monk Grissom."

"You go on back with Mary," Jim said. "Me and Clay'll see to it that those two's murdering days are over."

Satisfied, Lettie stepped back and looked at the two brothers, both tall and strong. Then she smiled at Jim and said, "You be careful. Don't do anything foolish."

Jim didn't reply but flushed slightly as he turned away, only to confront Clay's wide grin, which caused his blush to deepen in color. He knew there would be additional conversation on the subject of Lettie Henderson.

Chapter 14

Jack Pitt wasted little time preparing for the war he knew was coming. As soon as he and Fry pressed their exhausted horses back to Jed Springer's cabin, he pulled his saddle off and threw it on one of the fresh horses in the tiny corral. Directing Fry to do the same, he hurriedly explained. "We might have to get the hell outta here. I wanna have a fresh horse under me."

Fry didn't respond right away. Instead, he stood seemingly stupefied, staring at the slash across the cantle of is hand-tooled saddle, the result of Jim Culver's rifle. In a moment, his eyes crinkled in anger. "I paid a lot of money for this saddle," he fumed.

Pitt had no time for Fry's lament over his fancy saddle. "Would you rather have caught that bullet in your ass? To hell with that saddle. We've got to get moving."

Fry didn't reply but immediately did as Pitt suggested. Without looking to see if Fry was following his instructions, Pitt charged into the cabin and started stuffing food and supplies into two canvas saddlebags. Following behind him, Fry duplicated his big partner's actions. "Take all them extra cartridges," Pitt said, "and that salt pork." Fry didn't ask questions. When it came to fighting, Pitt was boss.

Picking out the two best horses left, they hurriedly tied on their sacks of supplies. After the packhorses were loaded, they led them around to the back of the cabin and tied them with their saddled mounts. Confused at this point, Fry asked, "What are we tying them up for? We'd better get the hell going."

Pitt cocked his head sharply and squinted at his partner. "Hell, we ain't running. We'll wait right here and see if those son of a bitches come after us. I'll make sure it costs 'em if they do." He gestured toward a window on the side of the cabin. "That's as good a spot as any for your rifle."

Fry was confused and not at all comfortable with the idea of being holed up in a cabin with someone shooting at him. It was not the same as it was back at the church, where he and Pitt had the others pinned down. "I thought we were going to get away from here while we had the chance. What did we pack up the horses for?"

Already watching the ridge east of the cabin for signs of pursuit, Pitt shifted his eyes briefly to give Fry an impatient glare. "It's gonna take a little more than that little set-to back at the church to make Jack Pitt run. We got the horses ready in case things go bad. I ain't planning to have to use 'em."

"Damn, Pitt, I don't know if that's a good idea

or not." Fry was fairly certain he had correctly read the handwriting on the wall, and it told him it was time to save his ass. "We're outnumbered pretty bad now. I think it's time we get ourselves away from here."

Fry's whining was beginning to irritate Pitt. At that moment, he wished Caldwell or even Trask were here instead of Fry. Fry was supposed to be the brains of the partnership, but he wasn't much good in a gunfight unless all the odds were stacked up in his favor. Pitt turned his attention away from the ridge for a few moments to explain the situation to Fry. "In the first place, maybe you ain't noticed, but the snow's already ass-deep in some of those passes. We don't wanna be floundering around out there in the snow unless we ain't got no other choice. If we have to, the horses are ready. In the second place, we ain't really outnumbered. There ain't but two of those bastards we've got to worry about. The rest of them farmers ain't gonna help 'em. So get your rifle up to that window. If we're lucky, we'll get 'em both when they come riding over that ridge. And when we finish with them two, I'm gonna burn Canyon Creek to the ground." Satisfied that he'd done all the explaining necessary, he turned his attention back to the ridge and waited, knowing the two men would be coming.

At his position by the side window, Simon Fry sat waiting. His rifle ready, he stared at the stark white hillside some seventy yards in front of the cabin. Fidgeting nervously, he glanced at Pitt, who was gazing intently at the ridge. *Stubborn fool*, he thought. Fry wasn't comfortable with Pitt's assessment of their situation. He felt cornered, and Fry never enjoyed being cornered. Sometimes Pitt didn't have enough sense to know when the game was up and it was time to run. The minutes passed, and it seemed that everything just became more and more quiet. The wind that had moaned without pause throughout the night suddenly ceased, and there was no sound at all outside the cabin. It was as if the valley had died. Fry suddenly received an urgent call from his bladder. "I've got to take a leak," he announced.

"Take a look at the horses while you're out there," Pitt said without looking around.

Cradling his rifle on his arm, Fry pushed the snow away from the door and went outside. "We're going to need more firewood, too," he called back to Pitt as he rounded the corner of the cabin, his eyes still concentrating on the silent ridge before him. It had stopped snowing during the night, and, looking up, he could see a break in the clouds. It would be sunup pretty soon, with a definite possibility that the sun would actually break through. Hours had passed since he and Pitt had fled from the church. *Where are they? Maybe they're not coming after us.* He discarded that notion immediately. They would come. Maybe they were getting organized, waiting for daylight. There were enough of them to put a ring around the cabin and shoot it to pieces. *I'll bet Pitt never thought of that. Damn stubborn fool. If they're waiting for daylight, we ought to be hightailing it out of here, leaving them nothing but an empty cabin to shoot up.*

Propping his rifle against the wall of the cabin, he proceeded to relieve the pressure on his bladder while constantly looking left and right, alert for any sign of attack. The horses stamped impatiently, complaining about standing all night with saddles and packs, watching the man to see if he was going to remove their burdens. The dark sky was already beginning to fade to gray, and still all was deadly quiet. Then, off in the distance, the quiet was penetrated by the mournful howl of a lone wolf. It seemed to strike a death knell in Fry's mind. *To hell with this,* he thought. *Pitt's crazy. I'm not going to wait here to be executed.*

His decision made, he untied the horses. As quickly and quietly as he could, he hitched both packhorses to one line. Then, leading his saddled horse, he led the packhorses away from the cabin. When he was far enough to feel that he had not been discovered, he stepped up into the saddle and guided his horse down along the water's edge. Several hundred yards up the river, with still no sound of alarm behind him, he kicked his horse hard and headed for the pass at the upper end of the valley. "All right, Pitt," he uttered aloud. "Be sure you hold them off for a good long time." Feeling gratified that he had made a prudent decision, he urged his horse to pick up the pace. Pitt was a handy man to have around, but he had outlived his usefulness. Fry always felt that the best way to handle trouble was to be somewhere else when it happened.

Clay Culver crawled back down from the crest of the ridge to where Jim waited with the horses. "I reckon they're in there. There's a fire going in the fireplace. There's some horses in the corral, including the ones they rode off on. But the saddles are off. They mighta threw their saddles on a couple of fresh ones. Probably around back of the cabin; I could see tracks leading around there."

Jim nodded. He looked back over his shoulder. Already thin fingers of sunlight were finding their way through the scattered clouds to light the tips of the tallest pines. They wouldn't have much longer to wait until the sun climbed over the eastern slopes of the valley, casting a brilliant glare across the snow-covered ridge. With that blinding light behind them, the two brothers planned to move down the ridge on foot, hoping to advance to within a few yards of the cabin before having to take cover. While they waited, Clay offered his brother a strip of dried venison. Smiling, Jim accepted, and the two of them chewed away at the tough, leathery meat as if the coming fight were no more than a rabbit hunt.

While they waited, Clay pressed Jim for news of the family, especially their parents. "I kept telling myself I was going to go back to see the folks," Clay confessed. "But it seemed like something always kept me from going. And now it looks like I'll be scouting again for the army come spring, what with the Sioux getting riled up over the wagons going through their territory to the country above the Yellowstone."

"Ma and Pa are getting pretty old," Jim said. "Pa took sick two years ago, and he just never seemed to get over it. John pretty much runs the farm. I guess it'll be just him and Stephen now, since I don't aim to go back to face an army trial."

"You said that lieutenant shot at you first. Surely they won't charge you if it was self-defense."

"Maybe," Jim allowed. "But they were coming after me for horsewhipping the son of a bitch in the first place, and I'm not willing to trust a bunch of army officers with my life."

Clay was in the midst of telling Jim about the two years he had spent living with the Blackfeet when the sun's light suddenly burst forth across the hilltops. "It's time," he announced. "We'd best move on that cabin while the sun's right behind us."

Inside the cabin, Pitt squinted against the blinding light of the sun as it reflected off the snow-covered hillside. "Damn," he cursed, trying to scan back and forth across the ridge. He realized then why the two riflemen had waited. "They'll be coming soon," he called back to Fry. *What the hell is he doing out there?* "Fry," he yelled. "Better git your ass in here. They'll be coming soon." He turned his attention back to the ridge, but, when a few minutes had passed with no response from his partner, he yelled again. "Fry!" When there was still no response, he began to worry. Maybe he had been wrong. Maybe they weren't waiting to have the sun at their backs. They might have snuck up behind the cabin and caught Fry outside.

Seized by a new sense of caution, Pitt backed away from the window. His rifle held ready to fire, he tiptoed to the back window. Being careful to keep his body to the side, he peeked through the cracks in the closed wooden shutter. Although his view was limited, it was apparent that there was no one behind the cabin. Sudden anger overcame caution, and he flipped the latch on the heavy shutter and flung it open to verify his immediate suspicion. "That low-down, thieving coward," he growled. Fry had run, and he had taken both packhorses with him. Pitt caught a flicker of movement out of the corner of his eye and turned to aim his rifle at a stand of willows near the water. Just in time, he realized that it was his horse ambling in the trees, stripping willow leaves from their branches. *You're gonna rue the day you ran out on Jack Pitt*, he silently promised Fry. First, there was this business to take care of here. He hurried back to his post by the front window in time to catch a glimpse of Jim as he dived for cover behind a lone pine halfway down the ridge.

"Dammit!" Pitt swore, angry at having been caught away from the window. He rose up and shot at the pine but was forced to duck back immediately when two quick slugs from Clay splintered the window frame inches from his head. He scrambled to the other side of the window, trying to see where Clay's shots had come from. He searched frantically, trying to make out some irregular shape in the glistening hillside. *There he is!* But he was not quick enough. Before Pitt could draw a bead on him, Clay disappeared from his view, blocked by the corner of the cabin. Pitt tried to see around the edge of the window and was immediately dusted again—this time from Jim's rifle behind the pine.

"Gawdammit," he roared in angry frustration and rolled over to the cabin door just as another slug whined overhead, passing through the open window. Worried about Clay, who had disappeared from sight around the side of the cabin, he nevertheless had to watch Jim behind the pine tree. Pushing the door slightly ajar, giving himself just enough room to see the pine, he was alarmed to discover tracks leading from the tree down toward the other side of the cabin. They were on both sides of him now, out of his field of vision. He cursed Simon Fry for leaving him in this position. He knew that he couldn't watch both sides at once while they gradually closed in on him.

He could see how this was going to end if he stayed in the cabin. While he fired at one of them on one side, the other would move in closer. The two would alternate back and forth until one of them was close enough to stick a rifle through the window and cut him down at point-blank range. He quickly decided his chances were better on the outside. If he could surprise the one who had been behind the pine, he might just be able to hit him before he realized he was being attacked. Also, his horse was in that direction, feeding in the willows. If he got to his horse, then he could ride around the other man, maybe come up from behind and get a clean shot at him. *Then*, he promised himself, *I'm going after Fry.*

After making sure the magazine of his rifle was fully loaded, he pushed the front door open. Moving slowly and with great caution, he eased his body outside, pausing for a few moments with his back planted flat against the rough wall of the cabin. As he had figured, if he couldn't see them around the ends of the cabin, then they couldn't see him. Everything went totally quiet as he inched his way along toward the end of the cabin, his eyes riveted on the corner, ready to fire in an instant at the first sign of motion. For what seemed a long time, there were no shots fired on the cabin, and Pitt

could only guess that the two men were quietly
working their way into position to release a bar-
rage. *Only I ain't gonna be there*, he thought. All
was still quiet when he reached the corner of
the cabin and dropped down on one knee. The
only sound was that of the horses in the corral
snorting softly as they cocked their heads to
watch him. Very cautiously, he eased one eye
past the corner of the building. What he saw
brought a smile to his grizzled features.

Reaching the bottom of the slope, Jim paused
before making his next move toward the cabin.
There were no windows on this end of the
cabin, so he decided to try to work his way up
to the back. Before leaving the cover of two
small pines opposite the back corner of the corral, he hesitated, puzzling over the lone horse
standing in a patch of young willows near the
river's edge. Saddled, including a packed saddlebag, it was not hobbled or tied but seemed
to be wandering at will. As Clay had seen from
the top of the ridge, there were tracks leading
around behind the cabin. But Jim had a clear
view of the back of the cabin now, and there
were no horses. *Damned if I don't believe one of
them took off.* When he gave it more thought, he
realized that all the shots fired from the cabin
had come from the front, even though both he
and Clay were shot at.

He couldn't tell where Clay was, but he decided it was time to move in close. Leaving the
cover of the two trees, he ran as best he could

manage in snow that was almost knee-deep. Off
to his right, he heard the horses in the corral
snorting. Glancing in their direction, he saw
their heads up, all looking toward the cabin. He
was immediately alerted. Without wasting time
to think about it, he dived into the snow, bringing his rifle up at the same time. He heard the
sizzle of a bullet as it snapped over his head.
Not waiting to take dead aim, he cranked two
shots out in rapid succession at the rifle barrel
protruding from the corner of the cabin. In the
confusion of his own shots, he didn't hear Clay's
shots from the other corner of the cabin. With
nothing but snow for protection, Jim lay in the
open, his rifle ready, when Pitt suddenly
stepped out from the cover of the corner. Jim
raised his rifle but didn't pull the trigger. Pitt's
glazed eyes told him that the big brute was a
dead man. Pitt took two steps toward Jim, then
crumpled in a heap.

"Reckon there ain't but one left," Clay commented dryly as he walked around the corner
after Pitt.

Jim got to his feet, dusted the snow from his
clothes, and walked over to stand beside his
brother. "He was a big son of a bitch," he commented, gazing down at the late Jack Pitt lying
face down in the snow. Two bullet holes were
placed neatly between his shoulder blades, no
more than two inches apart. "It's a good thing
you were there, 'cause he caught me out in the
open. I must have gotten off two or three shots,

but I didn't have time to aim. I didn't hit anything."

"I wouldn't say that," Clay replied dryly, the hint of a smile forming at the corners of his mouth. "I counted two shots, and you hit the cabin with both of 'em."

"At least I didn't hit you," Jim said. "I guess his partner kind left him in a bind, didn't he? I'll get the horses."

Steadman Finch, alias Simon Fry, was on the run from justice once again. This time justice came in the form of two deadly avengers whom Fry feared more than the law. He had already been tried and sentenced. These two were the executioners. As near as he could estimate, he had covered close to three miles when he heard the shots behind him. *Pitt's catching it now*, he thought.

He felt no twinge of conscience for leaving Pitt with no one to watch his back. Those were the breaks, as far as Fry was concerned. His primary concern was for himself, just like always, and he had a bad feeling about the two strangers with the rifles. He had a feeling that Pitt was facing more than he could handle. That was the reason Fry felt justified in taking both pack-horses. Pitt was going to have no use for supplies in hell. *You did provide one last useful service, though, partner. You delayed them long enough for me to get away.* It was rough going, plodding through the snow. Fry felt confident they wouldn't be able to make any better time than he did, and he had a sizable lead. His only concern now was how high the snow might have drifted in the pass. *I'll get through somehow. I always do.*

A long ridge led up to the narrow gap that was the entrance to the valley the settlers had named Canyon Creek. As Fry approached the trees at the foot of the ridge, he pulled his horse to a stop and listened. The shooting in the distance had stopped. It was all over at the cabin, one way or another. Maybe his gut feeling was wrong. What if Pitt had managed to kill the other two? Then he would be coming after Fry with murder on his mind. He turned in the saddle and stared back at the frosted valley behind him. *He's still got to catch me*, he thought and turned to face forward again.

It was a solid blow, like someone had punched him in the chest with a fist. Startled, he jerked his head back in surprise. At first, that was the only sensation he felt: a heavy blow to the chest. It happened so quickly. Confused, he felt another blow, this one lower in his abdomen. But now there was a deep, fiery pain scorching his insides. Fry looked down and recoiled in horror when he saw two arrow shafts protruding from his body. Now the pain became intense, and his head started to spin. He could feel himself falling, so he tried to dismount, barely getting one foot out of the stirrup before his balance failed him, and he went crashing to the ground. The impact with the ground caused him to scream in pain as the arrows shifted in his organs.

He lay helpless in the snow, gasping for breath that was reluctant to come, his stomach periodically heaving in an effort to vomit the blood that was rapidly filling it. His eyes barely registered the blurry image of the half-breed boy walking slowly toward him, another arrow notched on his bowstring. He tried to raise his hand but found that it was suddenly too heavy to lift. "Please," he choked. "Please, help me."

"I'll help you," the boy replied softly and laid his bow aside. Moving deliberately, he drew a long skinning knife from his belt and moved toward Fry. Kneeling, he grasped a handful of Fry's hair and jerked his head back.

Unseen by Simon Fry, Katie Mashburn walked her horse unhurriedly out of the thicket of young pines and dismounted to stand behind Luke. She did not turn away from the grisly ritual as she had done when Wiley Johnson was scalped. Fry's blood-curdling scream when his scalp was lifted only served as balm for the consuming desire for vengeance that raged inside her. Taking Luke by the arm, she pulled him aside so that Simon Fry could see her. Gazing down at the dying man with eyes as hard as flint, she spoke. "This valley is my home. I'll not be driven out of my home by scum like you."

Fry stared up with eyes rapidly glazing over as he looked upon approaching death. Too far gone to know who was talking or what was said, his only sensation was one of excruciating pain and horror. "Help me," he sobbed, fearful of what might be waiting beyond the dark doorway that loomed before him.

Luke waited silently beside her while Katie stood impassively watching the final moments of the man responsible for so much pain in her life. She made no move to back away when he reached out for help, his feeble hand grasping her boot. After a few moments, she slowly drew her pistol and, in a deliberate motion, aimed it at the center of his forehead. Then she pulled the trigger. She remained standing over the body for a long while before finally kicked the lifeless hand away from her boot and turning to meet Luke's solemn gaze.

A little more than a mile away, Clay Culver held his hand up and pulled back on his reins. "I thought I heard something."

"I heard it, too," Jim said. "Sounded like somebody screaming." A few minutes later, a shot rang out.

"Better keep your eyes open," Clay advised. With a gentle pressure of his knees, he signaled his horse to continue.

They had not ridden far when they spotted the source of the sounds they had heard. It appeared to be two men standing over someone on the ground. There was no one else in sight. As Clay and Jim approached, the two men turned but made no move to run. They just stood there, watching the two riders approach. Closer now, Jim could see that it was a young man and a woman. The young man was holding a bloody scalp in one hand and a skinning knife in the other. Jim started to draw his Winchester from its holster.

"Hold on," Clay said. "I know them." Then he called out. "Luke, Katie, it's Clay Culver."

There was an immediate reaction of relief on the part of the woman as she recognized the big mountain man. Clay and Jim pulled their horses up before them. Glancing down at Simon Fry, Jim said, "Looks like you folks don't need any help from us."

Luke seemed to be in a daze as he stood there for a few moments without speaking. He glanced back and forth at the faces of the two brothers as if trying to place them. Finally, his gaze settled on Clay, and a light of recognition flared in his eyes. "Mr. Culver," he said.

"That's right," Clay replied. "You remember me, don't you? I ate supper a time or two at your place."

"Yessir," Luke said. He took a step away from Simon Fry as Clay and Jim dismounted. "You got whiskers now," he offered as an excuse for not recognizing the big mountain man at first. Looking down at the body before them, he said, "Him and his men killed Monk Grissom."

"I know," Clay said. "This one's the last one. The rest of them's gone under." Looking down for a moment at the body of the man who had brought death to the peaceful valley, Clay then turned to Katie, who had suddenly been drained of emotion. "Are you all right, Katie?" Although she looked about to wilt, she picked up her chin and nodded. "I saw where they burned you folks out," he said. "Who's in the grave under the cottonwood?"

"Pa," Katie replied, eyeing Jim with curiosity.

"I suspected as much," Clay said. Then, noticing her scrutiny of Jim, he said, "This here's my brother Jim." Figuring that was introduction enough, he went on. "Folks in the settlement figured you two might be dead."

"I expect we might be if we hadn't run," Katie said. When Clay expressed surprise that she had come back to the valley knowing Fry and his men were still there, she explained. "We knew we would be safe in the Shoshoni village, but I had no intention of letting that collection of riff-raff drive me out. We stayed with Luke's people for a couple of days, just long enough for Fry to think I was gone for good. I figured it would be easier to get a shot at some of 'em if they didn't know I was looking for 'em." She paused to glance at Luke. "Of course, I had plenty of help. He watches over me like a mother hen." The look in her eyes revealed the pride and maternal admiration she felt for the boy.

Clay shook his head in wonder at the woman's spunk. Monk Grissom had always said that Katie Mashburn was worth more than the rest

of the folks in Canyon Creek combined. Clay
was beginning to appreciate Monk's regard for
the young woman. "Well, like I said, Fry's the
last of the bunch. There ain't no more *Montana
Militia* in Canyon Creek."

"The bastards burned my cabin down,"
Katie said.

"I'm afraid so," Clay replied, "but I reckon
we can help you build a new one."

"Thanks. I appreciate your offer." She smiled
for the first time since they had ridden up. Then,
gesturing toward Jim, she asked, "Does that in-
clude him? He looks like he's got a strong
back."

Jim grinned. "Yessum, that includes me."

Nodding contentedly, she looked from one
face to another. "All right, then. We've got a lot
of work to do." She stepped up in the stirrup.
"We'll just let this buzzard lay right where he
is. Luke, grab onto his horse." Turning back to
the two brothers, she asked, "Did anybody find
my cow?"

Clay couldn't help but laugh. "Yeah, I think
Horace Spratte's got her." He turned his horse
toward the settlement, shaking his head in
wonder.

Lettie Henderson stood in the doorway of
Nate Wysong's little store, watching the trail
that led past the church and on toward the north
pass. Behind her, the Wysongs, the Sprattes, the
Lindstroms, and Whitey Branch were crowded

around the stove and in the midst of an earnest discussion about the future of their little community. Horace Spratte was concerned by their recent proof of vulnerability and openly wondered if they all weren't insane to stay in the isolated valley. He admitted that he and Effie had already been discussing the possibility of pulling up stakes and leaving. Reverend Lindstrom was doing his best to discourage this pessimistic talk, Canyon Creek having long been his dream. But there was a sense of worry that hung over the tiny gathering. The discussion was interrupted by a comment from Lettie by the door.

"Somebody's coming," she said. "It's Jim and Clay, and there's two people with them." Her remark prompted everyone to get up and come to see for themselves.

"It's Katie and Luke." Nate was the first to recognize the two riders following along behind the two brothers. He pushed past Lettie. The others followed.

While the others rushed to greet Katie and Luke, Lettie took only a moment to look at the new arrivals before walking to the hitching rail. Hands on hips, she planted herself before Jim and demanded, "He got away, didn't he?"

"What makes you say that?" Jim asked.

"Why, because I don't see him with you," she retorted.

"Well, you see his horse, don't you? He's dead. I didn't think I had to bring his carcass back for you," Jim said as he stepped down from the saddle.

She relaxed her stern countenance. "Is he really dead?" He nodded. "I can't believe he finally got what he deserved," she said, her voice suddenly losing its edge. Jim thought for a moment that she was about to wilt. But, just as suddenly, she pulled herself together and announced, "Well, that's that."

"I reckon you'll be heading back east when the weather lets up," Jim said.

"What are you going to do?" she asked.

"I don't know. Stay here for a while, I guess. I told Clay I'd help him build a new cabin for Katie Mashburn. After that, I don't know."

"I might stay here a while myself," she said, nodding her head thoughtfully. "It's a long time till spring. I'll just see how I feel then."

Overhearing the conversation, Clay was forced to smile. *You'd better watch out, baby brother. That young lady looks like she might be making up a halter to slip over your head.*

Mary Wysong interrupted the fuss being made over Katie Mashburn long enough to introduce her to Lettie. Katie gave the young girl a good hard look before extending her hand. She decided at once that Lettie was the kind of person Canyon Creek needed when Mary explained that Lettie had traveled clear across the country to find her father's murderer. "Welcome to our community," she said. "We need some strong women."

"I kinda figured you'd be thinking about moving away from here," Horace Spratte commented to Katie.

"Why would you think that?" Katie asked, surprised.

"Why, after what you've lost . . ." Horace started.

Katie snorted. "It'd take a helluva lot more than that to run me off." She looked at those around her. "Why, hell, we're just getting started. Ain't we, Reverend?"

"Amen," Lindstrom replied. "We're just getting started." He turned to look at Horace Spratte.

Horace was too sheepish to respond, but Effie spoke up. "Amen. We're gonna be here."

Reverend Lindstrom's smile conveyed his satisfaction; his dream of establishing a bona fide town was still alive. He felt the need to make a statement. "Friends, I think I speak for all of us when I say we owe Katie Mashburn an apology. We should have listened to you and Luke, Katie. I'm sorry." Katie acknowledged his words with a simple nod. Raising his voice then, Lindstrom said, "I think we ought to celebrate a new beginning tonight. You're all invited to my place for supper." His invitation was met with a rousing cheer.

Jim Culver looked around the crowded cabin and realized his brother was missing. He walked to the door and looked out to discover Clay

standing near the corner of the cabin, gazing at
the snow-covered mountains that surrounded
Canyon Creek. Hearing the door open behind
him, Clay turned and smiled at his younger
brother. "It gets a little too hot in that crowded
space with everybody so close, doesn't it?"

"Yeah," Jim replied. "I figured you were getting smothered in there." He walked over to
stand beside his brother. "You've been living in
the mountains too long," he teased.

"When spring comes, we'll build that cabin,"
Clay said. "Then I'll show you the heart of the
mountains. If a man has a soul at all, he'll find
his religion in the Rockies." He pointed to the
closest mountain, its peak veiled in a misty
snow cloud. "Beyond that mountain the real
world begins. I warn you, little brother, it'll get
a hold on your soul."

It couldn't happen soon enough to suit Jim.
But first he would have to wait out the winter.
He and Clay planned to camp in Monk Grissom's cabin, Katie and Lettie could do just fine
in Jed Springer's old place until spring. While
he might be anxious to see the mountains, the
thought of seeing more of Lettie had its attrac-
tions, too. Hearing the door open again, they
turned to find Luke Kendall coming to join
them. Without a spoken word, they all felt a
bonding. They were three of a kind.